# Niq Mhlongo

# *The City Is Mine*

Kwela Books

Kwela Books,
an imprint of NB Publishers,
a division of Media24 Boeke (Pty) Ltd
40 Heerengracht, Cape Town, South Africa
PO Box 879, Cape Town, South Africa, 8000
www.kwela.com

Cover design by publicide
Typography by Nazli Jacobs
Set in Bookman

Printed and bound by CTP Printers, Cape Town

First edition, first impression 2024

ISBN: 978-0-7957-1024-7
ISBN: 978-0-7957-1025-4 (epub)

'Niq Mhlongo is one of the most high-spirited and irreverent new voices of South Africa's post-apartheid literary scene.'

Rachel Donadio, *The New York Times*

# 1

Of all the fights I have had in the past with Aza, this was the most bitter and painful one. I could not take it any longer. I knew I had to leave her before I did anything stupid and used my anger as an excuse.

One hot Friday in April, a few months ago while cleaning up our bedroom, I discovered a title deed hidden on the bottom of a drawer. It was inside an envelope, carefully attached to the bedside drawer so that you could not see it unless you removed the whole drawer. I became aware of this by mistake. While trying to use a feather duster, I pulled open the drawer until it unhooked itself and fell to the ground. The A4 brown envelope fell to the floor and caught my eyes as I tried to put the drawer back.

Aza was not home yet. Anyway, she always came back late from work on Fridays. Curiously, I opened the envelope and found two startling revelations. The title deed and the fake lodger's contract from Davidson Properties were both folded together inside the envelope. The title deed confirmed that the house we had been living in together as tenants for about eight years actually belonged to Azania Nene, my fiancée. She inherited it from her dad when he passed away thirteen years ago. That was way before we met. Aza and I have been together for the past eight years. We had been trying to have a baby, but suffered miscarriages twice. That's how close we were.

Now, her failure to disclose this important information about her ownership of the house was not my only worry. What made me angry was the fact that I had been paying the rent for the same house for the past eight years. She had even forged a lodging contract between us and the so-called non-existent Davidson Properties. All along I'd been thinking that we were paying the rent to a genuine owner of our three-bedroom house in Linden. That was what devastated me the most.

I was overwhelmed with resentment. Did I sacrifice my own family for this, I asked myself as I felt the tears of anger that weighed heavily within now pressing against my eye sockets. I remembered when my mother died two years ago in my home village of Moletji. I could not even afford to bury her. I had to choose between contributing towards her funeral or risk being chucked out of the house by the fictitious Davidson Properties. As a result, I had since become a black sheep in my family. I had even failed to contribute to my mother's tombstone. Before she died, when she was sick because of her diabetes, I could not afford to drive to my village to see my mother during critical moments. But when Aza's mother was sick, we drove all the way to Heidelberg every weekend to see her. At some point I was forced to take a loan from the bank to pay our rent. I'm still struggling to repay the bank even today.

My eyes darted around the room, as if searching for anything that might be out of place. I began to spray and wipe down the rest of the bedroom surfaces and wardrobe handles. Inside I was burning with helpless rage and fury. The anger was stronger in me than my physical pain. As if to make sense of the title deed again, I put it on top of the bed. I then knelt beside the bed with my elbows on the mattress. My face was very close to the title deed as I read it again and again. My upper lip became hostile when I saw her name, 'Azania Nene', in bold letters. I was shaken and puzzled. I stood up, sat down, walked around the room, blew my nose and wiped my face. I felt numb.

In my predicament, useless thoughts crowded my head. Maybe I should burn down the house before I leave? I had a malicious thought of leaving the gas stove on. But what would I achieve by that except going to jail? I couldn't even go home to Moletji and talk to my two sisters and tell them what I had discovered. They had both warned me a long time ago that Joburg City was only for work and not to find a wife. Neither of my sisters considered Aza as their makoti. Besides, I'd not been home since my mother's burial. I could not even afford to send money home because of the seven thousand rand rent I was paying every month. My family held Aza responsible for my no-show in all our family commitments. They thought that all of my money went to her and her family, which I'm afraid was partly true. One of my sisters, Puleng, even concluded that the reason we didn't even have a child together was because she was living an expensive life. This hurt me a lot and caused more of a rift between my family and me.

The truth was, I loved Aza. Another fact was that I was living a high comfortable life with a demanding girlfriend, now fiancée. She did her hair and nails every weekend. I was living beyond my means and was certainly earning lower than her. She also drove an expensive car – a Volkswagen Touareg. I voluntarily sponsored all those exotic desires and her craving of money.

# 2

Shock has a habit of digging holes in our memory. I stayed on the couch half-asleep all night, waiting for Aza to arrive. At regular intervals I was woken up by hunger, or kept partially awake by anxieties and unclear hopes. Questions reverberated endlessly through my mind, echoing a deep loneliness, a void that no amount of praise and attention could fill. My throat ached and my eyes stung with sweat. Each breath I made was like inhaling fire. All I wanted was to sleep but I couldn't. A heap of unanswered questions accumulated in my head. I thought about the threatening tone of the creditors' letters. I had also accumulated speed fines for my car for which I had not been paying the instalment for about three months now. On top of that, I owed the bank about eighty thousand, which was the loan I took just so that our accommodation was guaranteed. In my mind I was convinced that the life I had built with Aza both in reality and imagination was very risky and costly.

I used to earn fourteen thousand a month as a salesperson at GroundDeco, our vinyl tiles and sheeting manufacturer company. I had worked there for the past ten years. The title deed discovery and subsequent fight with Aza happened at the sad time when our company was on the brink of collapse. Our manager, Mr Daniel van Zyl, was found guilty of channelling the company funds into his own account. He had swindled over fifteen million, resigned from the company and moved to Dubai. At that moment there was a protracted legal battle between the UAE and South Africa over his extradition. This came after he had pleaded guilty to twenty-five counts of corruption and twelve of money laundering. Mr van Zyl was scheduled to appear at the Specialised Commercial Crimes Court in the next few months. Due to his corruption, GroundDeco was restructuring and relocating to Cape Town. My future was uncertain.

At one in the morning Aza was still not back home. I could feel my mouth quivering with rage. My shoulders had gone numb. I went to the fridge in the kitchen, grabbed a beer, and drank it straight from the bottle. I waited for her until I sank tiredly into a kind of reverie, sitting there with my mouth open. An hour later I went to the bedroom, and gradually, I began to fall asleep. But before I surrendered completely to sleep, as I lay in bed and closed my eyes, I saw my past and future with Aza racing towards me. My memory brought back all the good and sad things I had experienced with her in our eight-year relationship. It took me to the first time I met her in 2010. She had come to buy the tiles at our company in Main Reef Road, Langlaagte. She was hoping to convert her house into a BnB and sublet it to the soccer fans who would be coming to South Africa during the World Cup. Since the country was going to host the tournament in June, Aza was expecting to make a fortune by renting out the whole house. She then charmed me into using my employee discount. I was still not experienced in dating city girls then. I had come to the city in 2008 to study Electrical Engineering at the University of Johannesburg before I was financially excluded at the end of that year.

I began to take Aza out to dinner and movies a few months

after we had met. Little by little the line of demarcation between friend and sweetheart blurred. I remembered taking her to lunch at Rosebank News Cafe on her birthday which was in April. She ordered a gin mojito which the waitress took a bit longer to bring. She complained throughout the waiting time, which was less than ten minutes. When the waitress finally brought the drink, Aza took one sip of the cocktail before she grimaced and complained to the waitress. She said that her drink didn't have enough gin in it. I was embarrassed when she told the waitress to take the cocktail back and put in more gin. But when the waitress came for the second time with the cocktail, Aza claimed that the cucumber slices looked thick and old. The poor waitress must have been sent back about four times before she started to cry. Aza started to shout at her and demanded to speak to her manager. To avoid the prying eyes of the other customers, the manager apologised and gave Aza a drink for free. What Aza didn't know was that I had secretly arranged to pay for the drinks and even gave the waitress a good tip of twenty per cent.

You see, by nature I'm shy, with a reticence comprised of both modesty and dissimulation. That is why my sisters, Puleng and Mpho, thought Aza and I were a mismatch. They had noticed during one of our few visits home that Aza was accustomed to calling the shots. I grudgingly agreed with them, but deep down I knew they were right. Taking control was something Aza did unconsciously and reflexively. She always spoke with my village sisters with that tone of entitlement that royal and city breeding brings. She could be generous and caring, but she had a darker side as well. This was characterised by her impatience and her forthright and unwavering self-absorption. These qualities seemed to have intensified through her years studying Business Administration at the University of Johannesburg.

It was in those instances and others that I thought maybe I was with the wrong person. I think these were the early signs that I should not have ignored. When I was growing up in Moletji I used to hear my elders talk about what a good woman looked like. It was generally accepted in my village that a good woman should be restrained in temperament but wild in bed. Aza was none of that. But I loved her and that was why we were engaged. I'd also bought her a ring that cost me about fifteen thousand. We were already discussing wedding dates. We had even started paging through magazines together to choose furniture and decorations, even though the date was not set yet.

She came home around three in the morning. My weakness is that when something bothers me, I do not come right out and say it. I keep it to myself, harbouring my resentment, letting the bad feeling build and build. That is me. I measure myself and those around me by an impossibly rigorous moral code.

I was lying there, trying to sleep, when her drunken voice came out of the dark.

'Babe, are you asleep already?'

I was not sure if she was talking to me or our dog, Popcorn, as she barked twice. I clearly had no idea how I should behave so I pretended to be fast asleep. I had absolutely no plan for how to cope with the situation. The memory of the last time we had sex and the scene in my dream floated in front of my eyes, jumbled together in the dark room. I tossed and turned. Very soon I was listening to her snoring and she talked a little in her sleep.

# 3

The morning air inside the house was thick with betrayal. I opened the curtains and sunlight filled the bedroom. Aza had just returned from the bathroom and was still standing by the door in her floral pyjamas.

'How could you do this to me? After all these years you don't tell me that you actually own this house?'

The voice that issued from my throat was thick with rage. My discovery so startled her, she took a step back from the door.

'What did you expect?' she said with no trace of arrogance. 'I have to make sure I'm good and covered in case you leave me.'

I was nonplussed by her peevish tone.

'What? Who told you I was going to leave you? You don't trust me?'

'You can never know with men these days.'

'We are supposed to trust each other, remember? We promised each other.'

'Trust is a double-edged sword. Besides, I'm your woman. You are supposed to take care of me.'

She threw up her palms, her tone informing me that she didn't think for a second that she was wrong. I felt as though I might cry.

Her eyes followed me with such a strange look in them.

'But isn't taking care of you what I have been doing all along? I have been struggling to make ends meet for us so that we are good. But you were busy taking from me.'

'So you were expecting to live here for free and not contribute, is that it? You wanted a comfortable life like in a hotel without paying? How do you think I pay for the lights and for the Wi-Fi in this house?'

'But you …'

'But what? What are you going to do about it? What did you expect? Living for free? You have to take care of your woman, not only through your dick.'

'After everything we have been through together and now this dishonesty?'

'You can't complain about a lousy seven thousand rand a month. It can't even buy my makeup and nails or maintain my hair. Your age group maintains their women by giving them fifty thousand pocket money every week, but you are here complaining about a lousy seven thousand? Seriously? Who do you think I am?'

'But that's all I can afford.'

'How do you think I maintain this beauty that attracted you in the first place? I'm different from your average village girls that you used to date. Let that sink into your head.'

'You should have told me. It's not right the way you just took a decision to make me pay seven thousand.'

'Yeah, it happened. So, what are you going to do about it? After everything I have done for us, you can't be crying for a lousy seven grand per month. If we break up today what do you expect me to do? You expect me to be poor and homeless? Hell no. Don't act like I stole from you because I didn't.'

I looked into her eyes to see if she was feeling ashamed. Her smile withered. I guess when you don't have the truth on your side, attitude is your best friend.

'So, you're already thinking of a break-up plan even before we get married? Is that what you're telling me? What about our marriage plans, huh?'

'Mangi, don't be naive. In any plan, no matter how carefully thought out, there are always two to three unavoidable risks.'

'You failed to disclose it. You lied to me and to our relationship. You hid close to half a million for yourself while you watched me suffer. You kept a secret behind my back. That's called betrayal.'

'A point of correction. It was not a secret. You just didn't know about it.'

An uncomfortable silence followed. She dropped her glare after looking up. Her face twitched and her eyes flickered from me to the wall behind me. I felt too weak to even speak to her. A little sadness crept unexpectedly into my voice.

'You betrayed me.'

'I don't care,' she said. 'Do what you want to do.'

'Oh my god! We are struggling and you know very well. I can't believe that a person who had assured me that she knew all about my obstacles and dangers is likely to be my traitor.'

'It's not my fault that you are short-sighted,' she retorted, shoulders hunched, hands now buried in her gown pockets. 'That money is supposed to be ours. Stop this ranting of yours because I'm not apologetic for doing what I had to do. What if you leave me today? We are not even married yet.'

'That's my point. We are engaged,' I said quietly, defeat in my voice. 'The reason we don't have a date yet is that I'm still trying to save some money for the traditional wedding which you and your family demanded from me. Besides, our company has let go of me and a few others.'

'Be a man and stop getting mad about your duty as a man. You're my fiancé. Start acting like one instead of sitting on your scrotum the whole day watching TV.'

'Is that how you think of me?'

'What do you want me to say? That's all you do since you have been laid off.'

'Aza, this is serious. I now ask you in all seriousness for a full explanation if you are the kind of wife I would like to have in the future. Why didn't you tell me that this house is yours?'

'If you have to know, I'm paying some of the bills with the money that I get from you as my future husband. Besides, I need to do my nails and hair to look beautiful for you. Real men pay for their ladies to look beautiful. I'm only twenty-nine years old. I don't want to look older. You have expectations for me to look beautiful, but you can't even maintain me. You must pay.'

'This is denial, deceit!' I shouted. 'You have a severe allergy to the truth.'

'I think you take me for granted. There are many guys out there who want to give me what I deserve. You're not growing. I can't look at you as a great man any more. You must blame yourself for that.'

'You must go to the psychologist. I think you have too much ego to be part of another person in marriage.'

Aza snapped her tongue against the roof of her mouth, making a noise of contempt. Her nostrils pulsated and her lips trembled. Filled with fury, she focused her gaze on me with such intensity that I almost felt afraid, and stopped what I was about to say. For a long moment thereafter, she was silent.

Then she blurted out, 'You must be crazy!' She pointed her finger at me. 'You thought you could just bring a penis in this house without any money? Is that what you thought?'

'What do you mean?'

'You thought I'm so desperate for your penis that I would just allow you to live in the house for free without paying anything? For your information, a penis is not hard to get. I can't be living with someone who sits around all day scratching his balls while playing video games.'

As she spoke, she made an obscene gesture with two fingers and slammed the bedroom door so hard it rattled on its hinges and banged open again. She then sat down on the bed. I felt hurt, humiliated, rejected, lost. What she said and revealed made me think and question. I tried to speak, but I managed only two words.

'Fuck it.'

We stared at each other with what seemed painfully close to hatred. A raw feeling travelled up my throat. I was sweating. Aza puffed her cheeks to signal she was very angry.

'Don't ever talk to me in that tone of a voice again,' she said, her eyes widening as she sucked the air into her cheeks. 'No one talks to me like that. Do you even realise how aggressive you are towards me?'

'You don't deserve my kindness.'

Her eyes were narrow and angry. She stood up and started to pace the room, touching a TV, opening the wardrobe doors and glancing at a few women's magazines lying around. She was still not looking at me. But then she scowled at me, and with cold calculation, cursed me. Her voice was high-pitched and aggressive.

'Fuck yourself, masende akho,' she said, twisting her lips to give the isiZulu word for testicles a measure of its horror. 'Your only claim to being a man is having a penis. Otherwise you're not a useful male. You're a dumb, ungrateful and arrogant world-class arsehole.'

18

I walked to the sitting room and just stood there. I was wretch-ed and helpless, horribly paralysed and I couldn't help it. Tears streamed down my face. I felt defeated and so emasculated that I leaned against a wall to keep from falling. The deep sadness was lingering in the house. Everything within me, and outside, was abandoning me.

# 4

There is a place in Joburg City Centre where single, divorced, engaged, married, angry, and non-committal men meet every day.
No one talks about it in public. You might have passed the place
when you were last in the city without being aware of it. Unfortunately, you'll have to discover this place on your own. We angry
men are ashamed of it during the day, but proud of it at night or
when we are inside. The best way to discover this place is when
you feel lonely like I was at that moment.

That's right. You could be lonely as hell in this city except
inside a brothel. To be specific, I'm referring to The Royal Park
Hotel on the corner of Nugget and Leyds streets in Hillbrow. This
is a classic hotel that boasts an adult entertainment venue, bar,
night club, snooker and pool, casino and brothel. I discovered
The Royal a few years ago when I was a first-year student at the
University of Johannesburg.

Back home in Moletji, I used to hear elders say that men are
raised differently from women when it comes to sex. It's only now
that this statement makes sense to me. It is true that men like
me do not have the same shame that is placed on women for
needing sex. As a man I could simply walk into any brothel to
satisfy my craving, especially since I had not had sex with Aza for
almost a week and a half. But, for a woman, like the sex workers

at The Royal, to be open about their cravings, society would label them a prostitute, whore or slut. These stereotypes lay there under the covers of darkness within our psyche.

I arrived at The Royal in the afternoon before five and I paid the fifty-rand entrance fee. After five, it is double the cover charge. At the entrance door I was searched by the bouncer whose veins on his neck and head were as taut as ropes. He also had a scorpion tattoo on his neck and almost all his fingers had gold-plated rings. He wore fake gold jewellery around his neck too. As he searched me, I instinctively looked at his ringed fingers. I then gave him a nice nickname, the Lord of the Rings, behind his back before he allowed me in.

Upon entering, I turned to the left towards the entertainment hall and bar. The three upper buttons of my shirt were undone. Around the corner, a man's hand was under a lady's short skirt. Her muddy makeup looked as if it had been finger-painted on. By the glass door was a huge poster of a naked girl with the captions:

*Dying to please YOU*
*Doggy*
*Missionary*
*Cowgirl*
*69*
*Wheelbarrow*
*Holding up legs*
*Spooning*
*Reverse cowgirl*
*Oral*
*Anal*
*Tabletop*
*Hand job, spank and fuck my mouth*

There was something comforting about The Royal and I thought it had something to do with the kind eyes of the sex workers who filled the space. The noise was like a beehive. The light was hazy with cigarette smoke. On my right were a few pool tables and slot machines where patrons were busy playing. I passed a few Thai ladies who used only their hands to communicate to me their massage business which included a blow job package. Some ladies sat on the big bar stools drinking Savanna Dry. They made some sexual gestures at me and I responded by shaking my head and smiling politely. One of them had a wide mouth and her lower lip was pushed out like a sad child.

Beyoncé's 'Ego' was playing loud and three half-naked strippers pole-danced to it. The men's eyes devoured them. They cheered as each stripper climbed the stairs, slid down the pole and up again, legs up, head down. The girls' eyes peered at each man's face. Another one looked at me, her forehead wet, and there was dampness all round her eyes. It felt as if a part of me had come back and that people here were horny twenty-four/seven. When I ignored her, she fixed her eyes on a man with a cleft chin in front of me.

Around the bar, people looked on while drinking their cold beers placed in front of them on the counter with slushed ice. I walked around looking for an empty seat; there was none. As I surveyed the place, a large buttock was pressing against me. It was that of a lady who was dancing erotically behind me. Men were ogling her well-rounded thighs and breasts.

The atmosphere nourished my dry soul. It took my mind away from my present situation with Aza. It also excited a part of me that hadn't been roused recently, except one night when Aza had come home drunk. I would not even credit that as sex.

As soon as one song ended, a new one started with a new pair of strippers on stage. It looked like each one of them had requested the DJ to play their own song to make their entrance. I walked towards the end of the bar full of men. 'Emotional' by Carl Thomas was playing and a group of men were cheering on the dancing ladies. From their stools at the bar, men multitasked by drinking from their beer bottles with their lips and ogling women's cleavages with their eyes.

I ordered a Windhoek Draught dumpy, and as I waited for the waiter to serve me, a lady came and stood next to me. She was in her mid-thirties, I guessed, with a round brown face and wearing red lipstick. Her gold earrings were in a bold African design with a matching pendant around her neck. Her perfume was strong, and she was warm, with soft eyes which said she was eager to mix. She was beautiful, but at first I didn't like the splotches which she had tried to cover with thick makeup on her face. At least not when I was still sober.

'I think we've met before, you know,' she said to me while searching my face.

That was the kind of line that makes a guy with my kind of urgent need pay attention to a lady in a brothel. While I was trying to respond to her, another drunk, half-naked woman tried to grab me from behind. She tried to hug me as if she knew me from somewhere and actually clung to me. I pulled away, waving a hand in refusal.

'This handsome one is with me,' said the lady while frowning at the intruder. 'Please don't disturb us.'

The opportunistic woman simply gave a vulgar laugh before taking a swig from her bottle of Savanna Dry. She then walked away. The other lady came very close to me. Since the bar area was nearly full, she had all the excuses to stick to my chest, her breasts rising and falling, her heartbeat sounding in my head.

Her eyes were deep-set, bright and friendly. We hit it off immediately.

'My name is Mangi. I'm not sure if I met you before?'

'I'm Boni. Is it your first time here?'

'Not really. But I have not been here in a long while – that's why I don't think we have met before.'

'And how long ago is a long while?'

'Maybe nine years.'

I was right. The last time I was at The Royal was a few years ago, maybe ten years ago when I'd broken up with my ex, Neli. That's when I used to frequent quite a few brothels, from Little Rose to Diplomat Hotel and Summit Hotel. From those experiences I have learnt that being in a brothel you have to acquire a special kind of attitude. You have to be careful, cheerful, bright, good-humoured and grateful to fit in.

'Welcome back. You came to the right place at the right time. I personally give nice times to broken hearts.'

'I'm already walking on that difficult journey of a broken heart as we speak,' I said as if it were a joke.

'Don't worry. Today you're in good hands. After today you will come begging for me, I swear. That's how good it gets down here with me.'

'Work' by Rihanna was playing. Every lady inside looked bewitched by it as they started twerking and swaying as best as they could. The tension that I had been feeling quickly faded. I had an impulse to stay with Boni, to embrace The Royal, to be protected and cherished by its walls.

'Can I buy you a drink?' I offered.

'I would love that. Thanks.'

'What's your poison?'

'Savanna Dry.'

I talked for about ten minutes with Boni, punctuating our stories – especially the sad ones – with a laugh. At least I'd found the first person I could talk to about my problems.

'You need to release that stress.'

'How do I do that?'

'Come with me to my room upstairs. I will give you a good time at a good discount.'

'How much is your discount?'

'Well, you seem like a very nice person. Normally it's two hundred rand for BJ and one round. For you it's one-fifty an hour.'

'That's fair. Let me finish my beer first.'

I licked my lips and cleared my throat. It was the first time that I had such things said to me. I felt like a celebrity. My pride, like someone relaxing in a steam bath, stretched out languorously, surrendering completely to the warmth of her words. A group of women surveyed me with their flirtatious eyes, shouting to one another quite openly as I followed Boni up the stairs.

# 5

Coming out of The Royal at around ten in the evening, I was a happy man. The rain was pouring down in solid sheets. The wet pavement was lined up with vendors selling their wares under their umbrellas, from barbecued chicken feet to traditional medicines. As I walked past them towards the parking lot, I could read the labels of the different kinds of African sex medicines displayed. There was anything from mpesu, amafutha enhlanhla, bheka mina ngedwa, imphepho, moringa, mvusa nkuzi, shibhoshi madubula, maqinisa nduku, mhlabe azesuze, phakama, velabahleke to isiphephetho. The rubbish bins next to the vendors were filled with cabbage leaves and orange peels and other discarded things.

I walked into the rain and let it soak my body. I felt a shiver of satisfaction passing through me. The rage that had consumed me earlier that morning was suddenly transformed into some kind of jubilation. I was cured. Indeed, sex workers are noble humanitarians and therapists, generous in nature and greatly skilled. They possess a wonderful healing touch, I thought as I reached my car. Sex workers assist men like me to develop a layer of immunity against threats from women like Aza. It was as if the skin around my tortured soul was now thick enough to face Aza's insults. That moment with Boni inside her room was spe-

26

cial. It had allowed me to veil the truth about the emotional abuse I had been subjected to all this time by Aza.

I drove slowly through Wolmarans Street, fascinated by that part of the city's ugliness at night. It was one of the dirtiest and most populated parts of the city that not even a broom of a political party could sweep clean, I thought. Maybe it was because of the many taxi ranks around the area, I tried to reason. The traffic ran slow. In the street people walked about staring in different directions, clutching their belongings, their faces focused but empty. The street vendors were also packing up their stalls and returning to their homes. A man was pushing a trolley filled with his belongings. He walked with wide steps and his heavy long overcoat swung rakishly above his shoes. A homeless person was lying in the middle of the pavement, facing the concrete. He looked drunk, or maybe he had taken too much of the cheap nyaope drug. I was disgusted to see two men taking a piss against a building that used to be a post office near Joubert Park. A couple of sex workers in miniskirts and leather boots kicked their way through a pile of rubbish while flashing their thighs at the oncoming cars.

'Take Your Love and Keep It' by Steve Kekana and Nana Coyote was playing on the car stereo and I instinctively sang along. Sometimes music speaks what you feel inside. I guess I needed to express my soul's healing through singing. I was driving more from reflex than concentration, reading the road signs with a mix of skill and intuition. My mind was occupied by thoughts of Boni. I'd even promised her that I would be back soon and asked for her cell phone number. In my mind I could see her lips that were coated in red. At the same time I was replaying parts of the conversation we had. I guess I was just tired of all the humiliation I was enduring at home.

'No marriage succeeds without a good sex life,' Boni had said, her soft hand stroking my back with its fine nails. 'Otherwise a man will start shopping around outside for willing women. That was the reason you came here today.'

She was right, I thought. I was experiencing unemployment problems and a bad love life with a sharp-tongued woman. Aza only smiled when she saw money in her bank account. Since I had been laid off from work it seemed she was very dissatisfied with me. She was always finding things to criticise in me. I was forever being unfair to her and it seemed I annoyed her with every breath and step.

As soon as I turned on to our street in Linden, my mood changed. Strange visions, each weirder than the last, paraded endlessly before me. My mind went over the things Aza had said that morning, one at a time. I tried to remember them, to complete meanings, so as to create for myself that part of my existence which I had lived during the years with her.

I parked the car next to hers in the carport and walked slowly towards the house. The lights in the dining room were still on. The rain-sodden earth emitted its mortal odour. I put my ear to the door and heard Popcorn bark. I felt at the handle, it was not locked. I tapped lightly at the door and opened. Everyone stopped talking. It seemed as if I had disturbed an intense conversation. 'Sentimental' by Alexander O'Neal was playing softly from our JBL boombox and somehow, for a second, it reminded me of Boni and The Royal.

I was greeted by Aza's eyes, her three girlfriends' and a guy's. It seemed there was a party inside the house and I could smell fried meat. I knew two of the ladies. They were Aza's colleagues at the Cell C cell phone company where she worked. One of them never wore a bra. The first impression I had when I saw her was that her boobs were too small. Aza had told me their names a few times, but I didn't catch them and didn't care.

As I closed the door behind me, I caught Aza staring at me. Her weave was long and a lustrous black. I thought that she was going to smash my skull into a pulp with the wine glass that she was holding from the way she was looking at me. I immediately remembered the important rule of our house – I hadn't wiped the soles of my shoes on the doormat before I'd entered the house. My Aza was germaphobic. I still remember the embarrassment I felt when, a few years ago, my two friends, Andile and Tebza, came to visit me. Instead of greeting my friends, she told them to go outside and wipe the soles of their shoes. She said that her house smelled of dog shit because they entered without wiping themselves. Since then, I never brought visitors inside our house.

I greeted everyone as a group politely. Aza rolled her eyes as if to tell me to relax in front of her friends. She had a tipsy glaze in her eyes. Avoiding further eye contact, I walked straight in the direction of our bedroom.

'Hey, babe, you're back. Come on, join us,' Aza said with an exaggerated wink.

I was not that surprised that her attitude had changed one hundred and eighty degrees. Aza always had a way with people. I figured she was caught up in a dance of public image. But I was also happy that she had lost all her rage and reproach against me. I knew my fiancée. When drunk or tipsy, she had a heart of gold and I preferred her that way.

I clenched my teeth and turned my back, leaning on the wall and jerking my head towards the bedroom. I then twisted my lip in uncertainty.

'I'm tired. Let me sleep,' I said, feigning a yawn. 'I will see you in the morning. You guys enjoy yourselves.'

'Please, babe, just for thirty minutes and you can go.' Her happy expression collapsed. 'Don't be rude to our guests.'

I looked at her pleading expression. Grudgingly, I obliged to avoid any confrontation. Aza's anger meant two days of silence between us, not even giving each other the time of the day. Sometimes she went on an emotional rampage that lasted for about a week. So, I sat down on the couch and listened to their conversation.

'Okay, but I won't stay long,' I said while looking at her.

She turned her gaze to me and smiled.

'Shall I pour you a gin or will you drink beer?' she asked while looking straight into my eyes, as though she had forgotten she was in a room full of people.

'A gin is fine, thanks.'

She poured the gin and tonic that was already on the table and put in three ice cubes. I closed my eyes briefly and rested my head against the back of the couch. Popcorn came and laid her head on my hand before licking it. I scratched her neck in return. I picked up the glass of gin that Aza had just poured for me, inhaled it, and then took a sip, my hands engulfing the glass. I could feel my limp penis sticking uncomfortably to my thighs. Somehow I became afraid that Aza would notice the vague smell of sex on me. I was glad that from where she was sitting, she couldn't see my facial expression as we were facing the same direction. But what if she asked about it? What lie would I tell her? Should I tell her the truth about what I'd done with the sex worker and apologise? Conflicting emotions crashed over me as Aza started talking while looking at me.

'Babe, this is my friend Vumani.' Aza pointed at the man sitting opposite us. 'And this is my friend Sonto. Of course, you already know Nozi and Carol.' She turned to the guests. 'Everyone, this is the man of the house, Mangi.'

'Again, hi, everyone.'

They all said hi back and Vumani smiled at me. The small wrinkles around the corners of his eyes were those of someone who laughed a lot. His sharp eyes were almost fierce, topped with thick eyebrows, and he wore circular glasses that seemed to be a part of his face.

'I'm happy the man of the house is here to join us. This debate is very interesting.' He turned to me and laughed at his own joke before he continued. 'These ladies were overpowering me before you came in. They were taking advantage of the fact that I was the only man among them.'

'Oh, I see. Hopefully I will catch up with your debate.'

'Yeah, feel free to join in. These ladies centred everything around them and are very sensitive to the issue of relationships that we are talking about. Maybe selfish is the right word.'

Vumani had a high-pitched laugh that was funnier than the joke itself. Aza sneered at his words. I knew that warning sign well and I took the cue before things turned ugly. So, I simply shrugged to avoid any confrontation that may ensue. I could not say a word. Shrinking back and taking another sip of my gin, I decided that twenty minutes was the minimum period before I could politely slip away.

I knew Aza very well. Besides her dictating the way I dressed up, there were also things I could not say in front of her family and friends. She had warned me a couple of times that I should not talk to her or her friends when drunk. I was also not allowed to dance to music when drunk as my movements were embarrassing to her. Defying these rules meant three days or more without talking. That was the reason I had developed a talent for ignoring my feelings around her.

'No, Vumani.' Aza shook her head. 'You've got it all wrong. We women aren't really complicated. We are very simple. We are literal beings and we usually mean what we say. The problem is that you men spend hours analysing what women have said when it is so obvious.'

'You see that, my outie?' said Vumani, looking at me for support. 'That's exactly what I don't believe. That's exactly what I'm talking about.' He tilted his head to the side and laughed. 'Women! You can't have a healthy argument with them before they accuse you simply because you were born a man. They have a hate/love relationship with a penis. For them every male is an embodiment of the men who humiliated them.'

There was a clear and deliberate discontent in his voice. I tried to make sense of what they were talking about, but I failed. I had to put on a cloak of indifference when Vumani stared at me for affirmation. The whole talk sounded like a game of sweet and bitter words that made it difficult for me to make meaning out of. But it was clear that Vumani thought that I had ceremonial responsibility to side with him. Instead, I decided to keep my mouth shut, to speak only when spoken to, and to make my answer to all their questions short and artless.

For about twenty minutes I remained silent, producing only a few monosyllables from time to time, coupled with a few nods and shaking of my head. As a result, I acquired the reputation of being a terrible bore from the group.

'The truth is that the tendency with you and other men *is* to overanalyse everything women say or do or don't do,' said Aza's friend Carol. 'That is why you are incapable of love.'

'You're right,' Aza chipped in. 'The world will never find peace until men like you fall at the woman's feet and ask for forgiveness for misunderstanding us.' Then she looked at me. 'When a good man holds a woman well, she becomes a queen – his queen.'

'No, no, no. The problem here is that a woman won't tell you the truth about what is going on because she herself does not understand,' Vumani countered, his head thrown back, his eyes screwed up, laughing with his whole body.

'But that's because men's ears are less suitable to make them believe than their eyes,' Sonto said, her hands sketching ideas in the air. 'Men do not believe in what they have not seen. They are the biblical doubting Thomas who refused to believe without direct personal experience.'

'Men are never satisfied,' Aza said. 'Nothing separates them from the beast.'

All the women nodded enthusiastically. Sonto gave Aza a thumbs-up. She looked at Vumani, pursed her lips, and pushed back the wisps of her weave. At this point I could not control my eyes and I dozed off. But, on the edge of sleep, it was as though a hand jolted me back into wakefulness. It was in fact Aza who'd nudged me to stay awake. My hand unwittingly pushed my gin glass from the table. The sound of it smashing on the floor jolted me violently out of my sleepy state, interrupting the debate that was still going on.

A shadow of disappointment crossed Aza's brow when I looked at her instinctively. I covered my eyes with a palm.

'Eish, I'm sorry,' I said while looking at Aza to see if her eyes held judgement, but she smiled at me.

I tried to scoop up the broken glass but she winked playfully and gestured at me to stop. She looked strangely different that night.

'Go to the bedroom and stop snoring on the couch,' she commanded.

I stood up, said bye to everyone and went to bed. Vumani smiled crookedly and shrugged as Aza held my hand and led me to the room. The high heels she was still wearing made her a little taller. The soles of her shoes gave a sharp click against the floor. Without a word she pushed me gently inside the bedroom and closed the door from outside.

'Good night,' she said, her tone soft while I felt a twinge of guilt for breaking a glass. 'We are still sitting.'

I had never seen her in such a tender mood, I thought. It was like seeing the sun shining one last time over the Joburg hills before winter came and buried its warmth under a grey cold.

'Night,' I replied to the closed door.

In the early hours of the morning, she finally joined me in bed. She snuggled closer to me and I pretended I was already asleep. I just felt no excitement touching her. Although she tried to guide my hand, I pretended I was too drunk and in a deep sleep. The flames of passion had died down, perhaps from lack, perhaps from excess fuel. Maybe I had overspent my passion at The Royal.

# 6

I woke up around nine the next morning. I could not sleep peacefully. There had been a mist early on, not a thick mist, but enough to announce the cold weather to come. My chest felt tight, my throat dry. I got up and went to the kitchen to drink water. It was stuffy and dirty in the kitchen with dishes scattered all over, leftover food, wine spills on the table, unfinished drinks in lipstick-stained glasses and empty bottles. The smell overpowered my nostrils. Red wine had been spilled on the floor and had been allowed to dry, making the surface sticky. The kitchen was also dark and smelled of instant coffee and roasted meat and marijuana. The combination of smells hung heavy in the air. I opened the window. Popcorn was sniffing around, licking here and there.

I opened the door to take Popcorn out for her morning pee in the yard. The sky outside was blue and the sun rays filtered through the tree's yellow leaves in our small garden. The busy brown birds shrieked on the branches. Autumn leaves had gathered on the ground. Popcorn inspected the area, snuffling around before squatting to take a shit. I scooped the shit into a small plastic bag and threw it into the bin.

I went inside again and I could feel the odour of yesterday's fried meat reaching deep into my stomach. I used the vacuum cleaner to trace pieces of yesterday's broken glasses in the dining room and in the kitchen.

Aza came to the kitchen just as I had finished the vacuuming. My discomfort mounted. I switched off the machine and silence encircled us. I could feel the unresolved tension in the air. I was just not sure on which side of the bed she'd woken up that morning – whether she was going to be kind or cruel. In my mind I was waiting to be scolded for breaking her five-rand glass last night and embarrassing her in front of her friends. Even worse, I might have made some noise using the vacuum cleaner which had woken her up from her peaceful morning sleep. I avoided Aza's eyes, instead staring down at the plate I was now washing.

'Morning, babe,' she said.

'Morning. Did I wake you up with the vacuum cleaner?'

'Not at all. I was woken up by thirst and a small headache, not you.'

'You want some Grandpa for your headache?'

'No, not really. It's just a little irritating thing. It will be over soon.'

Ah, thank god, she got up on the right side of the bed and was not grumpy this morning, I thought. Even though she did not have her makeup on, she had a beautiful face that was kept youthful by comfortable living.

She opened the fridge, took out a cold Savanna Dry. She drank it all in one go with an air of impish innocence.

'I shouldn't have drunk so much last night,' she said while touching her forehead and letting out a sigh. 'My head is spinning with babalas. But it will be over soon, I know.'

'The key to drinking is to say no, or enough,' I said with a touch of irony.

She nodded her head in perplexity rather than in agreement. Popcorn lowered her head between her forelegs and rubbed it with her paws.

'Lesson is learned.'

She seemed worried. I refrained from asking her what time she'd come to bed last night. There were little beads of sweat on her brow as though she had been through something strenuous.

'I'm sorry I was rude to you yesterday morning,' she said while standing near the sink. 'I've been an ass to you. I don't know what demon got into me.'

We exchanged a glance of regret. She looked harried. Her eyes were wide and dark and clotted with makeup. She looked at me thoughtfully. Her feet, as always, were impeccably cared for, with no hard skin on them. Her long fingernails were filed flawlessly.

'Don't worry about it. It's okay.'

There was some uncomfortable silence. I thought back to the insults she'd hurled at me and it made me a bit nervous. My reflections were interrupted by Popcorn, who came and stood between my legs. She started scratching me lightly with her paw, possibly warning me that she was thirsty. Aza remained silent for a few moments, as though looking for a lost word.

'No, it's not okay,' she said in a worried tone. 'I know I should have told you this, but my mother was diagnosed with diabetes and needs regular drugs and food to keep her alive. I need the money for her medical expenses.'

She was quite emotional about it. Her eyelids twitched and narrowed as if winking slyly. I was not sure I had the energy for this conversation right now. There are some things that are better left unsaid, untouched, unbothered.

'I'm sorry to hear such bad news. I was also surprised because rudeness never suits a beautiful woman like you.'

'I should have been open with you about it. My mother's diet and medication is expensive. I have to make sure her diet is balanced by buying veggies and fruit for her every week. I spend lots of money on snacks and vegetables with less calories.'

'I now understand.'

She stretched out her hand and our palms pressed together. I realised that she was not wearing her engagement ring. Now was not the time or moment to take issue with her or chastise her for not telling me about the rent money and her mother's illness earlier. Instead, my eyes wandered across the various familiar objects in the kitchen and fell on the empty Savanna Dry bottle on the table. Through the window I saw a black bird fly past. We stood like this for a moment. Popcorn was nosing around for crumbs.

'I'm really sorry.'

'Don't worry. What happened has happened. We have to move on.'

'I didn't mean what I said yesterday. I was stressed out,' she said while she poured some water from the tap into a glass.

'I figured that out.'

I hated her mood swings, which affect my own mood so badly. A moment ago, I had been completely demoralised, but now things had suddenly brightened again. The only thing I appreciated was that she seemed to have lost her air of superiority and condescension. She sat on the chair looking miserable with a glass of water that remained half-full.

'You're right,' she said after taking a sip. 'Let bygones be bygones.'

She stood up and put her arm around my shoulder, pressing herself up against me. Her face was close to mine, an arm around my neck. To me it felt less like a sign of affection, more like strangling. Her mouth still smelled of yesterday's cigarettes and wine. She played down the fact that she had not brushed her teeth and gave me a sort of half-kiss on the mouth. As she removed her hands from me, I saw a tear run down her cheek. I would have liked to wipe it away, but I restrained myself.

I forced out words that I didn't mean: 'It will be alright.'

We exchanged a knowing look. I concentrated my eyes on her little birthmark like a beauty spot over the left corner of her mouth, a mouth that sometimes smirked, giving her a mischievous look when combined with a raised eyebrow.

'Strangely, I dreamt about her last night,' she said, wiping a tear from the corner of her eye.

'Who are you referring to?'

'My mother. I wonder what that dream means. She was very angry about something I had done.'

'Sometimes dreams help us to deal with traumatic experiences and memories. It is essential for our survival. A dream is equivalent to a hope.'

To be honest, I wasn't sure if I still felt any love for Aza. It was clear that the two of us were dancing to the music which had long stopped. Love had clearly left the house. Maybe she was trying to rekindle it that morning when she put her arm around my shoulder. But it didn't work. I was cold, jittery and dysfunctional around her. Until the title deed discovery the past Friday, she had constituted my whole universe. Now I felt like a hostage of false definitions.

'When did it happen? I mean about your mother's sickness? Is it a recent thing or something that your family knew all along?'

'It happened a few years ago. I know I should have told you. My dad never cared about my mom, you know, and that is the reason they divorced when I was a young baby.'

'Oh, it makes sense.'

I nodded, but my mind was elsewhere. Each time the words came out of her mouth, my irritation and disbelief mounted. In my state of apathy, I did not ask further questions. I was not even sure whether she was telling me the truth. To me, as from the past Friday, her life was nothing but a tissue of lies with which she'd enveloped her greed, to veil it from the world. In fact, what this revelation did to me was to make me angrier. It was like there were levels of mothers. Her mother appeared to be more important than mine. We never did anything for my mother when she was still alive. When she died a year ago at the age of seventy-one, Aza didn't even stay after the funeral. My mother was buried a day before her own mother's sixtieth birthday. She had succumbed to the attacks of epilepsy that left her paralysed and heaving for breath. I felt it was some-thing I could have prevented if I'd had enough money to send her to a hospital. Instead, I was busy paying rent to my so-called fiancée. And yet, for the first time yesterday, Boni, a sex worker, had shared my pain over the loss of my mother when I'd told her in passing that she had died. That was something that Aza never did.

I decided at that moment to recoup some of the money I had lost by stealing her engagement ring that she was no longer wearing anyway. I knew she had put it inside her jewellery jar.

# 7

I had no illusions left that I had not sworn my fidelity to alcohol, The Royal and sex workers. Boni had telephoned me in the morning, declaring herself ready for me. Christmas comes once a year anyway, I convinced myself. If I missed it, I knew I might not get it anytime soon again. After the call, I replayed our conversation in my mind and drove to The Royal.

'Would you like some company today?' she had asked.

'Well, it's a Sunday and I was planning to take it easy at home. What do you have in mind?'

'A lot of beautiful things and a guaranteed orgasm. You know it's mandatory for a man even on a Sunday to live an abundant, happy and healthy life.'

'Are you saying what I think you're saying?'

'Just come and you will see and feel for yourself.'

'Okay, I'm on my way.'

'I bought you plenty of your poison – a six pack of Windhoek Draughts.'

'I can't say no to that. I'm on my way.'

It was best to go somewhere where there were no lies, I thought as I drove to Hillbrow. I had suffered enough. Now my moment of triumph was here. Love and affection, so long repressed in Aza's house, flowed freely in me when I thought of The Royal.

I had succeeded in pushing Aza to the back of my mind. She had told me she was going to a baby shower somewhere in Midrand and I didn't care. A fairly believable rumour had it that she was cheating on me with Vumani.

By two in the afternoon, I was entering The Royal. After having been body searched by the Lord of the Rings, I did the usual and walked towards the bar. Everyone and everything seemed saturated with happiness inside. Moloko's 'Sing it Back' blended with the sound of drunk voices, obnoxious laughter and the stench of cigarette smoke. I walked around, waiting for Boni to come down. She had been busy with a client upstairs; she had told me via sms it was the last one for the day.

To kill time, I went to the bar to buy a beer. While I was waiting to be served, a woman with wide tunnel-like nostrils playfully slapped me on my ass. Her hair was dyed pink and she was wearing white shorts and a pink T-shirt with 'EGO TRIP' printed on it. She gave me a lewd laugh when I jumped as though I were whipped. She moved past me with a confident smile and a drink in her hand. That brought my soul back. It was like coming out of the darkness and into the light. Joy and laughter was in abundance at The Royal. All I had to do was to look at a pretty face or a round full ass, or full lips. But that Sunday was for Boni.

I waited for about ten minutes before Boni found me at the bar. She walked towards me, bringing a strong wave of perfume with her. She was wearing a tight-fitting white blouse that showed her navel and simple silver hoops in her ears. I was mesmerised by the whiteness of her long nails. They were lustrous and almond-shaped. But the useless thought that intrigued me more was how women with such long nails wipe themselves after doing number two in the bathroom.

'Here you are. Standing like a pimp and enjoying your beer?'

she said, stretching her arm across the back of my chair and giving me a shoulder squeeze.

'Should I take that as a compliment? Pimps all around the world don't have a good reputation. They seem like brutal people.'

'I guess you're the type that reads a lot of crap. If you knew what the word "PIMP" stands for, you would be happy that I elevated you to that high status.'

'And what is that?'

'It means Power In Manipulating People, especially beautiful women.'

'So, you think I'm manipulating you?' I asked with a smile.

'I have no doubt about it. It's very rare that someone like me calls a particular guy on a beautiful Sunday just for a nice time together.'

'I think it is the other way round,' I said jokingly. 'You look pretty by the way.'

'Stop lying to yourself,' she said with a smirk. 'I'm only a sex worker.'

'That makes you even more sexy.'

'Don't forget, God promised men that good and obedient wives would be found in all corners of the world. But then He made the earth round and put the brothel in the centre. And He laughed at stupid men who didn't read His trick so well as they went searching for these women in the corners of the world.'

'Did God mean to make the world like this, with such disorder and confusion, you think?'

'I think so. But only to trick stupid men.'

'I'm glad I came straight to The Royal.'

'The meaning of life is in living it. You're one of the few rare species of clever men who came directly to the source of happiness.'

A brief thought of Aza absorbed me, then faded.

Boni cut short our conversation and laid a hand on my shoulder.

'Finish your beer and let's go upstairs for the real royal treatment.'

I stood up abruptly. 'Gypsy Woman' by Crystal Waters was playing with patrons dancing and singing along *la da dee*. I would have loved to linger there, to stretch each day into a year, each year into a decade, and a decade into a century just to watch the beautiful lust facilitators inside The Royal.

The passage was filled with worried faces. We took a lift to the sixth floor. From there, it looked like Joburg was going about its Sunday business as usual.

'Welcome back to The Royal. Make yourself comfortable.'

'Thank you.'

The first thing she did was to give me a cold Windhoek from her small fridge. She glided around, exuding pride of ownership, touching and straightening things on the small table and wardrobe. Artificial flowers in a jug decorated the table.

The two three-quarter beds with matching sheets were put closer together to appear like a king-size bed.

'My roommate, Dee, goes home every Sunday. We normally go together, but this Sunday I said no because it's dedicated to you.'

'I'm honoured. Where is her home?'

'East Rand, Tsakane. We attend church together there every Sunday.'

'Oh, I see,' I said as I opened the beer.

'Sorry for keeping you waiting downstairs. I thought I was not working today, but then there was an emergency.'

'I enjoyed waiting for you downstairs.'

'I know. Every man does. The Royal is like a tree of life that brings forth many different kinds of women.'

44

'I absolutely agree.'

'I'm glad it was worth the wait. In a place like this, a man, at least, is free to explore all passions and all countries. Our motto here is to help men to overcome their problems while indulging in the most exotic royal pleasures.'

'Of course I enjoyed waiting for you and didn't feel the time moving. I know the laws of the jungle very well.'

'I don't think I'm following you ...'

'I mean, even in the jungle, the male lion has to rely on the lioness for food. Did you know that the lioness is in charge of hunting, but the lion always eats first?'

'Well said. I was hunting for you.'

I had a wild, highly erotic vision of what she'd said. I waited for her to take the initiative, but she stayed where she was.

'So, you just decided not to work today?'

'Sometimes I do on Sundays so that I can go to church and study.'

'Study where?'

'UNISA, Business Admin second year.'

'Oh, I see. And which church do you attend?'

'I'm Catholic. You don't believe a sex worker goes to church and studies?'

'I'm not judging. I'm not a churchgoer either. I'm also a UJ dropout.'

She gave the briefest of smiles and then shifted the conversation in a direction she was more comfortable with. Next door, the conversation I had heard before through the thin wall fizzled out and the grunts took over, eventually fusing with sounds of a woman's moaning.

'Yesterday I had this rich client. I was at his house and when I came back, Dee was already gone.'

'Ah.'

'And he had a stomach that matched his bank balance.'

I laughed. I was not sure if we were close enough to talk about our personal life or just general things. I did not dare question her, but, realising how experienced she was, I told myself that she must have made the night pleasurable for the man. I took a swig at my beer.

'I can only imagine.'

'What is it that you can only imagine?' She smiled. 'Oh, I see. His dick?'

'Well, that too.'

'The reason most people in the world suffer and are not happy inside is that they are not having a real orgasm. People like me help them to reach their heights.'

'I guess you're right.'

'Life is an adventure to be embraced with an open mind and loving heart. Now, allow me to make you happy.'

She began to undress slowly. She very neatly folded her dress and put it on the chair next to the bed.

'Now it's your turn.'

I started to take off my clothes as she looked at me from my chest, down to my belly and legs. It made me a bit uncomfortable, but I could not complain. She was already lying down on the bed, supporting herself on one elbow.

'You have a beautiful body. Come.' She pulled me to the bed.

She placed her leg over mine and kissed my lips. Her mouth tasted as if she had been eating honey and every part of me itched in a nice way. She then ran her fingers over my testicles and tickled me. It was like I was possessed, and I made several moans and groans. I then burst out laughing. Our legs pressed together and slowly rubbed against each other.

'What?' she whispered into my ear. 'You mean no one has touched you on the gearbox before?'

'No.' The word left my mouth too quickly.

She hooked a leg behind my buttocks to draw me closer. She then gently took my hand and placed it on her breast. I fondled her breast, mechanically. Each millimetre of our touching skin was like a declaration that we were going to fuck, not play. She shifted positions and moved her head below and began to lick my penis. She first touched it with her lips and then she tickled my crotch with her fingers. I shivered with excitement. We hypnotised each other.

'You really have never been touched here?'

'Not in this beautiful way.'

She smiled at me and the small dimple in her right cheek surfaced.

'Just close your eyes and see.'

# 8

It was over before it even started. Once my hormonal whirl was spent, I found myself staring at a complete stranger in Boni. She released me from her tender, perfumed squeeze. I felt relieved and free of stress. The love I felt for her at that moment was a mixture of trust and excitement, tranquillity and intensity. Her magic touches had managed to calm my nerves effortlessly.

We were silent for a short while. It was not a hostile silence, but something that suited us both and allowed me to think. I'm always like that after reaching my orgasm, I'm not fit for human society. I need a bit of space and silence.

Boni threw me a towel to clean the mess between my thighs. She opened the fridge and handed me a cold beer. While drinking I was thinking about The Royal blessing. This is a place, I thought, that was made for guys like me. Here, there was no need to explain myself to Boni for having an orgasm in ten seconds. Common lies such as, *Oh you are too fresh, that's why I came so early,* or, *I'm stressed, my dog died when I was twelve* are not necessary here inside the brothel. The sex workers were here to heal our stress. Here, we were stress free.

Boni was already freshening herself up and I was getting dressed. She then opened the window and looked at the sprawling city buildings while putting on her red lipstick. I looked at her and saw that she was smiling and blinking at the mirror in her hand. Her eyes were large and long-lashed, her neck slender.

'Thank you for the royal treatment,' I said. 'I'm not used to this lively and highest display of affection. You just know which buttons to press on me.'

'I can see your eyes shining with joy. A good orgasm is satisfying; a great orgasm can be a revelation of your deepest being.'

'I believe you. It was the nicest short trip to paradise.'

'I know. I've been in this business long enough to know that all men want are orgasms and not conversation, let alone a relationship.'

'Excellent observation. I wish my woman was as open as you. Some of us are cursed with resentful and hostile women. Women who only look after themselves and their side of the family.'

'Well, I guess in every grade of life there are always two sides to every matter,' she said, pencilling her eyebrows. 'Most women are lacking in their orgasmic bank accounts.'

'Good point. It's like you know my home well.'

'It's a common occurrence and not only in your home. Some women fail to take responsibility for their actions. In turn they blame their men for their own devious acts.'

'Well said.'

'It does not make sense when some women compete with their mothers-in-law and sisters-in-law.'

'You nailed it. But how do we avoid this?'

'Simple. Find a partner who wants the best for you. Let a woman deny man sex and he will go find it somewhere very cheap, like here at The Royal where we give them royal treatment. Same applies to a man – a woman can also find sex anywhere. And that will be the end of their relationship.'

We talked for nearly fifteen minutes. She surveyed her face several times in the mirror while I drank my fifth beer. She looked serious, probably unsatisfied with her eyebrows. She then sat down and started filing her nails, whistling. She dipped her forefinger into some oil bottle and began administering it, first below her eyes and then upon the nostrils, then upon the mouth, and lastly upon the soles of her feet. Suddenly, we heard a commotion outside and the loud voices of a man and woman.

'No, you cannot leave until you pay,' I heard the woman say. 'This is The Royal, there's no free sex here.'

'But where is my wallet? You stole it!' a man's voice insisted.

'No one stole your fucking wallet. Don't come up with stupid excuses and stories.'

'But I heard someone come inside the room while we were busy. You guys are thieves.'

'Maybe it was in your dream. It was you who came inside me and not someone else.'

'You stole my wallet, I want it back.'

'Stop playing games, whoever you are called. I want my money. I'm here to work and not to be your free ride. Give me my three hundred.'

Boni ignored the commotion for a while. She trotted to the mirror and got out her lipstick again. Suddenly we heard the rushing of people on the stairs. Then we heard a man crying and it disturbed me for a while. The commotion grew louder and louder, punctuated by shrieks.

'It happens all the time – clients not wanting to pay for The Royal service received,' Boni said nonchalantly. 'It also happened to me a few times. Don't worry, you are safe.'

'It sounds serious though.'

'Yeah, it happened twice last week. It's amazing how like animals all men look when they are consumed by basic desires for sex,' she said while looking approvingly at her image in the mirror. 'But once they get The Royal service, they take advantage of us because we are vulnerable. They even call us names.'

'That's an anti-climax, a disappointment.'

The commotion gained momentum. Boni and I came out of the room to witness. Two broad-muscled bouncers were roughing up the man. One bouncer grabbed him by his lapels. He lifted him up to the level of his eyes.

'Dude, are you going to pay or maybe you would prefer being sent to your ancestors from here? I'm being serious.'

The man leaned on the railing and looked down. He was filled with fear. His eyelids trembled and a deep sigh shook his chest as though he were about to begin crying again.

'I swear they took my wallet inside her room.'

'Don't fucking lie. We know the likes of you.'

The man was solidly proportioned. He was wearing wire-rimmed glasses that gave him a disgraced professorial demeanour. He was dark-skinned with square shoulders. The woman I'd seen earlier with pink hair was standing against the wall by the door chewing gum. She was wearing a short skimpy black skirt that barely covered her red panties that kept peeping out. Her blue blouse's top buttons were open and she had on large pearl studs. She was also fair-skinned with a small nose and mascara-crusted eyelashes.

'I swear there is a lady that came into the room while we were busy,' the man insisted. 'She's the one that took my wallet, I swear to God. They took my money, cell phone and cards.'

'There was no one in the room. Stop lying,' the woman insisted.

The second bouncer had a small jutting forehead and a broad nose that took up most of his face. He looked eager to throw the man down to the courtyard. The man's pants were hanging around his buttocks with the belt unbuckled as though he were caught in a sexual act. As if to bring himself back to his senses, the man struck himself on the forehead with the palm of his hand.

'Please don't kill me,' the man pleaded while he was suspended in the air. 'I swear to God this lady robbed me.'

The bouncer shook his head impatiently. His eyes crackled with mischievous malice. The man's hands were shaking and he was coughing rapidly. He sobbed like an adolescent.

'Where is my money?' the woman asked with flaring nostrils and trembling lips. 'You won't get out of here alive if you don't pay my money now.'

The gum-chewing movement of the woman's jaw was earnest and fast. The man stared at her, then at the bouncers, before he chewed his lower lip to stop its trembling. He began to spit out the flecks of blood that he had been swallowing. With the tip of his tongue, he felt along the inside of his lower lip where there was a bleeding cut. Eventually he rubbed his bleeding mouth with the tip of his fingers.

'Okay, stop,' Boni pleaded, making calming motions with her hands. 'He was actually here with me earlier and forgot his wallet and money in my room.'

'Are you sure about that?' asked the bouncer while looking at Boni.

'Certainly,' she said, her eyes darting around with worry.

We all looked at Boni with great astonishment. The bouncer let go of his grip on the man. The man's eyes shone with a final hope. Beads of sweat fell from his forehead. He covered his face with his hands, plunged into a swirl of embarrassment and rage. The lady lit a cigarette and started smoking with slow, mournful intakes of breath. The smoke curled upwards and made her squint.

'You see how you were taking chances and lying about me? You cowardly piece of shit. You accused me of stealing your wallet.'

Her tightly folded arms were rigid. She continued chewing her gum revoltingly while flicking the corners of her mouth with her tongue at regular intervals. She raised her head to take a long pull on her cigarette from time to time. Somehow, I felt pity for the woman. I followed Boni as she went into her room and took money out of her drawer.

'Why did you do that?' I whispered.

'You didn't see it? Those guys would have killed him. He was just one leap away from eternal peace with his stupidity.'

'They will think you had something to do with it.'

'That is not the point.'

'What is the point?'

'The point here is that there are places where there is no wrong or right. Where your anger comes from is less important than what you do with it.'

'But that's his problem and not yours.'

'Listen, I saw those people throwing someone out of the window not so long ago. Imagine dying for not paying for sex. Some men can be stupid.'

'You think that stubborn guy should walk away without paying?'

'Not at all. But I also know those ladies. They have a bad reputation here and they work with the bouncers in tricking customers.'

'Oh-kay, I see what you mean.'

As Boni went out of the room to give the money to the man, I was also busy reflecting on her personality. Meeting such a woman with a heart of gold at the brothel was one of the remotest occurrences I could ever dream of.

# 9

I came out of The Royal at about six-thirty. Its outlines blurred in the evening glow and a few lights twinkled from the windows of the nearby flats and on the street. The Joburg sky exploded with noise and colour. A crowd was walking in and out of the stores and streets like ants around spilled sugar. I looked at my cell phone; I had several missed calls from Aza.

In the parking lot, before I even started my car, I tried to call her. The calls went unanswered and I gave up. Other messages I received were from the bank. They were reminders about the car instalments that had not yet been paid.

Despairing thoughts of every kind darted through my mind as I drove west through the city in the direction of Melville. The sound of Kassav's 'Ou Lé' floated vaguely in the background on the radio. As the song ended, and the DJ started to talk, the heaviness of the past few days suddenly weighed down on my eyelids. Just like that, my thoughts drifted off to Aza. For the past few weeks, everything about her exasperated me – her face, her clothes, what she did not say, her entire being. Her very existence. All this filled me with malice and a desire for revenge. I had become withdrawn and irritable around her. It was as if I were just buying time to still be with her.

Arriving home in Linden, I saw Vumani's car in our carport. I told myself that I was not going to pretend that day and sit with them for drinks if that was what Aza's missed calls were all about. Anyway, I was already tipsy. I decided I should wait for a few minutes and compose myself inside my car. It was also important to strengthen my voice for the conversation that surely lay ahead, so I cleared my throat a few times.

As I entered the house, Aza was circling the kitchen like a vampire looking for blood. The look that she gave me was intense and it seemed to chill my blood. Vumani was standing against the wall next to the fridge. Popcorn came running to me and caressed my leg with her tail.

'You only come now? Where have you been all along?' she asked me. 'I have been calling you many times. You didn't even bother to answer or call back.'

I realised that I hadn't prepared a story about where I had been. The task of putting together something persuasive was daunting and there was no time to do it now. Instead, I deliberately decided not to answer that part of the questions.

'But I did call you later when I saw your missed calls and you did not respond.'

'Where have you been?' She was glassy-eyed and angry. 'You see what the thieves did?'

I shrugged. I have learnt that a shrug is sometimes a powerful reply to a question. And a shrug is also an easy way out of a lot of things. I looked at the room, from the broom that was propped in one corner to the dirty dishes and pots in the sink.

'I was hanging out with friends. What happened?'

'My clothes are stolen, the TV is gone, my laptop, too. My Burberry and Louis Vuitton handbags – everything is gone.' She paused for an instant, composing herself. 'How I'm going to replace my things?' She breathed in deeply before letting out a dramatic sigh.

I fought a twinge of guilt and walked to the bedroom.

'Don't touch anything there. The police are on their way,' said Vumani, looking at his watch. 'I called them about thirty minutes ago.'

The bedroom was in a jumbled state. My shoes, most of my clothes, the bedroom television set, the boom speaker and my laptop were all gone. I then came back to the kitchen where Aza was still pacing up and down.

'If you didn't go out to your girls this would not have happened. Did you even lock the doors properly when you left, or were you in a rush to meet up with your girls?'

She was shattered, breathing hard through her open mouth. It was impossible to tell what she was gazing at in the distance through the open window, or what her secret thought might be. She then focused her gaze on the frail plants wilting in their pots on the windowsill.

'You're not useful in this house. Sometimes I ask myself why I'm still with you. Everything in this house is me. I fix the leaking geyser, I replace light bulbs, I fix blocked toilets. I repair the vacuum cleaner. I do everything. All you know is to cook the food I buy. I'm tired.' She paused as if on the verge of adding something. 'I'm really tired. It cannot go on like this.'

Of course that was not entirely true. I mowed the lawn; I washed the clothes and dishes and other important things. Even though I had been laid off from work, I still managed to have the rent money with a bit of money that I got from my former employer. But last month was the last time I received that money. Even if I had money, though, I would no longer contribute towards the rent since I'd discovered that I had been lied to all along.

'I think you have been waiting for this to happen because you don't care anyway,' she continued. 'Things cannot go on like this. I want someone to take care of me. If you can't, just let me know so that I can go on with my life.'

I was both disgusted and ashamed that she'd mentioned all of these ugly things in front of Vumani. To speak ill of those we love always requires a certain degree of detachment, I thought. We stared at each other, not speaking, almost as if stunned at seeing each other for the first time.

'I will be outside,' said Vumani, looking embarrassed on my behalf.

I always find it hard to gaze directly at people who mean every word they say, but this time I did. The sudden impact of her words, as they clattered into my consciousness like a bullet through the heart, made me shudder. My first instinct was to bow to her and apologise. Instead, I gave her a cool look, not hostile but not friendly either.

Several thoughts were busy racing inside my head. What if she had done this to the house herself? But for what reason? To force me out? Really?

'What am I going to do now?' she went on, her voice flat, her tone resigned. 'And I know you have been sleeping around.'

# 10

The police arrived an hour later. After giving a statement, Vumani left. He told them he'd been called by Aza when she got home. Aza corroborated that she had come from a baby shower. I told them I had been with friends watching a soccer match in Florida.

'So this is the door they broke into?' asked one of the two police officers with big teeth.

'Yes. It seems like it,' Aza replied in a low voice.

The other police officer had a deep, smoky voice; I guessed he had partied a lot in his previous life. He looked at me and at Aza.

'Anyone you suspect?'

We both shrugged simultaneously. Aza bit at her pinkie nail and examined it, ignoring my gaze. She kept her calm demeanour, probably only because of the presence of the two police officers. Inclining her face towards me as if to keep me from looking around, she answered the policeman with a voice admittedly trembling and uncontrolled.

'No one in particular,' she said, shaking her head with wide eyes.

'Is the house insured?'

'Yes, but only for some items.'

The light from the bulb overhead shone over her brow as if over polished marble, down to the arch of her eyebrows.

'This place has been a target of late. Last week alone we had seven reported cases of robberies. The nyaope kids that hang at the park are suspects. We are monitoring them very closely. Please let us know if you hear or suspect anything.'

'We will,' I said.

The officers left their contact numbers after taking fingerprints at the door, wardrobe, walls, everywhere.

'Can we talk about it?' I asked after the police had gone.

'What is there to talk about? Is that going to bring my things back?'

She slammed the kitchen door shut and tossed a magazine she was holding onto the couch. It struck Popcorn as she was about to sit in her favourite corner. Aza then directed a curt nod towards me and without a word she walked towards the room, disappearing inside before she slammed that door too.

That night I slept in the other room in the single bed. We started to communicate in monosyllables and only when the conversation was totally necessary. My only friend in the house was Popcorn. I began to feel the emotional pain. Aza's silence was infinitely more menacing than a flood of her threatening words. During this time, Aza had made Lira's 'Hamba' her official soundtrack to our current situation. She would play that song loud and more than twenty times a day on her cell phone while fluffing up cushions and fondling blankets. The song had become my most irritating earworm. I knew she was grudgingly dedicating it to me to make me leave. She would sing along to the song loudly enough for me to hear from the bedroom, especially the part which tells the partner in isiZulu that even if they left now, she wouldn't cry, that she'd had enough. Every time our eyes met she looked away, demonstrating she didn't want to give me the time of day. She would close her bedroom door and act like there was nobody in the house. Sometimes I would hear her talking on her cell phone and from her tone it would be obvious that she was talking to a man with whom I suspected she was on intimate terms.

I had hope that this behaviour would end soon just like in the past, but it dragged on this time around. Any woman can be talked around, I thought; I only need to be persistent and take a lot of nonsense from her first. The truth was that I just didn't have the strength to lose her, and I began to feel contempt towards my own weakness.

# 11

I dedicated the month of May to applying for jobs. I didn't go out, not even to The Royal. Since I no longer had a laptop, I would go to the internet café down the road to use their computers. The entire month, Aza and I were not on speaking terms. When I tried to have a conversation with her, she simply turned her back and went to her bedroom which I was no longer allowed in. The unanswered questions, the blank stares, the silence – it was all too painful. I pretended not to notice, not to be bothered, not to be annoyed. I acted as if I were busy reading and hoped that the books would protect me from my growing loneliness.

The thing about women like Aza is that they can keep a low profile for months before laying their cards on the table. By June, she began the mornings with tirades about everything I did wrong in our relationship and in life in general.

The trigger came one Thursday evening in June when I got a serious tongue lashing for something I considered unimportant. After using the loo, I had forgotten to put the toilet seat down after taking a pee. That was a cardinal sin. She found me in the kitchen having just come into the house with Popcorn.

'You must stop behaving like a child. How many times must I tell you to put the lid down after peeing? I'm not your mother.'

'I don't appreciate your words and their tone. I'm an adult.

Besides, you have no right to invoke my dead mother's name in that way. Let her soul rest in peace.'

The whole house smelled of the antiseptic that she had used in the bathroom. Damp spots covered the walls and bathroom ceiling.

'If you think you are an adult then you must start behaving like one. Adults don't behave like you do.'

'I have taken you for quite a sensible lady, but you seem set on indulging in a bizarre array of moods lately.'

'Why don't you just pack your things and go,' she said in a loud voice, with her face towards me so that I could read her lips. 'I'm tired of telling you the same thing over and over again like a big child.'

She was right; I didn't know why I was not leaving her. I think I was like those who believe that heaven will fix everything. It hadn't yet come to my attention that I can't always trust that luck would favour me one day. In this case with Aza I also needed to factor in bad luck and move on.

'Someday, one day, after I have left your house, I hope you will learn to thank the people around you, even for their smiles, touches and nods,' I said to her and I didn't recognise my own voice, which sounded like I hadn't used it in ages. 'Unfortunately we will be living apart then and I will not be with you to remind you of my words.'

Aza looked at me with a frown creasing her brow. She gave me her classic exaggerated look with pursed lips and plenty of side-eye.

'What are you waiting for? Just go now. Don't forget to close the door properly when you finally leave this house for good.'

She slammed down the mug of tea she'd been holding with such a force that I thought the kitchen table might crack. Popcorn stood up on hind legs and, in her panic, started to lick her paws. I ignored Aza and went outside again. Aza followed and started needling me. Her patience with me on that day seemed to have reached breaking point. She was shouting loudly, drowning out the neighbour's loud house music.

'I have no more use for you here any more. You're a burden. I don't even trust you. I would not be surprised if you organised your goons to break in.'

The words, one by one, stabbed into me and there was nothing I could do to prevent them forever changing the course of things.

'How could you say that to me? You're being unfair and unreasonable. They stole from me too. They took my laptop, clothes and boombox.'

'I hate to have a man who uses up my breathing space for nothing. I want my freedom.'

I don't think she understood the full venom of her words. I closed my eyes as a wave of irritation overtook my body. Maybe my refusal to accept that I should go was animated by my selfish love and fear. It was clear that her bitterness towards me had accumulated in her soul, each day, like muddy water gathering in a Joburg pothole.

From then on, I was even afraid of using the loo at night because she would complain about the flushing noise. If I didn't flush, she still got angry. The best way was to control myself no matter how much I needed to go.

But how long was I going to continue living like this? Every day I turned the idea over and over in my head. I was hurt, shaken and exasperated to the point of madness. I found that I was no longer dealing with the woman of my dreams, but an enemy. A disturbing thought kept recurring to me that the Aza that I had fallen for, never happened, that she was in fact a lie, a phantom, a dream or a nightmare that had come to my life one suffocating dark night, and when I opened my eyes to the sunlight, she would be nowhere to be seen.

# 12

Whatever was holding Aza and me together just let go and nothing we did could hold it. The gulf between us had been made deeper. One day in mid-July, after two months of trying to act normal, I woke up one morning and decided to leave and never to come back. Aza had gone to work.

Popcorn watched me as I paused at the kitchen door with one of my backpacks over my shoulder and another in my hand. They both contained my remaining clothes that the thieves had left behind. I smiled bitterly at Popcorn as she moved a little of her body under the kitchen table as if to acknowledge that she was awake and guarding the place while I was gone. I petted her head for a few minutes, thanking her for being a great friend. I would miss her for licking my feet in my sleep each morning, for farting while sleeping, for jogging with me in the park, most of all for keeping me company while Aza was out drinking with her buddies or not talking to me. I hoped Aza remembered to feed her, take her out to relieve herself, and walk her. I then took a final look around the place that I had thought was ours, opened the door, locked it from outside, slid the key under the door and left. I guess in this business of love it is important to manage your exit. That was how I exited our Linden house, the place I had come to call home for the past eight years. And if the world ever allowed me to love again, I hoped it wouldn't be with a person like Aza.

The sky was clear, with just a hint of clouds. As I drove out of the driveway for the last time, I was seized by a frisson of fear. It was the fear of the unknown, the thought of leaving everything familiar behind me. I was not sure how I felt – whether I was happy to be away from Aza or whether I despaired at having found a false hope. I was satisfied that my finally moving out was not due to malice on my part nor to any disloyalty I needed to apologise for. Perhaps it was a kind of loyalty to myself, a drastic but necessary way of changing my life. I knew at that moment that I would do anything for happiness, even if it meant finding a short-term pleasure. I wanted to spare both of us from heartache. I wanted Aza and me to be happy and carefree in our separate ways.

My fear gave everything a strange thrill. I usually avoided fear, but this time it gave me pleasure to take a risk. I wanted to approach the edge of things, where the sky was the limit. But fear had already deepened into something I could not name. I felt like a bird that had just learnt the joys of how to fly but at the same time was afraid of flying far from the comfort of its nest. It was as if all my life I had been led by the hand like a small child and suddenly I was on my own and had to walk by myself. I had Aza to thank for helping me to reimagine this world in front of me, the world not yet in existence.

I had no plan of where I wanted to go. At least I had one thousand two hundred rand between myself and poverty. I was driving instinctively in the direction of Joburg City Centre, but then I decided to stop at the Melville filling station to think. Slowly I began to prize hearing my own thoughts. Where was my home? I could not go to my ancestral village, Moletji in Polokwane. My sisters would never help me without extracting an emotional price so great that I would have to turn into a child again to count on them. Besides, I didn't have enough money. Also, my relationship with my relatives was not good. So, I couldn't go home even if I wanted to. I didn't have money to help out then and I most certainly don't have money now. They probably still haven't forgiven me anyway.

Thoughts buzzed around in my head. Not to be lonely, not to be scared, I had decided that these were the important things in life as a homeless person. I was tempted to go to The Royal to breathe the pure air of freedom, but then the incident that had happened the last time I was there when the man was nearly thrown from the sixth floor put me off. I had also been ignoring Boni's calls with the hope that I might be able to straighten things out with Aza.

I sat in the car for an hour or two, doing nothing, periodically changing radio stations while scrolling on my cell phone to check whom I could call. There was a smell of petrol in the air. I tried to read the news on my cell phone but had a hard time finding a story that interested me. I watched a YouTube video with girls in it but I could not concentrate. I spent the entire time wracking my brain, thinking up every conceivable kind of a lie, unable to rid myself of the mental image of Aza. Gradually I began to convince myself of how much happier I would be without her, how her frantic energy had sapped my life, how her wild fantasies had deprived me of any life of my own.

A new thought suddenly flashed through my mind. I hear many people say that your first love does not end, especially when you have broken each other's virginity. Mine was not the case with Kamo. I didn't break her virginity, but I tried to go back to her anyway.

She answered my call on the third ring.

'Hey, babe,' I tried to be calm.

'Hi, Mangi.'

'How are you?'

Interest flickered in my eyes, then died when Kamo took her time to reply. This helped me to cast my memory back a little as I pictured her. She had a voice with a peculiar sound which made you feel sorry for her. She also had a bad habit of nodding unnecessarily.

'Are you there?'

'What do you want?' she asked in that brusque and commanding voice.

There was no trace of friendliness in her voice. All the words I wanted to say closed my throat and stopped my mouth. In fact, they crowded my mouth without coming out.

'I was thinking maybe …' I paused midway through my rehearsed speech. 'Is this a bad time to call? Sorry, I should have asked first.'

'Yes, I'm just surprised that a person who disappeared for so many years now suddenly comes calling me, "babe". What do you want?'

'I was just passing by your hood here in Roodepoort and thinking of you,' I lied. 'Do you still live there?'

'Yes, where else would I go?'

Her full picture came into my mind. She had a beautiful face with wide black eyes in which sadness mingled with shyness.

'Can I come see you?'

'What for?'

'To catch up with you.'

'Listen. If your dreams still make sense after you have woken up, maybe that is because you have not woken up yet,' she said.

'After such a long time. No, don't come. A cheater is always a cheater.'

She dropped the call.

I tried to call again and she didn't answer. She had every right not to talk to me. Somehow her reaction made me realise that I can't always play the victim. I had also hurt others in life. Just like Aza, I had been an ass, too. I had failed to think of the little bits of adversity that life kept at the ready, things that could not be predicted and that made a mockery of any calculations.

My brain randomly started to regurgitate images of Kamo and me when we were still together. We had been together for two years before I became serious with Aza. I actually started my relationship with Aza by cheating on Kamo before she finally left me. During that time I experienced commitment to one woman as an imprisonment. In fact, I used to lie to myself that I didn't leave my village home for a life of freedom and adventure in the city to end up chained to one woman. That was me then.

When I was still together with Kamo, every passing day was like an embrace uniting us more closely, more completely. She wanted to have my baby so badly, to settle down with me, to love me. I had put up no resistance to her proposal that maybe we should be together.

After we broke up, she had gone through a bout of depression. She was very close to my mother and sisters, and they liked her. She was so desperate to get me back after we had broken up that she even took a bus to Moletji to ask my mother and sisters to talk to me. When that didn't work, she sent me messages threatening to kill herself, hoping that I would feel guilty and take her back. But that was when my new relationship with Aza was flourishing. We were the best couple, travelling together to Durban, Blyde River Canyon, Maputo and Victoria Falls, and other exotic places. That was before Aza developed a bad tongue. Everyone in my family believed I was obsessed and that Aza possessed a love potion which compelled me to love her.

So, after what I had done to Kamo, I naively thought she'd only reflect on our early days together. It was clear that time was over.

The second ex-girlfriend I called, Naledi, responded with yeses and nos as though she knew well that I was prattling, filling the silence. She had nothing to boast about as far as looks were concerned so I didn't pursue her. Anyway, her body tilted too forward when she walked.

Really, I was afraid of being hurt and rejected, and I would avoid anything that hinted at that possibility.

It was only towards the evening that panic took hold of me. It was the loneliness. It's amazing how a homeless life outside the comfort of four walls makes one more alone. There I was, face to face and alone with myself. The impulse to call Aza and the reluctance to believe that I had finally walked out of her house dominated my thoughts.

As darkness fell, I decided to drive to Rosettenville where I used to live before I met Aza. I was surprised by how easy the act of leaving was and how good it felt. The fear of not knowing where to sleep can sometimes give you incredible strength, if not a pair of wings. I was on the M1 and I felt a gentle vibration of my Hyundai i30. My hands clenched around the steering wheel as I stepped slightly on the accelerator. The needle went up to a hundred and thirty kilometres per hour. That short trip felt like I was flying. My ears were full of the buzzing of a swarm of invisible bees. The trees and streetlights lining the road lost their shape as the car sped up. My field of vision became narrower the faster I drove. But the new idea took hold of me, filling me with energy. I wanted to be away from people who may recognise me, far from ever meeting Aza.

When I stopped at the filling station, the glorious Rosettenville night greeted me. I relaxed in the seat and tried to sleep, but I couldn't. Instead, I stared at the moon and it felt like it had a hole in the middle. The absolute loneliness of the moment was made even starker by the cold winter night.

# 13

The first week I spent sleeping inside my car at the filling station was very stressful. Those were the longest nights of my life and it changed me forever. I felt as if the weight of the world were compressing my chest. I could no longer think with my head but with my heart. My freedom was forgotten and compromised. I often thought of people's faces. I didn't want anyone to see that I had no place to live. At the same time, I thought about my ex-girlfriends, friends and relatives I hoped would call and offer me a roof over my head, even if just for one night. But if you come from Moletji village like me you don't have relatives in Joburg City. My only uncle who used to work in the city had since retired and gone back to the village. Besides, Joburg was now part of me and I was part of the city. Once you live in this city, it touches you more than hands can ever do.

Well, there was no time to wallow in self-pity. I had to survive – that's all that mattered. A memory of Aza came to me. It enhanced my view of her and the place I had just left behind. I realised how much of me was lost along with those memories. I looked at my cell phone many times and wished Aza would call me and beg me to come home because she missed me. She was always in my thoughts, hovering like a great, unseen shadow over my thinking process. Almost every day, the memory of her and how she'd chucked me out of her house, came flooding back to me. Her face, which I had memorised every morning, noon and night for over eight years, hardened before my eyes. The sad part was that I could not bear the torture of this recollection. It penetrated the emptiness in my new life and emptiness became my constant companion.

During those first days of homelessness, my hungry stomach, my empty pockets, not having a roof to live under, and my broken heart taught me the most valuable lessons in life. In my head I had registered a list of ten potential filling stations in and around Joburg with friendly petrol attendants where I could sleep without being harassed or chased away. I wanted to make sure that my suffering and homelessness was at least dignified. To achieve that, I made sure that I didn't sleep in one filling station two nights in succession. As a result, no one suspected I was homeless and unemployed. I also avoided the risk of being banned from filling stations. Often, I would come to a filling station late in the evening pretending to be too drunk to drive; therefore, I appeared to be a responsible citizen who didn't want to risk other people's lives.

Filling stations are relatively a safe place with good security to park a car at night. If I went somewhere else I would have risked my life and the car that I was still paying off. But there was a risk of being seen as a potential suspect by SBV cash-in-transit cars and their armed security personnel who came to collect the money at the filling station for banking. There has been a reported rise in cash-in-transit robberies and ATM bombings by the criminals in Joburg. Anyone like me seen near to or inside a suspicious car was a potential robber. It was only after SBV had left that I was able to gather my terror in my two hands and possess it.

With every passing day, the tide of hope slowly began to ebb. It was as if, with every step, I were trying to pull my feet out of thick mud. My little money dwindled very fast. Somehow, I felt oppressed by the vague sense that I did not belong in this city, or anywhere else in the world. I could only charge my cell phone by switching on the engine of my car. I was reluctant doing so because this exercise tended to finish the little petrol that I had left to move to the next filling station. Unlike when I was still living with Aza, this time around I had to forget about dressing neatly, ironing my few clothes and taking a shower or bath. I had to adapt to a new lifestyle of wearing the same clothes for a week without showering, often using public taps and toilets to refresh at the filling stations that I slept in.

As the cold winter advanced with the precision of a serial killer, the city further disorientated me. I unwittingly became a seasoned insomniac. I knew that sometimes the way to beat sleep-lessness is to outwit it, to pretend I don't care about sleeping. This also meant that I had to get used to the sounds of the engines and the permanent smell of petrol. Because of this, I discovered voices I'd never heard before in my head. Sometimes these voices took on that bitter, stubborn tone. They were voic-es that pointed out my isolation, disorientation and instability, linked to betrayal and abandonment. My mind was full of sen-tences and moments, as if waking from sleep with a heaviness caused by unremembered dreams.

Well, life was like that, I told myself tentatively. It was about highs and lows, blanks and glimpses, and now and then maybe that awful flash of pain. I had to delete all negative thoughts, release the past, and look to the future with positivity and the lightness of a man unencumbered by emotional baggage. That way, I would cope.

# 14

I woke up with the first rays of sunlight at the Shell on Siemert Road in Doornfontein. The sky was still a dark shade of blue. The end-of-July morning sun was blinking through the gaps of buildings from the direction of the Ellis Park Stadium. The succession of identical days had begun. On an average day, hours went on and on, numberless, always the same, bringing nothing.

I went to the toilet, splashed water on my face and armpits, and then changed into new clothes. I felt the sun begin to rise, the air still breezy, before the city clogged up with heat and fumes. The first thing I did was read my messages from my cell phone. I had a missed call and a long WhatsApp message from Aza:

*The car people came by yesterday and the day before. They say they have been trying to reach you and that you have not been able to pay your instalment for six months. They want their car back. Call them or arrange to pay with your bank. You can drop the car here if you want. They have been coming here almost every day and I'm getting sick and tired.*

A momentary flush of anger passed over my face. Joburg, the city I loved so much, was suddenly silent. I felt that I either had to fight this emptiness or put an end to my life. I could no longer bear to watch my life in the city's sad streets.

My heart started to beat wildly and my throat was dry. I felt anger and animosity towards the whole world. I was exhausted by the hardship that beset me and the anxiety that had dogged me. The fear of loneliness, the prospect of losing the car, all welled up in me. Then, about twenty minutes later, I received that dreaded phone call.

'Is that Mr Mangalani Mangena?' a lady asked.

Looking at the number, I realised she was from the car people and decided to compose my voice. My legs and hands shook violently. My lips trembled and I opened my water bottle to drink from it.

'No, this is John, his friend. Mangi left his phone by mistake here before he left for Qwaqwa yesterday.'

'Do you know when he will be back?'

'Yes. After two weeks.'

'Please tell him he must return the car. We have been trying to communicate with him without success and he does not answer our calls or return our emails. Please tell him this is serious and there will be consequences if he does not return the car by the end of the week.'

Beads of sweat trickled down my face. My entire face felt sticky, the sweat now running into my eyes. I opened my eyes and saw many people but yet no one. Just a great nothingness all over the city.

'Where must he return the car?'

'Woodmead, Wesbank Repo Cars. He knows the place. He must call us. We've sent him emails.'

'I will let him know.'

'Tell him it's very urgent.'

'I will tell him.'

'Do you perhaps have his alternative number?'

'No, I don't.'

'What is his relation to you?'

'He is just a friend and former colleague.'

'Do you have an address of where he lives or where we can find him?'

'I only know his house in Linden.' I closed my eyes and sucked in air between my teeth. 'I forgot the name of the street.'

'That's the one we also have on the system.'

'That's also what I have.'

After ending the call, I plunged into a great emptiness. A guard paced up and down outside the convenience shop. Everything in my consciousness, every memory, every idea, was bursting forth in a single spurt, like the thousand flashes of a firework on New Year's Eve.

Despair engulfed the world around me. I had to do something quickly to make the feeling go away. I opened the car bonnet, unplugged the battery, just in case these people tried to trace the whereabouts of the car through the tracking device. But I knew the tracking device had been disconnected the moment I failed to pay Tracker about six months ago. I was disconnecting the battery just in case they had a means of connecting to it.

I would have gone to The Royal if I had money, but I was penniless. So, I left the car and walked towards Joubert Park. At least on that day the sun was very hot, even though it was still winter. I had not shaved in more than a week, so my beard helped to disguise me. My fake Ray-Ban sunglasses further protected me from evil eyes. All of a sudden, I felt joy in staying close to danger. As long as I was hopeful of surviving danger, the beast which that call had awakened in me would never go to sleep again. Yes, no sleep for the guilty, I said to myself as I shook my head.

# 15

The bright morning sun slid gradually over the high iron gate of the Ellis Park Stadium to throw narrow patterns of parallel shadows onto the ground before it. The Joburg heat filled the air in all its intensity. The breeze which had sprung up in the morning had died away like a ghost returning to the grave. As the sun burned down, sweat stung my eyes and I wiped it away on my shirt sleeves. At the corner of Beit and Nugget Street a homeless person stood at the faulty traffic lights with a board that said: 'LET'S DO LUNCH, YOU BUY, WE EAT'. His dirty shoes were falling apart and attached to his ankle with a dark string.

I smiled at the man before spending a moment exchanging banalities with him. His face radiated joy and he had a cataract-ed eye.

'My brother, how is life?' I asked.

'It only takes time, but in the end it will come together, my brother.'

'Heita daar.'

As he smiled at me, rivulets of sweat ran down my back, and my shirt clung to my skin. Before the traffic light, a motorist dropped a cigarette he was smoking on the ground. It lay burning faintly. The homeless man ran towards it, picked it up, and smoked whatever was left of it.

'We shall survive, my brother,' he said to me. 'Life has no plot while we are still living. Surviving means being born and reborn over and over again.'

'That's the word,' I said as I left him.

In front of me the city looked happy and loud, although there were signs of dirt, neglect, decay and ageing infrastructure everywhere. Nostalgia hit me as I crossed the railway line separating Hillbrow and the CBD. A black rubbish bag sailed from the train bridge onto the line below from a hawker, and it burst up, scattering rubbish between the disused railway lines. Big fat rats scattered and then regrouped before foraging the teared bag.

The deeper I penetrated the city, the more diverse the population. I strolled down the congested De Villiers Street, crossed Claim and towards the MTN Noord Taxi Rank. I became acutely aware of the rubbish on the street. The streets were filled with a world of languages. There were working men and thieves of various kinds. As I walked slowly, I might have heard all eleven South African languages and more than a dozen languages that I could not understand. In front of me a young homeless man walked round the edge of a pile of rubbish. The oversized dirty T-shirt that he was wearing made him look even thinner than he was.

At Klein Street I turned to the right into Wolmarans Street, passed the now-neglected Johannesburg Art Gallery building into Joubert Park. The July wind stirred up the black plastic bags before they got trapped by the fence next to the gallery. I couldn't help but move my jaw several times at the smell of the braai meat and at the sight of the flowing coffee at the shop next to the taxi rank. I sat on the pavement for several minutes catching my breath before I could get to my feet.

I wandered through Wanderers Street, enjoying the odd mix of feelings of nostalgia that showed their shadows, then vanished again in my mind. The city looked like it had changed a lot since I'd last walked its streets. There was no sign that it was once a city of gold. All I saw and smelled was rubbish everywhere, fake goods sold on the pavement, peanut shells, an odour of urine in the alleys, broken bottles, roasted and boiled mielies, squashed banana, mango pips, and dirty plastic bags thrown everywhere. Every building I looked at was old and neglected as if screaming out for a coat of paint. I slowed my pace and read the names of different shops like God's Paradise, Sweet Waters and Hollywood Guests. The smell of fish and chips frying wafted through the crowded street. It reminded me of my early days when I'd come to this city to be a student at the university, and how new and enticing everything about the city was.

Time was passing with unbearable slowness. I sat down on the bench at the Joubert Park and watched people play chess using the huge chess pieces and the floor chess board. The person I rooted for to win was an unkempt, agitated man who appeared to be around fifty. He had a bush-like grey beard and hair. The way he posed before he moved his pieces triggered a flood of distant memories and emotions in me. His opponent was light-skinned with a pallid complexion. The front of his head was bald, whereas the back sprouted a thick tuft of hair. He'd bury his fists in his armpits before he made a move. He would then start biting his lower lip quite hard when he sensed that he had made a costly move. Small drops of sweat travelled down from his forehead and he didn't wipe them away.

The sombre thoughts that had blinded me seemed to have vanished as I watched them play. I used to come to this place years ago when the park was clean and safe. I would sit in the same spot and watch people play chess, which was also one of my hobbies. Today, the park looked like a no-go area, especially at night. It was inhabited by thieves, prostitutes and druggies who had populated the city. I was astounded by how old I felt. All those memories that were re-emerging from my past seemed to be shaping my present. My dirty beard, Joubert Park, the nearby Wanderers Taxi Rank, Park Station, the flats – they all created a vast emotional distance on which I could look back, and from time to time I murmured with my eyes half-closed.

Joburg City used to be my home. It had taught me a number of survival skills ever since I got mugged in this city a few years ago. Walking in Joburg City Centre was like carrying my death on my shoulders. One must always watch out for pickpockets, cell phone and bag snatchers. Always pretend you belong to the city. Since the day I was mugged, I had not reconciled with this city. I had an ongoing abusive relationship with Joburg, just like with Aza. As I continued walking, I became extra cautious. Today, Joburg streets are yours; tomorrow, there's no guarantee. That's how disfigured this city was. It had been taken advantage of by tsotsis and like its neglected drug-addicted street kids, it has never regained its soul.

It was in the city that I met Aza and fell in love with her. For eight years until now, she had constituted my whole universe and together we had become ourselves. But ever since I got mugged, I look at this city with great suspicion, just like Aza. I had come face to face with its reality, its mental, physical and emotional poverty. No doubt, this city had turned me into a stranger, a foreigner in what used to be my own home.

# 16

It started raining at around eleven pm when I parked my car at the Engen by Empire Road. My petrol gauge was pointing to yellow, near empty. The parking area was full as motorists were waiting to fill up their tanks. At midnight the price of petrol was going up by a rand and five cents per litre. I was left with about six rand in my pocket, not even enough to buy a litre of petrol.

With the rain came a great hope for me as it lashed hard on the roof and misted the windscreen. I was happy because I thought I had already mastered how to be alone, which was the first step to successfully deal with loneliness. I had cut myself off from everything and everyone because of my poverty and also just to prove I was free.

I reclined my seat, watching the rainwater flow into the filling station yard and on to the street. I had bought a loaf of bread, half a litre of Coke and peanuts for dinner. I started eating the soft part of the bread and left the crust in my plastic bag. More and more cars came to the filling station and waited for the rain to abate. Suddenly, the mist grew thicker, making it impossible to see a hundred metres away. That's when I was able to fall asleep and I had a very strange dream.

It started with the tallest building in Joburg, the Carlton Centre, losing shape and tilting to the side. It was during the ANC election campaign. Somehow, I was a journalist, covering the election using my laptop that had been stolen a few months ago at Aza's house. President Ramaphosa was busy talking on stage and he was facing Small Street. The Carlton Centre in the background was branded with the ANC colours of black, green and gold. The whole area was cordoned off, from Carlton Centre to the now-derelict and abandoned Carlton Hotel and Holiday Inn. As the president was talking, the crowd booed him. That's when the Carlton Centre building started to fall, slowly. And then the nearby High Court building caught fire. Bit by bit it became obvious that the whole city was sinking. The politicians on the podium started to argue as to who'd got the tender to implode the buildings and the city. People screamed and panicked. Then, there was a huge explosion. The Carlton Centre, the former Holiday Inn, the High Court, all sank deep into the ground. Everything nearby was level. Joburg City became a huge lake of water with bodies floating all over. Aza stood at the edge of the lake with Vumani pointing at me. She emitted a soft scream, a sound I had never heard from her before and her teeth turned into fangs, like a zombie. I tried to run away, but my feet only ran in the same spot.

At dawn, the ground rumbled, and there was heavy thunder and lightning. I became watchful and tense, and my heart was pounding. Sleep was heavy on my eyelids. I kept wiggling my toes to stay awake as I was afraid of thunder and my bad dream. I stayed awake like that until about seven in the morning and it was still raining. Empire Road looked flooded with cars moving very slowly to join the M1 South.

I checked my phone. I had a few messages, from Boni, the car people and Aza. Boni wanted to know why I was not answering her messages that she had been sending. Of course she didn't know that I had no budget to see her since I was now homeless. I didn't even have the money to pay for The Royal entrance fee. The car people wanted their car back which was now my home, and they were threatening me with nasty legal consequences. Then I started reading Aza's message.

*They were here again yesterday and this morning looking for their car. Tired of explaining that you no longer live here. Return the goddamn car or pay the instalment. U can afford it since u no longer have rent issues.*

I was affected by the threat implicit in the messages I had read and listened to. I felt limp and drained, just like I always do after an attack. I found it hard to be alone with my own thoughts. Overcome by a wrenching loneliness, I put my phone away, slowly shook my head and kept my eyes shut. Of course, every experience in life has its climax, whether it be happiness, sorrow, sickness or hunger. I tried to convince myself that I had made the right choice by leaving Aza. Why did I expect to be happy when most people aren't in life? God had willed it so. Perhaps these thoughts of mine are just melancholy and confusion which will blow away like dust.

It continued to drizzle outside. While I was reminiscing about the horrors of my life, a petrol attendant guy knocked on my window. Next to him was a woman with an unfurled umbrella. As I opened the window, a sudden gust of wind that accompanied the rain blew her umbrella inside out.

'Sorry for disturbing you, but I was wondering if you could help,' the petrol attendant said. 'This lady and her kids had a problem with their car and was wondering if you could drive them home. This weather is not good for the kids to be outside like this.'

'Please, baba,' the lady pleaded with me. 'I have been trying Uber since four in the morning when our car broke down and I have three kids with me.'

'I understand ma'am. Where is your home?'

'I live in Pretoria, Lynnwood.'

A fierce gust of wind bent a small tree over and pushed the lady forward against the car. The raindrops drummed on the roof of the car. The leafless branches in front of the car swayed and made a whistle. Rustled.

'Pretoria? I would like to help, but the challenge is that I don't have petrol.'

'Don't worry about that. I will pay.'

'In that case we are ready to go. But be warned that my car is not clean. I was hoping the rain would clear up so that I can go to a car wash,' I lied.

'Thank you so much. God bless you. I don't care about cleanliness at the moment. As long as I get these kids home, I will be fine. Also, I need to be attending to something important at twelve and I can't be late.'

The woman gave me nine hundred rand and I put four hundred worth of petrol in the tank. The lady preferred to sit at the back with her three children. The car reeked of my dirty socks worn too long, the quintessential scent of a homeless man.

I joined the M1 North. The driving was slow because of the rain, sixty kilometres per hour maximum and there were a few accidents and stuck cars along the highway. I stole a glance at the woman from the rear-view mirror. She looked impatient as she shook her head up and down, sideways, crossed a leg, uncrossed, rubbed her hands, rubbed her thighs. Her face, although beautiful, reflected her depressed state.

'Thank you for driving us home.'

'My pleasure, ma'am.'

'Our car broke down on our way from Bloemfontein. A good Samaritan dropped us at the filling station early this morning. My friend was gonna fetch us, but she got delayed by this un-stopping rain. Thank God you were there. The petrol attendant and I were just trying our luck when we spoke to you.'

Sometimes a chance occurrence like this leads to endless changes and reversals, and the scenery shifts, I said to myself.

'I was also waiting for the rain to stop. Luckily, I don't have anything planned today.'

'Are you from Joburg?'

She was forever pushing her braids back into the rightful place every time she sensed they were collapsing onto her forehead.

'Yes, ma'am. I'm from Linden,' I lied again.

'I see.'


I dropped off the lady in Lynnwood about an hour and a half later, but didn't come straight back to Joburg. Instead, I loitered in Hatfield for a while. I decided to spoil myself with a decent meal. I entered the Pick n Pay and treated myself to a pap and steak. I ate inside the car that I parked on the street. It seemed to me that all the bitterness of life I'd experienced that morn-ing was served up to me on that steak. As I devoured it, I could feel a kind of stagnant dreariness clearing up from the depth of my soul. I also bought myself two six packs of Black Label beer at the bottle store.

The more I drank the beer the more I thought about Aza. Im-mediately, her beauty and all the pleasures our affair had brought me while we were still together came flooding back into my mind. Now I was acutely aware of all the small pleasures of being alive. Yes, sometimes beer and necessity bestows a man with courage he did not know he possessed. As the hours passed, the urge to see Aza grew in me.

# 17

I don't know how I drove in the rain on autopilot from Hatfield in Pretoria to Aza's street in Linden, Johannesburg that night. I only reflected once I was standing in the rain in her street. It's surprising how alcohol and circumstances can redraw a person's shape beyond recognition. It was past eleven at night, and yet at that hour, some inexplicable force compelled me to come to Aza. The rain was pelting hard and I was soaked as I stood and faced her house. I saw Vumani's car parked in what used to be my spot. That made me furious. Were we both in love with Aza, or perhaps that was the most delusional of all my delusions, I asked myself. Somehow I thought of her naked and bound, blindfolded and spread-eagled on the floor of her bedroom by Vumani. We often don't know we've lost laughter by being away from others, but as we lose it, something in our spirit stops working.

The street was quiet and the rain continued to soak me. It was as if I had travelled back in time in order to carefully study what had happened. Instinctively, I found myself whistling the same song that we liked together, 'Yellow' by Coldplay. The lyrics had remained imprinted on the bar lines of my past with her. I was suffering from a barb of lonely love. It seemed to me that I had spent my lifetime with Aza although we'd only met just over eight years ago. I thought of her body resting against mine in the TV room watching *Friends* with my arm around her.

I cursed myself for not having loved her enough. I stood there calling her name softly, blowing her tender messages with kisses that were scattered by each raindrop. I recalled how I used to rub her body with oil, massaging her temples and forehead. She would be lying on her back with her hands placidly over her breasts. I was seized with the longing to fling myself into her arms. I thirsted for her lips. I remembered the sound of her laughter, but could not remember when I had last heard it.

There was a shrill scream from two cats nearby. I knew she was afraid of cats, spiders and lightning. But what if Aza saw me standing there – what was I going to say to her? Maybe I would say one last thing I always wanted to tell her that would help me wipe away the bitterness, I thought. I would tell her that I loved her, and it made me feel terribly guilty to realise that I liked living without her better than living with her.

Maybe I must use lightning and the rain as an excuse to see her. I wanted to protect her from the elements. But no, I couldn't go back to her house. I was locked out permanently. However much I might plead, however much I tried, nothing could go back to where it was before. I was condemned to be out on the streets. That was my fate. The past had turned away from me. Like they say, one day you're on top of the world; the next day the world is on top of you.

# 18

It was a noisy Friday night in August and people were drinking beer in the streets of Joburg City. As soon as I entered The Royal, a lady greeted me as if she had known me at another time and did not remember me now. She was wearing a very short dress. It was so tight that it contoured the shape of her firm breasts and her broad hips. She also had thick thighs and wore pink nail polish. Her eyes made me feel so naked and her presence kept distracting me from the song 'Pony' by Ginuwine that was playing. Some fine-looking ladies were making sexual dance moves on stage.

We communicated without words and without anyone noticing it. The movement of her fist indicated that she wanted to perform an act of fellatio on me. She even lifted three fingers to indicate that it would cost me three hundred rand. Using sign language, I promised to come to her later. I continued walking around. I saw the light wink out of the lady's eyes to indicate that she would see me later too.

I surveyed the thighs and breasts of the women who were dancing to the song. They were gyrating in circles. I then melted into a dancing crowd at the bar and bought myself a beer. The men smiled with shining eyes and shook their heads, over and over again. In the corner I spotted Boni sitting with a man and I waved at her. She invited me with a smile and a nod to come join them.

'What are my eyeballs seeing? Is it you, Mangi?'

'Yeah. That's me.'

We clung together in an embrace.

'Well, well. Good to see you after such a long time. Where have you been hiding and ignoring my calls and messages?'

'I went to Limpopo for a while,' I lied.

'I guess they are right to say that where there is a vagina, there is a way. It means the umbilical cord that connects you as a man and the nice smell of the vaginas in The Royal can never be severed.'

'Not all men like a vagina, you know,' I said, trying to figure out what she actually meant.

'I know, but those who like it like you remain connected to it forever.'

'You look beautiful, by the way,' I said, trying to shepherd the conversation away from sexual matters.

'If I was, why didn't you come to see me or at least say it all along?'

'It's a bit complicated. Like you said last time I saw you, every man has a forgetfulness condition.'

I sat down and she introduced me to the guy sitting with her. Her fingernails looked like they never had dirt under them.

'This is Ndoda. Our stunt guy. I guess you remember him.'

I stared blankly at the guy and registered nothing.

'I don't think I do. Please remind me.'

'You don't remember the guy who nearly lost his life for not paying for sex?'

'Oh yes, I remember now. That was a long time ago and I think he was wearing glasses on that day if I remember well.'

94

'You have a good memory, my brother. I do sometimes wear glasses.'

'Nice to meet you, Ndoda. I'm Mangi, the man whose money she used to rescue you from those beasts that day,' I said jokingly.

'As you can see he is here again, just like you returned to this place today,' said Boni. 'Isn't life just a big circle?'

There was laughter. Ndoda's left eye was a little smaller than his right.

'So, you're my saviour too.'

'Something like that.'

'He is like a cat. He has nine lives,' Boni said. 'Even after escaping death here, he still comes back.'

'I can't help it. Just thinking of this place is enough to make me feel more of a man again.'

'Ndoda is right. I'm also here with one hope, to discover things I have forgotten about myself,' I said.

'On a serious note, I shall never forget the two of you for saving me from that criminal masquerading as a seller of passion. It took me a while to realise that some women here in this place are natural-born thieves.'

'You're a survivor.'

'My brother Mangi, make sure you avoid women from two provinces while you're here – Eastern Cape and Mpumalanga. Stick to KZN women.'

'And you are back here for more passion.'

'Yes, my brother. Like they say, passion is a moment of madness.' He nodded and grinned. 'Anything is possible after a man and a woman have laughed together and shared their nakedness.'

A young lady led an elderly man to the dance floor as soon as George Michael's 'Careless Whisper' started playing. They swung and floated into each other's arms. Her hips and breasts were ample. Ndoda looked at ease as he tapped his feet to the music. I sat on the chair next to Boni.

'Let me guess, your wife got hold of your cell phone password while you were taking a shower. She found out about me and warned you about it. You then promised her that it was a mistake that will never happen again. She started to keep an eye on you, if I'm correct?'

The question came easily, but I was not sure of the answer to it.

'How do you know? Are you a prophet?'

She rolled her eyes to the ceiling, feigning disappointment. Having been in her company on previous occasions I knew she enjoyed dousing everything she said with a healthy amount of sarcasm.

'I'm a woman, remember. All men are the sons of their wives, mothers and future wives.'

'You seem to have experience in these issues.'

'I have been in this business for a long time to know that men lie much more in cold months and raining days when they're covered in blankets with a lady by their side.'

'I actually broke up with my fiancée.'

She stood up, came closer to me and put her hand on my shoulder. Her eyes opened very wide and she hugged me. She then looked at me with such fierce intensity that I blushed and dropped my gaze.

'Oh, poor Mangi. You look like you are soaked to the bones with matrimonial stress,' she said, her hand on my forehead as if checking my rising temperature. 'Don't worry. Here, in this male clinic, the future is in the past, and the past is in the present. As you know, I'm your doctor.'

'Hard luck, my brother. Love and marriage is a gamble,' Ndoda's voice rumbled as if he had a damaged larynx. 'That's why you and I are here today. Love is like a game of dice. Breaking up simply means you gambled and lost. But in this male clinic we are all winners, especially if you have money. This is like a socialist country. Everyone is equal. You're handicapped, have mental issues, too short, long-tom tall, white, black, it doesn't matter. The question and answer as well as the price is the same.'

'He is right. Here, you will laugh again,' Boni tried to be honest with me. 'Sounds like you need to be properly fucked in order to heal, my dear.'

'That is what the whores are for, after all,' Ndoda chimed in jokingly. 'They are there to put up with the ecstasies of the unlovely like you and me. Here lust and honesty are all in one. If you want love and lying, go home or get married.'

'Be careful. Don't be ungrateful. Who are you calling a whore now?'

'I apologise, Madam Boni. I meant to say ladies who labour through their private parts.'

I laughed.

'Can I tell you a trick? The best way of forgetting about her is for you to think about the things you didn't like about her and list them, one by one,' said Boni.

'She is right, bro. It definitely works.'

'Let me start. What I didn't like about my ex-husband is that whenever he reached orgasm he always squeezed my chest so painfully hard that I developed bruises all over. The police believed me when I filed for abuse later.'

'Is that right?' I asked.

'Mine left because I didn't look into her eyes and tell her I love her while making love,' said Ndoda. 'Why is it always an issue to look at the woman in the eyes anyway? What does love have to do with eyes anyway?' he asked while looking at Boni and then at me. 'What do lovers see in each other's eyes anyway that other people can't see? At least here in the brothel they see money.'

'Sex and love are indeed awkward feelings,' I said. 'Very often, mental problems can be caused by people who mean well.'

'You're right. So, my second ex-girlfriend was a nice girl, but very frightened of sex.'

I tried to think back to when I was with Aza. At the same time, I didn't want to think about that, and I pushed the thought away. I let Ndoda and Boni speak, let their silly anecdotes take me up and carry me along. At the same time a male voice came from the speaker.

'Don't forget you're not here only for beer and music. Ladies are available too.'

There was laughter in the bar and I also laughed. For the first time I realised that laughter scared me these days and I quickly closed my mouth. Laughter seemed like a scarce commodity that belonged to someone else, not me.

'Let me go get a beer for you, my brother. What are you drinking?'

'Windhoek Draught. Or anything that you can get. A beer is a beer, after all.'

'Just don't disappear with a girl,' Boni warned him. 'We are watching you.'

'Don't worry. I've fucked every woman in this place. They no longer make me horny. When are they bringing beautiful new stock from Rwanda and Ethiopia anyway?'

'File a complaint with management if you're not satisfied.'

'Yes, I've been meaning to do just that. Until then, I beg you to believe this, my dear: I shall always remain deeply devoted to you.'

# 19

In their skimpy, colourful skirts, three ladies danced, and they looked like they were half-naked. One of them flung herself about with a detached expression on her face. She began to dance a slow sensuous movement as men reached out to touch her.

'Ndoda is a funny guy. I like him,' I said to Boni.

'He is, isn't he? He paid me double the amount that he owed me for bailing him out from those guys who wanted to kill him.'

'He seems reliable. Is he your pimp?'

'My pimp? Hell no. You can't fuck your pimp. Besides, there are no pimps here. Biggest pimps in the world are at home and they are our parents.'

'What do you mean by that?'

'Parents always choose who is the right partner for their sons and daughters. My own parents wanted to pimp me out to an old rich man in the village in KZN. He was a traditional healer with lots of cattle and five wives.'

'Is that how you ended up here?'

'Yeah, I ran away from my two pimps, my own mother and father.'

For a moment I was left speechless, frozen. I sneaked a sidelong look at her as she took a last sip of her almost-empty Savanna

Dry. The look was to give her a little encouragement to say more perhaps, but she seemed not to have noticed.

'I thought you came here voluntarily?' I said, trying to dig more.

'Of course I came here voluntarily. But the majority of these women you see here, like me, have a history of abuse in common. We all dreamt of being in a good relationship, having a family and children. I sometimes miss cooking for someone and sharing my inner secrets with them.'

'I have also accepted my fate after separating from Aza.'

My words were meant to prod and push her until she released what she was withholding about herself. In fact, we were helping each other to unravel our lifetime of conditions, beliefs, habits and rules that were suffocating us.

'In what way? You mean you're not going back to her?'

'Yes. I mean, I have come to realise that you can't fight against fate. You can't resist the smiles of angels.'

'I'm also tired of this, here. I also want to be myself for twenty-four hours.'

'I can only imagine.'

'Yeah. I can no longer have a fake personality at this brothel where no one calls me by my real name. I want to have my real name back, not only when I'm at home in KZN. You know what it takes to shut off my real identity when I'm here?'

'No. But I reckon that it must be hard.'

'I also want money, stability and family. I keep telling myself that maybe I will meet the right person.'

I pitied her so much that I tried to comfort her. Her eyes looked straight ahead as if extending her thoughts to me. I could not get a chance to ask her what her real name was because I saw Ndoda coming with beers. It looked like he was a big cat at The

Royal judging by the way he walked nonchalantly and talked to every single lady in his sight.

'You will definitely meet the right person. One day, sooner or later.'

'It's easier for you to say that as a man.'

'Maybe you're right.'

'You guys often have a more immediate concern, which is whether a woman will sleep with you when the calling for sex arises in you. Unfortunately, we women are constantly trying to find out who is dateable.'

'But we also do that as men.'

'It's not the same. Belonging to most of us women lies the thorough search for a man.'

'I'm not sure that I'm following you.'

'What I mean is that as women, we have the responsibility to be thorough in our search for the right men because we want more. You as a man can meet your partner anywhere, including here.'

'But it's also important to know that relationships don't complete us, we complete ourselves. I'm also learning a lot after my separation from Aza. If we don't have the power to complete ourselves, the search for love becomes a search for self-destruction.'

The smile on her lips froze and turned into a grimace, and she quickly averted her eyes. Ndoda stood in front of us. He handed me two open beers and a Savanna to Boni.

'Sorry I took a bit long. There was a long queue at the bar. This is the only thing I don't like in this place.'

'I don't believe you. I know what you have been up to. It was the girls.'

'At least I was giving you time to catch up. I will be right back. Excuse me,' he said and went back the same way he had come.

102

I watched Ndoda as he disappeared into the dancing crowd. There was a man at the corner who had just come in and he was staring at us. He was fidgety and kept looking across at us with bulging round eyes. He had a face that made me stop my conversation with Boni and think about him for a second. Upon seeing Boni smiling back at him, the man came and greeted her. He was a short, fat man of about sixty, with a broad forehead, broad nose, broad lips, and broad hands. He had one pierced ear and a young boyish face with big round cheeks, beardless as a baby's butt.

'Are you ready?' he asked, laying his hand on Boni's shoulder.

'Yes,' she nodded.

'Let's go.'

A small gurgling noise came from the bottom of Savanna bottle as she slurped the last of her cider.

'Duty calls. I will be back later,' she said to me while standing up and taking the man's hand. 'It was nice catching up with you.'

I was left sitting alone. A woman wearing a lilac blouse, black leggings, and possibly two large heads of lettuce stuffed in her giant bra came over. A man sitting on my right greeted her gleefully as she jiggled her buttocks and adjusted her bra. It was as if she were dancing to a song in a manic sort of a way.

'Do you wanna go up with me?'

'No,' I said firmly.

She was leaning only a nose-tip away, her eyes upon my face. I felt her breathing hot against me and gently pushed her back. She gave me a contemptuously lewd look, as if she could not allow herself to accept rejection. She went to the man on my right and the two had a conversation. Then I saw Ndoda coming towards me with two women.

'My brother, your fuck is on me today,' he said. 'Consider it a payback time for what you did a few months ago.'

'You don't have to do this, my brother.'

'I swear by the horny spirit, yes, I'm serious. You can use this one. The blacker the berry, the sweeter the roots. The more slender the body, the deeper the roots.'

The woman was beautiful, with a little nose, red lips and long legs, unbelievably clean and tidy. She must take three baths a day, I thought.

'Not yet my brother.'

'I swear she gives good service, my brother,' he said before facing the other woman. 'Or this sweet thing here. She is famous for her cowgirl sex position. The choice is yours. All paid for, courtesy of me. Which one do you choose? Storm on my right or Beast on the left?'

'Give me a moment to think about it.'

'Sex is my mother tongue, baby,' said the one Ndoda called Beast. 'I'm dying of impatience to have you in my bed and corrupt you with good sex.'

'My brother, there's no way you can allow yourself to miss this hot piece of ass. Come on now. Make a decision.'

Her eyes never left my face. She winked at me. She had short blonde hair and was wearing shorts. She then flashed me a smile and lifted her shorts to show me her thickish thigh.

'I have a good idea. How about Beast and Storm together? Yeah, both of us,' said Storm. She wore a velvet miniskirt with red stockings and a pink wig.

'Did you hear that, my brother? When money talks, it is women who listen. Both of them are listening now because they can hear money talking in our pockets. I tell you what, why don't the four of us go now.'

'That's an excellent proposal,' Storm said while making sexual gestures with her mouth.

The lady pressed her leg against mine. That encouraged me to accept the invitation. Besides, I was conveniently drunk. The four of us took a lift to the fifth floor. I had learnt not to care about love any more, or even a relationship for that matter. But I was eager to get all the possible benefits from one and move to the next. It's amazing how our happiness depends on sex, not coffee and whiskey as I had previously been misled to believe.

I left The Royal around one am. The early morning air cooled off my heated body. A homeless man was standing in the middle of the pavement, one hand holding a small plastic bag, the other begging from everyone coming from The Royal. I tossed a two-rand coin into his open palm and went to the vendors. The trees loomed huge in some darkened streets where there were no lights and made a rustling noise. I breathed deeply, feeling the air cooler and softer than ever before on my face. I bought two hot dogs from the vendor and drowned them in mustard and tomato ketchup. While eating the first one, I thought of the next filling station where I could go and sleep. I settled on BP Smit Street, Braamfontein.

# 20

Sunlight streamed down from directly overhead, although it was not yet hot. I was awakened by a rude knock on my car window. I sat up and yawned, ran my hands over my face and wiped sleep from my eyes. A hefty white guy with an unfriendly face was standing by my door and pointing at me to roll down the window. My first instinct was that he wanted to hire me, like the lady I'd drove to Pretoria the other day.

I was wrong. When I looked around, my car was surrounded by three people. There was also a car behind blocking me from reversing. A black guy standing next to the passenger seat was pointing a gun at me. I was cornered. My eyes widened with astonishment at that realisation.

'Are you Mr Mangalani Mangena?' asked the white dude.

'Yes, I am. What's the matter?'

He looked at me for a second as if this disclosure of my name had suddenly created animosity between us. Then he surged towards the door and tried to open it. I stared in surprise.

'I'm here to repossess the car,' he said with some irritation. 'We have been looking for this car for almost three months now. You have been hiding from us.'

'What do you mean I have been hiding from you?'

'We have sent you messages on your phone and email. We

have also visited your last known address. You have ignored our calls too.'

I looked up at him, as if wondering what he meant. My eyes started to blink rapidly. I tried to summon up the small handful of courage I possessed, feeling the sweat prickle my skin.

'I have never received your messages and I don't have a phone any more, so where did you send the messages?'

'We also left many messages with your wife, Azania. She told us she delivered them to you.'

'She is not my wife and I don't know what you're talking about.'

'Stop wasting our time, sir. Get out of the car,' he said while looking at his colleague on my left carrying a gun. 'We need this car now. Give me the keys.'

A few people had gathered around us now. Some recorded what was happening with their cell phones. Lips stopped in mid-sentence, heads turned, and eyes narrowed with keen interest. My heart was beating as if waiting for a miracle to save me. There was a perpetual noise in my ear and I raised my hand like I was swatting away an irritating fly.

One by one the eyes of the people turned towards me, and I remained rooted to my seat. I decided I would play my part with a degree of self-denial.

'I don't owe anything for this car.'

'That's not what the papers are saying,' he said, the conde-scension clear. 'Actually you have not been paying for this car for months now. Unless your name is not Mangalani Mangena.'

'What if there is a mistake?'

'Come on. We can't go back and forth like this. Do you want to do this the simple way or the hard way?'

I then stretched my eyes wide open to match his gaze. The look that he gave me was unsettling and it chilled my blood. He also sounded like someone with a very quick temper and I didn't want to risk a beating in front of all those people who were busy filming. I kept my head down to hide my shame.

'Give me the keys now.'

'You have no right to harass me.'

'I'm warning you. Don't make me lose my patience because it will get ugly. Would you like to remove your stuff before we take this car?'

'This is wrong.'

'You have yourself to blame. We can make the whole process go a lot faster and with a lot less drama if you just give us the keys. The other option will be too rough and I don't even want to go there.' He gestured to my old backpack and a few clothes lying on the back seat. 'Take your belongings and leave the car and the keys. We can call the police if you prefer and that will be too costly for you.'

Donning a disinterested air, I surrendered my car key to him. The spare key was somewhere in the boot.

'But what you're doing is harassment and you are treating me like a criminal,' I tried to reason.

'Maybe you are a criminal. You have been running away from us.'

'It's not like I have robbed the bank. You have no right to point a gun at me.'

'Not paying what you owe to the bank is like robbing the bank. You know very well you failed to pay and that your time has long expired.'

I ran out of breath and there was a long pause. I felt life was changing too fast in front of my eyes. I stepped out of the car. For the first time I smelled the mixed fumes of battery acid, petrol and old oil.

'This is not right.'

'Feel free to report us to the police. Now, are you going to re-move your things or not?'

I watched the man's mouth as he talked. His brow glistened with a sheen of sweat. The tone was quieter now, dropping to its original iciness as he signalled at the others to start inspecting the car.

'You know I can sue you for this?'

'Stop wasting our time. We are working here,' he said with a voice that had a brutal harshness to it. 'Are you going to remove your belongings from the car, or will you come get them after you have sued us?'

'Yes, let me take my things out,' I said. 'But please tell me how you found me here. Did you put a tracker on this car?'

'That's none of your business,' he said, beginning to lose patience. 'Please remove your things. We have a lot to do. But before you leave, you have to sign a form to say that we have the car now.'

'What if I don't sign?'

'Then your bill will expand unnecessarily and you may find yourself in court. Basically, you are fucked already.'

They gave me a paper to sign. I read only the first paragraph of it, my heart hammering unpleasantly. A blur of minutes passed before I came to a page where I needed to sign.

'In case you want to continue suing us, the number and our address is here.'

They left me with a copy and drove away with my Hyundai i30. I closed my eyes, saw the blackness, and opened them to the waiting sun, which stung my pupils. The whole drama had tak-en about fifteen minutes. There was nothing I could do to resist the tears pouring down my cheeks. I didn't know that tears had such a comforting taste as I shook my head, defeated. The feeling of losing my car was like some parts of me didn't exist any more. My own tears offered me a moment of comfort and a needed intervention, which is something I often underestimated and never paid attention to. I sat down on the pavement with my two backpacks in an attempt to regain my usual composure. Some people were still filming me with their cell phones.

# 21

Humiliated, I left the filling station when I saw a man in the crowd laughing at me while talking to his friend. Maybe he didn't know the taste of humiliation. I walked with a slow gait, carrying my two backpacks. Sweat broke out from every pore. My feet made an unpleasant squelching sound as they trod through the mud at De Korte where the paving had been removed near the drainage.

The air in this part of the city had a sour taste. I also didn't like Braamfontein because it was full of students. The streets were full of nicely dressed young people who I felt looked at me as if I had just failed an exam. But I knew this was just my imagination after the embarrassment.

The sun was approaching the middle of the sky. The end dragged on. I didn't know where I was going, except I was going in the direction of Auckland Park via Jorissen Street. Taxi drivers hooted at me thinking that I needed transport, but I ignored them and continued walking. At the Braamfontein Cemetery, opposite the Wits University West Campus entrance, the palisade fence into the cemetery was broken. I paused, entered the cemetery and rested between two graves with huge tombstones. I felt myself growing drowsy. It was as if I had ended my life a long time ago. I had difficulty grasping reality and I thought I was becoming paranoid, near psychotic.

Tender memories, mingling with black thoughts, began clashing in my head. Right away, a new wave came over me. It was one of shame, of regret and yet still one of self-preservation. I felt desolate, lost, roaming haphazardly about in some unfathomable abyss.

By afternoon I became calmer, but still time refused to move. Every second was a century, every hour an age. Numb with exhaustion and hunger, I felt like an outcast from life's big feast. I no longer had any hope of getting out of my situation. The idea of the future, its bleakness and how to survive was my greatest entertainment, amusement and my time killer that afternoon. It is only when you have not paid much attention to the future that you suddenly realise how much the future normally occupies the present, how much of daily life is spent making plans and attempting to control the future. The future was a dark corridor with firmly closed doors at both ends for me. The two factors that helped me through that phase were hope and my desire to live. I was shaken but not broken.

As the city began to travel into the night, my optimism of finding a place to sleep also dimmed. My life as part of the city began to fade, little by little, without one half or the other half of me winning. I lay on my back, motionless, staring around vacantly. I saw objects only as a vague blur. A tear slid along my nose and remained there for an instant, hanging.

The sound of the city birds as they prepared to sleep in the trees punctuated the silence. Only the moon and my shadow were my company. The silhouette of the headstones and the cemetery landscape crowned by the trees made me feel a kind of dizzying energy rising up from my stomach. I would have preferred to hear nothing, see nothing, so as not to disturb the rapture of my recollections.

Then I heard the leaves rustling. I remained motionless because somewhere there was a low noise. Something was coming closer, moving along the graves and stomping. Every nerve in my body tensed up and froze.

The night became oppressive and the cold rose out of the ground. I put on more layers of my clothes. A surprising warmth came over me, but I was filled with fear and foreboding. It was a windy night, and the shadows in the cemetery moved back and forth in the sudden flashes. My eyes were stinging from staring into the darkness.

I thought I heard something again and lifted myself up to have a look around. I felt horribly drained. I gazed next to my bag with panic-stricken eyes. After a few minutes I heard the first scuffles and scurrying by the cemetery rats. I was relieved all my fears were groundless. The rats here at the cemetery were repulsive and huge. Maybe they feed on human skeletons, I thought. I'd seen a few during the day when I'd first arrived. They had horrible, evil-looking faces and the sight of their long, bare tails made me feel sick.

Sleep could not come. And when I was able to doze off a little, I'd quickly awaken, bathed in sweat. I turned my face up to the sky, squinting and breathing like the city was running out of air. Overhead a great mass of stars was wheeling up into the sky. Aza's name permeated my soul and I could not stop myself from thinking about her. Loving her had killed the dream that I once had. Her face would always reappear before my eyes, my ears filled with monotonous buzzing. These were not really thoughts. They were memories that came to torment me in my weakness and put me into a strange mood.

A little before dawn, the cold became severe. Like they say, away from home it's always very cold. I battled with every pulse of energy I could summon not to lose my grip altogether, not to give in, but to stay warm and alive. I stood up to examine my layered body. I smelled. Where did my body end and the air around it begin? Very often, we gain the boundaries of our bodies when we stink because no one wants to be near a smelly person.

Before I dozed off in the late hours of the morning, I began to contemplate leaving the city and moving back to my village. This city, Joburg City, Johannesburg, Johustlerburg, Johassleburg, Jozi, eGoli, whatever I called it, used to be mine. But now it had become elusive, mysterious, and above all, a place of utter alienation. All I could do at that moment was to put my hands over my ears, to shut out the past and focus on the future. That's if I still had the future.

# 22

In the morning, damp had penetrated right through my ragged clothes and my nose had been streaming snot for the past few hours. I decided to dry some of my clothes by spreading them out on a few tombstones.

The birds and insects had also begun their morning praises of the cemetery. I sat on one of the tombstones, just staring into space, not thinking, merely drifting and full of gloomy reflections. I was absorbed in drawing random circles on the ground and running my hand over my silver bracelet. The soles of my shoes were caked with mud caused by the rain of the previous days.

While waiting for my clothes to dry and removing the mud from the soles of my shoes, I switched on my cell phone. It was left with only two bars of battery. I had to be careful not to waste it if I still wanted to be connected to the outside world. Otherwise I had nowhere to recharge it since I no longer had a car. A message from Aza appeared on the small screen.

*Where did you think it would all end? I told you to return the car. Look at yourself now, you have gone viral because of your stupidity. You're trending. You're an embarrassment and I wish I had never met you. I want nothing that will connect me to you and I'm glad you are gone.*

A pain hit my spine and the nape of my neck. A fresh surge

of anger swelled up in me, threatening to drown out all my rational thoughts. I was overcome by embarrassment, guilt mingled with denial. I sat up on the tombstone, feeling terribly alone. Things I should have taken from her on the day I left crept into my mind. Maybe I should have taken her shoes, or even stolen her cell phone. The fact that I had managed to steal her engagement ring was the only consolation. I felt like I had rather repossessed it than stolen it when I found it abandoned inside her jewellery jar. I don't even think she'd miss it.

A lizard basked in the warmth of a rock nearby. I pressed my face into my hands. Great big salty drops were running down my face and into the corners of my mouth. I then stood up, walked about the graves, stumbling over the piles of dead leaves that the wind had blown around. Weeds and grass blanketed the graveyard. Aza's message had affected my confidence. As I sat down on one of the tombstones and opened the video that she sent me, I saw myself crying on the pavement.

I had thought I was finally learning about the trick of survival in that cemetery, of being able to hide in a silent place. I had convinced myself that I was unfit for any living human relationship, and that was why I had decided to live at the cemetery alone. I thought the Braamfontein Cemetery was a space to have my own private thoughts. But no, Aza's message and video had come back to haunt me. I realised that she was still a strong memory, a memory that was inside me, engraved within me. Nothing I could do would dispel it. Her memory came to me in fragments at first, but after a few minutes, it developed into concrete images and a definite theme. I felt panic and great bitterness. Even daylight seemed an unending thing at that moment.

Uninvited, the most distant memories as well as the most recent events started to occupy my mind. I remembered when

I went to The Banister Hotel in Braamfontein the other night with Aza and her pregnant friend, Ona. The place was nearly full as we entered and we scanned for a place to sit. I saw an empty chair and gave it to Ona so that she did not have to stand for long. That was a big mistake that nearly ruined our night and our relationship. According to Aza, I should have given her the chair first since she was my girlfriend and not Ona. I tried to reason with her that I had to give the chair to the pregnant lady first, but she was adamant that I was wrong. Her anger escalated to the point where we decided it was better to leave the place. Aza accused me of deliberately embarrassing her in front of her friend and the other people. I thought she was being petty, but we didn't speak for about a week after that incident.

But when she was in a good mood, Aza would shower me with loving words. She would also send me to the nearby Spar with a shopping list. At the end of that list she would write something like, *And we make passionate love if you come back within an hour.* She would then blow me a kiss, winking at me on my way out of the door. When I came back from the shop, she always kept her promises of passionate lovemaking. That was the Aza I'd fallen in love with. Even at this moment of hopelessness, I still smiled at a memory of that Aza. I'm still amused and often wince pleasantly at the affection that came with her tone of voice when she abbreviated my name Mangalani and called me 'My Mangi'.

Forcefully, I had to stop myself from thinking about Aza and decided to check on my drying clothes still on the tombstones. There was no use thinking about her. My memory of her had become the core of my despair. I needed to map out my plans for happiness that had snapped in the wind like dead leaves. I had to recoup my lost hopes, pick up the debris of life that Aza had smashed into tiny pieces. I had to get something to feed my unhappiness.

A thought ignited a glow in me and lit up my face. In an effort to recapture some sense of myself, I decided I should walk to Braamfontein Liquor Store for a bottle of cheap vodka. I still had about three hundred rand in my pocket, folded nicely with the engagement ring. But in Braamfontein I had to be careful not to be seen.

# 23

I quickly dressed in my hoodie, covered my head and carried my black backpack on my back. I left my clothes inside the other backpack on the sinking tombstone and started walking.

Jorissen Street was full of students and official-looking people hurrying to work with bags in which they probably had nothing more official than their lunch boxes. Some students walked by in their oversized jeans, jabbing messages into their cell phones and wearing headphones.

I was hungry and it seemed as if everyone I walked past was eating. I feasted my eyes on the food at the Braamfontein Centre. Aza's message from that morning kept playing in my head. It stuck to my mind like glue, torturing my imagination. It made me scrutinise every conversation from passersby. I began to assess people's opinions of me on the pavement, based on their facial expressions, their smiles, their frowns, their silences and their glances.

In front of Pick n Pay, a young nyaope druggie stood naked to the waist. His hands were covered with blisters and he was hurling insults while looking up in the sky and cursing no one in particular. People looked at him as if he had contaminated the entrance of the shop. Judging from his appearance he had not been on the streets long, though he was clearly homeless.

Inside the liquor store I bought myself a Smirnoff vodka for less than a hundred rand. I was surprised at how much I had missed my own voice when I gave the money to the cashier, shocked at the hoarse and agitated whisper that came out of my mouth. When a stranger in front of me turned to look at me and smiled, I was flooded with humiliation.

As I walked out, I picked up a used paper cup in the rubbish bin by the door. People looked at me sidelong – that's what I thought, at least, but perhaps they didn't even notice me. I avoided the crowded Pick n Pay and walked to the small shop at De Korte Street to buy some bread and Coke. My face was downcast, my shoulders slumped, my finger twirling a loose string on the hem of my hoodie. I didn't look to either side of the road or see very far. I was thinking that if people recognised me from the video, they would laugh at me and repeat spiteful gossip about me. In the small orbit of my thoughts, I felt like I was turning on my own axis.

I walked down De Korte Street towards the cemetery, stopping by the VW car dealership to pour myself generous tots of the vodka. A man in front of me lit a cigarette, another cigarette tucked behind his ear. Without hesitating, without making a face, like a studied drinker, with my bulging eyes and bobbing Adam's apple, I emptied my vodka from the paper cup. And the rage I'd been feeling was transformed into a kind of jubilation. All at once my desire for life came back and everything that I had promised myself before gave way in the face of that desire. I promised myself that I wanted to go on living at any price, so I couldn't burden myself with emotions that were out of place given the situation that I was in.

When I reached the cemetery, I sat on the tombstone, staring at my vodka. Even when tipsy, I made sure that I didn't step on any grave. My grandfather used to tell me that stepping on some-one's grave brings bad luck home. Stepping on someone's grave is like taking over that person's bad spirits, he would say. Your legs will rot while you're alive, my grandfather would warn me.

Scraps of my family history flashed before my eyes as I sat there drinking my vodka and eating my bread. The more drunk I became, the more I entertained my mind with my grandfather's stories. In my giggling drunken antics, the despair caused by Aza would get blurred. A fantasy induced by alcohol gave me a magical opportunity to escape from my real world and to enjoy a conversation with my grandfather who was already a history away. I would alternate between elation and despair while think-ing about him, my deceased mother and Aza. Another image that came to my mind about my grandfather was that his hair was white, his beard grey and long, and that he walked with difficulty. He never laughed and he prayed often.

My bottle of vodka and paper cup in hand, I decided to walk about the neat, straight roads of the cemetery. I had nothing to do, so I explored the designated religious sections: the Dutch Reformed, Church of England, Roman Catholic, Hindu, Muslim and Jewish. The sight of the neglected graves hurt me. Even here at the cemetery, the dead are divided according to their race and religion, I thought. With the crackling of the dried leaves under my feet, I continued towards the crematorium at the corner of the cemetery for Hindus, passing empty holes and broken plaques. I stopped at the Enoch Sontonga Memorial and poured myself another shot of vodka. It occurred to me to pray and this was the first time such a thought had visited me. I wasn't a religious person, so instead I took a sip of my vodka. It was as if stretching back into the mist of time. I remembered that during my History lessons in high school I had been taught about

121

the founders of Joburg: Von Brandis and Jeppe. Enoch Sontonga, who composed the country's national anthem, was buried here in the Native Christian section. I walked slowly while reading the names on the stones, like Schowl, Reinholtz, Reginald, Darrell, but I found not a single black surname in that part of the cemetery.

Many of the graves had been desecrated. The whole cemetery itself was desolate, lifeless, without movement, so lone and so cold-tempered that its spirit was not even that of sadness. I inspected the writings on the headstones. In my drunken mind I mapped out the history of the people who had died centuries ago and had been buried in that cemetery. Even a dead person has his place to sleep in peace, but we, the living, are homeless, I thought. I think the human race respects its members more when they are dead than when they are alive. Otherwise why do the dead have a place to sleep in peace while we suffer in the cold? Did all these dead people perish while searching for the elusive gold in Joburg City? Isn't this city built literally on top of a gold mine, I asked myself. Am I a mad person? Have I gone mad? Just because I don't see things people see or have things that people have, does it make me mad? The dead are not afraid. They don't get angry and hit someone, I told myself; that is why I prefer living among them.

I turned back to where I had set out from and began to retrace my steps, quite invisible, my feet having left no imprint in the earth to start with. I walked in deep shadow, but the flat rays of the sunset filled the treetops with light.

I reached my own part of the cemetery just after sunset. At first, I had been saddened by the vandalism in the cemetery. Then resentment had seized me when I'd realised that there was no African surname except for Sontonga. But the Braamfontein

Cemetery was where my city history education began. It began as a glimmer before it gradually became a solid awareness.

I felt imprisoned by the city. I was filled with the heedless violence of a man who had his lifetime cruelly wasted in the city. But what's that got to do with me, I asked myself. I'm from the village. I'm alive; they're dead.

That night, I dreamt of Aza. We were at a Jimmy Cliff concert at the Johannesburg Stadium. There was silence at the stadium and everyone lit their firelighters when he started performing 'Many Rivers to Cross'. He was shirtless, his chin overgrown with a beard, his thick dreadlocks dangling in wet tendrils around his ears. I was standing on top of a tombstone belonging to Enoch Sontonga, singing with tears in my eyes. Aza sat on the stone belonging to Johann Rissik and she was holding her firelighter. She came up to me, but just as I took her in my arms, she dissolved into dust in my embrace. I wanted to run away, but my legs refused me.

This tantalising dream opened up in me the hatred for her which was as powerful as my love and which was nourished by the same roots. In the same vein, this piercingly sweet vision remained in my memory as the most beautiful of all the possible dreams. Every time I was alone and dozing off, I kept striving to recapture its sensation, which still lingered in my mind.

# 24

In the morning, birds began their morning song and the sky lifted its curtains of darkness. The sun suddenly spilled out on the eastern horizon. I looked around to orientate myself. My thoughts were racing. My cheeks itched because I was not used to having a beard. Besides the hangover, I was in high spirits, thinking about Aza. Her face still came floating in and out of my mind like a butterfly. It was as if all my thoughts belonged to her. In a sense, it felt as if I were cheating on her if I failed to think about her all the time. Maybe it was nothing more than a bad attack of loneliness and fear. I knew I needed some closure with her, something that would help me not to think or dream about her like I had the previous night. I didn't know anything about happiness any more. I wanted to unload all the pain and hurt that I still felt inside me. That was the only way I could survive.

An idea grabbed hold of me that I should get rid of the two things I thought reminded me of Aza. My cell phone and the engagement ring. The thought of selling our engagement ring gave me a satisfying sense of revenge. I immediately retrieved it from my backpack, used one of my rags to clean it, and then put it in my jeans pocket.

At around eleven I left my things in the sinking grave again, grabbed my backpack and walked towards the city centre. My aim was to find a buyer, first at the few second-hand jewellery shops that I had seen along Bree Street Taxi Rank. If that didn't work out, I was thinking of walking to Fordsburg where there were cell phone shops and jewellery stores owned by Asian people. I had all the answers ready if they asked me where I'd got the ring from. I would tell them the ring belonged to my fiancée who had since died. I mean, it was not far away from the truth anyway. I had bought that ring at fifteen thousand rand for Aza and was hoping to recoup at least half that amount.

I was not in a hurry as I crossed Mandela Bridge, separating Braamfontein and the city centre, towards Bree Taxi Rank. The air was full of invisible menace, howling, whistling and hissing. My mind was full of Aza's image, as though I had activated a playback of my past with her, and she was in charge of it with a remote control. I thought about how often she would be angry at me for things that were beyond my capacity to fix at the house. What has my love for her ever done for me but disappointed me, I asked myself. Sometimes love is given too much credit. Love is an illusion. Sometimes in our lives we have to say no to love. I must banish it from my vocabulary from now on. Love makes you think you can avoid pain. Love and marriage are two comedies of deception. They are both bonds of sorrow, and it is a pretentious bond of compromise. As far as women are concerned, I have always lacked a simple quality known as caution – perhaps you might call it common sense.

I should have learnt a long time ago from Aza's actions that I was naive in love and wasting my time. When the washing machine or vacuum cleaner had a problem, she always expected me to fix it. When the kitchen unit fell, she expected me to be a carpenter; when the toilet blocked, she expected me to be a plumber. But when my friends and one of my sisters came to visit me, she always gave them an icy brush-off, conveying the clear message that anyone lower than the president or governor of the Reserve Bank had no real business dealing with her. She started hating my friends. I had never been a man for quarrelling and bickering, so I'd grudgingly never brought them in the house again. She never instructed me not to, but it just made life easier.

I tried to refocus my mind on something positive that we shared, but every attempt I made to conquer this negative feeling only served to strengthen it. Instead, my efforts to recall positive things about Aza gave me more reasons to despair and intensify my estrangement from her. It seemed as if the more she became aware of my undying love for her, the more she repressed hers, to keep it hidden, and also to weaken its hold.

The sight of a robbery taking place at the end of the bridge distracted me from my present thoughts. Two young men had snatched a lady's handbag at the traffic lights. She had stopped at the red lights with her car windows open and her handbag on the passenger seat. I cast my glance in the direction of the running robbers. A slight fear stirred in me, but really only very slightly. It was a rational fear, which was enhanced cautiousness. This episode briefly shushed my memory of Aza. But somehow, I wished it was her who had been robbed. My hatred for her had grown intense. I wanted her to fall down and break into pieces like me.

I passed two young women wearing matching denim cutoffs and baggy T-shirts emblazoned with the name of Wits University on them. As I walked past, one of them put her hand over her nose as if to keep out a nasty smell. My insecurity and unresolved anger had sharpened my sensitivity and I was convinced that she had smelled my disgusting homelessness. I sensed I had become a dangerous and bothersome existence to people. I was like an actor, and people walking by were like my audience. I had to pre-occupy myself with something – anything – to silence the voices in my head.

There was a nauseating smell of old cooking oil at the taxi rank. I could feel the sweat running down my arms, between my nipples and at the back of my knees. I decided to cut my hair and beard at the Bree Street barber for fifteen rand. I then entered the toilet, scrubbed myself hard under the tap, soap vapour making my eyes sting, while dark thoughts swirled in my head. Each time I lifted my armpits, I smelled the foul odour they gave off.

Freshened up, I put on a cleaner shirt that I had retrieved from my backpack. I peered into the mirror, trying to recognise my-self before I walked out of the bathroom, satisfied. I had grown thinner. My face was longer, my eyes large and nose flatter. Out-side of the toilets were many vendor stalls and I bought myself a cheap roll-on and perfume for my stinking armpits and body.

Walking slowly, I spotted a cell phone shop ahead. A homeless boy was standing by the wall, his hand pressed against it, as if he were fascinated by the coarse texture of the whitewashed wall on which he was rubbing his fingertips. His trousers looked as if they had originally belonged to somebody bigger than him.

I entered the shop and spoke to the Asian man behind a glass counter. He looked at me up and down, his glasses resting on the edge of his nose. He leaned forward and took his hands out of his pockets. He had a narrow gap in the upper row of his teeth.

'How can I help you, my friend?' he asked, his voice tinny, as though coming from a cheap radio.

'I'm selling my phone.'

'What kind of a phone? Let me see.'

I gave him my Huawei P30 Pro and he carefully studied it while punching something on the keypad. He looked at me directly for a while and I mentally begged him to redirect his gaze to the phone. He took a short breath, then smiled insincerely and blinked.

'Okay, I will give you four hundred.'

Negotiating a sale had never been one of my talents, but I decided the amount he was offering was too little for a ten-month-old phone. I tried to negotiate for more money, but the stubborn shop owner was in a take-it-or-leave-it mood.

'Give me eight hundred.'

'No. I can only give you four.'

'Are you joking? This phone is less than a year old and still costs more than five thousand in the shops. No, that's too little.'

I pretended to be walking out when the shop owner stopped me. I heard him talk to the man next to him in their own language, and I could tell the words were friendly ones. I knew they had reached some agreement when I saw his unshaven, pouchy mouth smile and heard his soft, gentle voice.

'Okay. I will give you five fifty and that is it.'

'Five fifty is better,' I sighed and bowed my head in assent.

I wanted to negotiate for more money, but my ignorance of how to do it drove the idea from my mind.

'You say it's not stolen?'

'It's my phone. Not stolen.'

'Okay. Give it to me. Where's the charger?'

'Here.' I searched my bag and gave him the charger.

When the moment came to part with my phone, my courage nearly failed me. Reluctantly, I removed the sim card and gave him the phone. The man forced a nod as he gave me the money.

Outside, the homeless boy's forehead was now pressed against the white wall as if to guard it from the heat. He stood unsteadily, rubbing his face with his hand.

For the ring I didn't have to walk all the way to the Oriental Plaza in Fordsburg to sell it as planned. I entered a jewellery shop a few blocks away and they offered me nine hundred rand, which I accepted. That sale made me temporarily feel free from some unseen burden. I knew I was a defeated man, but I stopped hating Aza, at least for a day. The anger that I had felt towards her melted. The money had enabled me to set aside my unhappiness. I was as happy as a person who had just managed to extract a bad tooth. From that moment, I told myself that I would begin concentrating on how to endure being alone. I was one thousand six hundred rand and some couple of cents richer. This included the few rands that I still had on me.

With the money in my pocket, there was only one place that I was thinking of, The Royal. And in next to no time, the dirt and stink that I had felt covering me dissolved. Without wasting more time, I hailed a taxi to End Street and got off at Nugget. I was full of hope, fertile with illusions of being rich.

Out of the blue I could hear the voice of my grandfather saying to me: *Mangi, life is like water; you can't grab it and hold it in your hands. You can only plunge into the middle of it.*

# 25

Inside The Royal you encounter two different systems of societies simultaneously. On one hand is a system of matriarchs who sit by the door and entice men to have sex with them even before the men settle in and have time to look around. These are mostly the experienced veterans of the place. They know the game well and are aware that their time as sex workers is nearly up. In this side of The Royal, women look like they are in control. They sit at the entrance with skirts or dresses hiked up and their blouses slightly open. Boni belonged to this system. She and her group of friends knew how to work on a man and give him a good time worth what he had paid for.

On the other side is the system of patriarchs who sit around the bar watching and targeting the young women with their miniskirts and tender flesh the colour of milk. In this system, men think they are in control because they can buy their power by getting a beautiful-looking young lady. This is where Ndoda belonged. This corner is right inside next to the pub. It is full of shapely ladies with incredibly round breasts and curvy asses. On the matriarchy side women dress up to charm you, and on the patriarchy side young ladies dress up to flirt with you.

What both sides have in common is that time is suspended by lust and jealousy. All the men inside The Royal respond by

130

resetting their clocks, usually in the early hours of the morning when they leave. This is also what I missed about The Royal. I liked the racy, adventurous feel of it at night, and the satisfaction that the constant attention from women fed to my loneliness.

I admired the way all the women at The Royal had a technique to make the first move. Once they knew who they wanted, they pounced like a hungry leopard. I liked the women staring at me from afar. That stare was like a dance

As usual, The Royal was full. 'Creep' by TLC was playing and the women were dancing so beautifully. I elbowed my way towards the bar. A lady gave me a suggestive look. She had straight black eyebrows and wide shoulders, but was too narrow-hipped and altogether too thin. My eyes locked with hers for a minute and she invited me with both her fingers to join her on the dance floor. I smiled but ignored her and walked to the bar. She continued swaying to the rhythm of the music and gently nodding her head at another guy who had just come in.

From the bar, with a beer in hand, I walked about, hoping to see Boni or Ndoda. I couldn't locate either of them in their usual seats. Opposite the toilets was a huge flatscreen TV set where patrons sat and watched the English Premier League game between Arsenal and Manchester United. I went to the loo. On the door was written 'size doesn't matter' in huge letters. The urinal also had the words 'Ctrl alt and delete'.

Coming out, I heard some noise. Strangers hugged and swung each other around as Arsenal scored a goal. For two hours I just roamed the bar, blind with alcohol and grim with lust. Like most men in there, I pretended I was in control, and most of the ladies assumed that I was.

I spotted Ndoda as he entered through the door. It looked like he had just arrived. He scanned around as if looking for someone.

His eyes darted about anxiously, hesitantly, to the right and left. Spotting me near the counter, his eyes focused on me with recognition. He then came to where I was standing. He laughed a bit, as if slightly shocked to see me. He was wearing a formal blue jacket and a shirt with 'SABS' printed on the breast pocket. He looked a bit agitated.

'My brother, I haven't seen you for a few days.'

'Have you been good?'

'Yes. Very good. I thought you had forgotten about this place when you vanished like a shadow,' he said as he jokingly poked me on the ribs.

'I was busy sorting out life.'

He stood still and looked up and down at the other patrons with his unwavering eyes.

It seemed he was not locating the person he was looking for anywhere. He continued to gaze about the place, scanning every person's face. From time to time he stopped to shake someone's hand or make small talk with them. He seemed to know a great number of people at The Royal, and they all looked glad to see him, treating him with special respect because of the way he was dressed up on that day.

'Who are you trying to find?' I asked.

'I'm looking for my colleague. We are late and we have to be at work. Have you seen someone wearing something like this?' He pointed at the SABS logo on his shirt.

'No, I haven't.'

'Okay, let me look for him. See you around.'

Less than five minutes later, he was back. He appeared fidgety while he waited in silence with his eyes averted. Lowering his gaze, he clenched his fists, then pulled off his glasses and looked at me from head to toe.

'Do you want to make a quick buck, my brother?'

I was startled and temporarily disconcerted by the straightness of his stare and question.

'For sure. What can I do for you?'

'Okay, come with me.'

'But what is the job about?' I asked as I followed him. 'I hope it's not about killing someone or robbing a bank. That, I cannot do.'

'No. You will see. It's basically nothing. You just sit around and not talk. That's your job.'

Outside, a Mercedes-Benz was waiting with two white guys inside. They were also dressed like Ndoda. The one in the driver's seat had a beard that ran into sideburns. Fine wrinkles spread all over his face like a spiderweb. The other guy was busy smoking. Both of their faces had an identical expression, a mixture of shock and curiosity.

'Where is Tom?' asked the guy in the driver's seat.

'I looked for him, but he is not there. But I trust my friend Mangi here.'

The driver looked at me again and frowned. 'Are you sure?'

'Hundred per cent.'

One of the guys gave me a curt handshake.

'I trust you. If he fucks up, it's all on you. Give him the uniform, then. Time is running out.'

'What is your shoe size?' Ndoda asked.

'Size eight.'

'And your trousers?'

'Thirty-three.'

The car reeked of cigarette smoke. The guy in the passenger seat was a chain-smoker, lighting a cigarette with the butt of the first one he was still smoking. When the driver talked to him in Afrikaans, he nodded vigorously.

Ndoda went to the boot of the car and came back with the uniform, the same colours he was wearing. I put it on as we drove towards Germiston. I still did not know where we were going and was afraid to ask. I also didn't know what was the proper way to act. When you have nothing to lose, you have more time for everything that really matters to you to continue living. You don't have much in the way of ordinary fear, but are afraid of death, of course, which is different because death is physical. The most important rule to learn when you're homeless is that it's about what you're made of, not the circumstances you find yourself in.

I looked at Ndoda as his fingers pulled absently at his scanty beard. There was a small knowing smile on his lips and his eyes looked into the distance ahead. I had been told by my grandfather in Moletji that before something great happens to you, everything falls apart. Maybe now was the time.

# 26

The car stopped in front of what looked like a shopping complex parking lot. The chain-smoking man got out of the car first and pulled out three files with papers from the boot. He distributed each one of them to us. Although his shoulders were not particularly broad, his jacket seemed tight round the armholes, and revealed, through the slits of his cuffs, sun-reddened wrists unaccustomed to being covered.

I was given a name tag on which was printed 'Mr Thomas Moloto. South African Bureau of Standards'. Ndoda helped me to clip it on my jacket after fixing his own.

'You look good, my brother,' said Ndoda.

'Thank you.'

'Yeah, sometimes you have to threaten poverty and enemies by just dressing up in a suit.'

'Thanks for the advice.'

'I mean it. You have to wear a good suit and cologne, walk into a car dealer with a briefcase with nothing inside and ask for the price of the latest Mercedes-Benz.'

'Okay, boys, let's get started with the stocktaking.' The driver spoke softly, rapidly, as though afraid the words would dry up. 'We only have until nine in the evening.'

The four of us walked into an Asian shop with a sign 'Afro Asian

International' on the entrance. The owner, a small Asian man, spoke little English. He first stared at the unexpected visitors, blinking rapidly, as though not quite believing his eyes. As the two white men spoke to him, he slowed down, his eyes scanning the nameplates on their jackets as though looking for something specific. At first, the Asian man's hands worked in the air, unhappily trying various lines of argument. Then I saw his head, half-nod, half-shake. His glance leapt between us. My heartbeat was a little faster, but my nervousness quickly vanished when I saw him shake hands with the white guy.

'You, Ndoda, will start on that shelf. You, Tom, on the left side until you meet in the middle. Ndoda, you will brief Tom on how to do this quickly. We don't have time.'

That was it. We were targeting shops owned by the foreign nationals. My job was to walk around the shelves with Ndoda marking goods that had expired or without the South African Bureau of Standards stickers. We recorded everything in the file that we were given. Ndoda even had a camera to take photos. At the clothing shops we checked the fake clothes on display mostly with misspelt names, Nike logos facing the wrong way, Adidas with double 'd' letters, a Lacoste logo with a crocodile that had a tongue, and so on. At the restaurants we checked the kitchen cleanliness, the adherence to safety protocols in case of fire, the number of foreign workers, and whether they had work permits, especially in Chinese shops and restaurants. We ended up at the KFC kitchen where, after doing our job, we were given two buckets of chicken to eat and some to take home with us. We might have checked about twenty-five to thirty shops with the two white guys doing the talking all the time. In each shop we spent no more than forty minutes. The two white guys would talk to the manager in the office and come out smiling and happy.

I was given one thousand five hundred rand for that day's work and my hope began to swell. The world was good and simple.

When they dropped us off in Hillbrow that evening, the white guys promised to be in touch again soon.

'Good job, inspectors,' the driver said, while the other white guy nodded encouragingly at us. 'We will see you next week. We will be working in the Rustenburg area.' He concentrated his gaze on my face. His hollow, dead eyes and dry lips seemed detached from the smile that played on them. 'We will communicate via Ndoda since you say you don't have a phone yet,' he said in a low voice, as though he was asking me a favour. 'If you want us to buy you a phone we can do so. But we will deduct it from your salary.'

'Not yet, thanks. I will buy it after the Rustenburg trip.'

Together with Ndoda, we removed our uniforms, putting them in the boot of the car before heading straight to The Royal. I had stuffed as much KFC chicken into my belly as possible, and now was the time to booze as much as I wanted, so that the passing hours without a place to sleep were not so empty. I was planning to stay at The Royal until the morning when I could walk the city safely.

'Are those guys real inspectors from the SABS?' I asked.

'Who cares, my brother. This country and this city is fucked up already. You need to use your brain and tactics in order to make it.'

'Well, I understand.'

'It's important for you to know that this city is divided into two types of people: the crooks and the semi-crooks.'

'I guess we are the semi-crooks.'

'Yes, and all the politicians and businesspeople are crooks.'

'It's survival of the fittest and bravest.'

'You're getting it now. This city we live in is a strange world, one in which some things matter more than your truth. It is only the rich who cannot afford to be smart in this world. You and I need to commit ourselves to something absolute in order to feed ourselves and our families. This world is governed by man-made rules.'

At the entrance of The Royal, Ndoda slipped a hundred rand note into the Lord of the Rings' hand. He was so happy and he thanked Ndoda with a smile. After some small talk, we were allowed in without being searched.

'I meant to ask, have you seen Boni?'

'No, my brother. Actually, the last time I saw her you were there too.'

'I wonder where she went to.'

'Maybe she has found a new man – it doesn't matter. You have to choose other women too and forget about her. There are plenty of them in there.'

'Maybe she is doing exams. She told me she was doing second year at UNISA.'

'Whatever, man. Good luck to her.'

I felt Ndoda was being ungrateful for what Boni had done for him, saving him from death by the bouncers that day. He tapped me lightly on the shoulder.

'You must get a new girl, my friend. You need a girl that can climb on top of you to straddle you like a horse. Boni is too old for that.'

As soon as we were settled next to the bar, a woman saw us. A wild surge of joy made my exhausted body quiver all over. She came over smiling and climbed onto Ndoda's lap, kissing him. She wore an orange dress that loosely fitted the curves of her body. She said her name was Rori. Her painted fingernails hung like pink flowers on her fingers. Her friend came and sat on top of me uninvited. Toni Braxton's 'Breathe Again' was playing in the background. The lady kept pretending to be pulling her right breast from under her loose blouse to entice me. There was no need for words; it was as if she could read my needs at that moment. I looked at her breasts, which were round and firm. She then undid the two top buttons of her blouse and strutted in front of me, showing off her cleavage. I wanted to lose myself in her, to cease to be a homeless me, to be transported to heaven on her borrowed wings. Within an hour, all four of us went to their rooms upstairs.

# 27

I left The Royal around six in the morning. With money still in my socks, I felt as if the future held a promise for me like a golden fruit dangling from some not-so-distant tree of life. I had spent about eight hundred rand the previous night on Rori's friend. It was worth every cent. It covered a few drinks, accommodation, a bath, which I took twice, and good sex. I was also allowed to use her towels, perfume, soap and lotion. Before I left, I asked Rori if she knew Boni. She said she didn't know her even when I tried to explain what Boni looked like. Rori was new at The Royal.

Leyds Street was already full of people coming and going, people who could be from anywhere. A cold wind smelling of rain blew across the street. I walked slowly, sniffing the aromas that came wafting out through the kitchen windows and doors of the different restaurants. At corner Claim and Wolmarans, people spilled out of a taxi. A smile of relief spread across my face when I saw the city busy again. I felt comfortable and satisfied.

My mind was not yet sufficiently clear for serious application of any kind. Walking helped me fight off the loneliness. Since I didn't have anything to do, I liked wandering around the city. It helped me to remember things and I was generally moved by the sight of people and the buildings.

Walking along Wolmarans, I passed Joubert Park on my left

heading towards Park Station. Interrupting the horizon in the distance was the tall Carlton Centre. I walked past the billboard which carried an advertisement of a man eating a slice of pizza. The road surface around there was worn out and full of pot-holes. I put each foot down slowly and firmly for the sheer plea-sure of feeling the stickiness of the tar and hearing it detach itself with a tiny sound like a kiss. I felt the sweat spilling out of my pores. The smell of oil or petrol wafted across me.

It was a grey morning and the sky looked dirty like it was going to rain at any time. The monotonous Wolmarans Street stretched with nothing to entice my eye. I passed a few ruined buildings and whistled thinly between my tongue and the roof of my mouth in disapproval. It was as if that part of the city were full of lost souls ready to be cleansed. A homeless man stood next to a shop collecting cigarette butts. He carried a cardboard sign with the words: 'Hiring someone to take care of me finan-cially. Full-time job.'

The idea seized hold of my thoughts when I saw people come out of the dilapidated building. Maybe it's one of the many neglected city buildings that have been hijacked by the city crim-inals, I thought. Discarded newspapers, rotten bread, watermelon rinds piled in a pyramid of rubbish in front of the building. The stink concentrated around the grisly overflowing bin was stifling. I covered my nose with my arm. A girl walked past, handing out leaflets, and she was met with a cold shoulder. A young man standing nearby dropped his paper after glancing at it for a second.

As I kept walking, I realised that sometimes solitude can be a good thing. I had all the time to think in the city. In the process of thinking, my memory of a clean Joburg was shattered. I strug-gled to remember the details of how I used to visit the Razzmatazz

Club on the parallel-running Smit Street. That was in the same year that I first came to Joburg. It was at the Razzmatazz where I first saw great musicians such as Mdu and Arthur perform. I used to frequent the Little Rose for cheap beer and sex during that time.

I thought of all my yearnings for luxury in the past. I remembered all the privations my soul had endured over the years, the degradation of my relationship with Aza, and my dreams of wanting to be an electrical engineer. All these dreams had fallen in the mud like a wounded bird. Everything I had longed for, everything I had denied myself, everything I might have had if I had married my high school sweetheart, Makoma, all these remembrances, came uncomfortably to my mind. They weighed on me heavily like a hiker's backpack that had been drenched by the rain.

The smell of vetkoek at the shop by Wanderers Street brought back a long-forgotten memory from my childhood. It reminded me of how my late mother back in Moletji used to bake vetkoek for us over Christmas. We would stuff the achar inside and eat it with Joko tea. But the name Moletji also conjured up images of watery cabbage for dinner, goats, cattle, donkeys, unemployment and poverty.

I went inside the shop, removed money from my sock, bought six vetkoek and instant coffee. There were a few taxi drivers inside who were also having their breakfast. In rapid succession, and with eyes watering with satisfaction, I gobbled up a vetkoek.

Outside, the first drops of rain pattered on the pavement, followed by white hail of stones falling everywhere. People started running to find shelter under the building awnings or inside parked cars. With the rain, the hailstones and the smell of vetkoek I found myself wondering how many other memories were hidden from me in the recesses of my own brain. All this filled me with wonder at the prospect of some day discovering a new world and life after this homelessness. I had existed in timelessness, no news filtering in from the outside world. My survival at this point was a hand-to-mouth affair that depended on my awareness. I had to readjust my expectations in life.

The rain was falling in large drops. Earth-shaking peals of thunder exploded again and again above the city. I was worried about my stuff that I had left in the sinking grave at the Braamfontein Cemetery.

A young boy stood near the door of the vetkoek shop, afraid to come in. His dirty trousers were rolled up to his knees. He glanced around uneasily before wiping the rainwater off his face with his hand and looked inside quietly. He had sunburnt skin that was peeling off his nose. I gave him two vetkoek from my packet and he thanked me profusely.

The rain continued to hammer down on the roof and hiss in the gutters. Without warning, my memory began to let me down badly by turning to Aza. Those thoughts, at first unfocused, wandered aimlessly, like city rats running in circles over the overflowing rubbish in the street corners. Then everything in front of me – the buildings, the street, the people – became so blurred and mixed up in my mind that I found it difficult to distinguish them. In the centre of it all appeared an image of Aza's face and there were many of her voices in my head. There was an infinite number of versions, an infinite number of realities of her that had formed inside my head. She was overly hateful to me.

*Are you going to eat all that? My ex used to say I love you in the mornings and you don't. You always do that as if you're a child, how many times must I tell you not to do it? You must man up. Do I look fat in this? Never mind, I'll do it myself. I'm used to doing things on my own. I can't live without you, babe. I'm not your mother, you know that. What's wrong with you? It seems I'm the man of the house. They have what you don't have. I downgraded myself when I met you. He treated me better than you. He spoiled me more than you can. You cannot dictate to me by telling me when is the best time to come home. I'm an independent woman. It's my money. You can leave if you want. I'm a grown ass woman. He knew how to talk to a woman, you don't. Maybe I made a mistake by being with you.*

I sat down, leaning against the window, so absorbed in thoughts of her that I heard nothing. Heavy rain battered against the windowpanes. The sour taste of panic rose in my throat and my eyes hurt from squeezing them so tight thinking about Aza. I was too immature to overestimate my resilience to her memory. But how could she take over my feelings like this, dwelling in the depth of my being, clinging to me? She had shattered my certainty in everything around me. 'Try to accustom yourself to it, Mangi. She is gone and life goes on,' I said, clapping my hands firmly together.

My eyesight blurred and I began to hyperventilate probably because of the heat inside the shop. My calves started to shake. I decided to walk out. There was still a drizzle. I stopped for a few minutes in the rain to let my nerves settle, and then stared up above the clouds. Feeling better, I trudged along the flooded Wolmarans Street, trying to numb my brain with the noise of the city, without being able to rid myself of the obsession hounding me.

The drain ahead gurgled. Two women in front of me walked under a tiny yellow umbrella. I walked with springing up and down motions to avoid puddles of rain that had formed in the

144

potholes. I felt my shoes getting submerged in the water. Aza's words halted as abruptly as they had come when a taxi's wheel splashed the flowing rainwater on me. I cursed, grinding my teeth in rage. Closing my fist, I straightened my middle finger and pointed it at the driver. The driver didn't even notice me. I was panting with anger. All I could do was stand there, shivering and hopeless.

# 28

The grass at Braamfontein Cemetery was still covered with water droplets, resembling tears on eyelashes. The bark of the trees streamed with moisture and the hailstones lay melting on the ground. In some places the surface of the path had been covered with mud. I had to step on large stones to get across. Most of the sinking graves were filled with muddy water. I found my bag submerged in one of the graves, like my hope floated off into oblivion.

It was getting dark and the whole cemetery looked spooky. The wind started to blow and the trees hissed. The rapidly quivering leaves rustled as the treetops gave their vast sighs, swaying endlessly back and forth. Drops of the earlier rain nudged off, falling with a ticking sound on me. The identical trunks of the trees planted in their straight rows stood out like dark ogres. I stared into the darkness. There was no way I could sleep there that night.

Carrying my wet bag, I left the cemetery and walked towards the city via Smit Street. I was halfway across when I felt the rain again. Out of the blue the sky just emptied itself in a terrible downpour. It began to fall all over my body, clinging to me, and there was a greater weight on my clothes and bag. It was already dark and through the lights of the slow-moving cars I saw a group of people running to take refuge under Smit Street bridge. There were about five people there, all males, circling around a fire. I turned a corner and stopped against the wall, my mouth dry and my heart beating miserably too fast. Paranoid thoughts began to form in my head. What if these are killers? What if they rob me of the money in my pocket? Will they strip me naked first, sexually violate me like I heard they do in jails?

After putting my bag down, I greeted them collectively with a smile, a hi and a wave of my hand.

'Hi, I'm Mangi.'

Surprised, they all looked at me and nodded. The older one seemed self-absorbed and moody. I was relieved to see two younger ones, they looked like they had rolled in the mud. These ones, I could easily defeat should a fight ensue, unless they had guns. The older one stared at me for a long time in silence.

'Welcome to our home. My name is Regulator. This is Bhoboza.' He pointed at the guy with a cyst on his forehead. 'And that one is Ghostface. Those two who fell in the mud are Seatbelt and Airbag.'

Regulator was short, thickset and round-faced. His unshaven cheeks were covered in stubble. His hair, some strands of it long and some short, stood up on his unwashed head. His eyebrows almost joined in the middle of his forehead.

'Nice to meet you.'

'Welcome to our city of broken dreams. Come and join us.'

They allowed me in their circle of fire. It was almost impossible to grasp the fact that there were human faces above those torn bodies, faces in which life went on from day to day under the bridge.

'Are you planning to be a citizen of our little city?'

'I'm not sure yet.'

'How long are you planning to be our resident?'

'Tomorrow when the rain stops I will leave.'

Regulator scratched his legs and looked towards the evening sky. The one called Airbag appeared to be the youngest of the group. Judging from the mud coating his shoes, they had walked a long way.

'Ah, so you are a resident in transit.'

'Maybe.'

'That's what this guy Airbag said the first time he arrived here seven years ago. He never thought he would be a permanent citizen of this city under the bridge.'

Regulator laughed loudly and the rest joined him. I was a little annoyed and embarrassed. Ghostface's laugh was as dry as his skin. It added up to some kind of genetic misalignment.

'It's just a temporary arrangement.'

Regulator nodded curtly at me with wide eyes. It seemed he already knew that I was lying and he made me uncomfortable. When I encounter a personality like that, I tend to step back because I don't know how to deal with it. Maybe I had developed a suspicious attitude towards people because of what I was going through. My hands started to tremble and I didn't know if it was because I was scared or if it was the wetness and cold.

'Okay, then. You look like a man who's got it all figured out,' he said sarcastically. 'Just don't forget us wherever you go.'

'I won't.'

'Where were you before you came here?' he asked, scratching his rough beard with dirty nails.

148

I didn't like the question; I felt it gnawing at my disguise, peeling back layer after layer to reach where I was hiding.

'In Linden.'

'As in Linden in the suburbs?'

'Kind of, yes.'

'Which house or park or bridge?'

I looked at the ground, as if the false answers in my head were written there.

'The one called Emma Park.'

'Are you sure? Because your body tells a different story.'

'What do you mean? What story?'

'From the state of your shoes, from the smell of soap when you first sat down, from your bag next to your feet, from your nicely shaved head, I mean everything about you. You can't hide it even if you try that you are new in the streets of homelessness. Have your rich parents finally cut you off their wealth?'

'I don't have parents.'

'But the way you look tells me that time has not yet lost all meaning for you, unlike us.'

I knew it was an ugly joke and made with the intention of wounding, intimidating and showing me who was boss. I kept quiet and continued to warm myself at the fire. The front of my clothes had dried, so I turned my back against the fire to warm the rest of me. The smell of decay grew and it was beyond description. It dawned on me that I was among the homeless. City poverty had created a new kind of human being in them. It was the kind who lived like outcasts under a bridge and I was about to join them. This realisation shook me.

Seeing sacks of their possessions cluttered on the narrow pavement near the entrance, red ants that ran, forming strange pictures on the wall of the bridge, I knew that my life was now out of balance. The politics of the stomach brought us all under the bridge of poverty, and the shadow it cast was as long as the time. I was at a fork in the road and luck wasn't running my way.

# 29

The rain pelted down, water streaming down the street. We could feel it beating hard on the tarmac, thrashing at the walls of the bridge, spilling itself ferociously over the city. At the same time Airbag took out a plastic bottle and poured some cheap liquor into a steel cup. He drank it with obvious distaste, and quickly, as though it were some unpleasant medicine. Then the cup went from one hand to another.

'We live under communism here in the city of broken dreams,' said Regulator after drinking his share. 'We share everything.'

'That's very nice to know.'

'All animals are equal. Ask our philosopher Airbag here. Like you, he came here smelling of soap. But within twenty-four hours he was disfigured like a true citizen of the city of broken dreams. I swear to you that everything gets disfigured on these city streets.'

Seatbelt rubbed his palms together in a gesture of joy and confidence after taking a sip. The cup was handed to me and I took a small sip. The liquor was very hard for me to swallow and I had to force it down as it burnt my Adam's apple. But it reminded me of my bottle of vodka that I still had from the other day. I took it out and everyone celebrated like it was Christmas. That was how the six of us cemented our new friendship on the first day. It was by sharing a cheap Smirnoff bottle which was half-full.

'Welcome to communism in our forgotten city of broken dreams,' said Regulator while pouring the vodka in the cup. 'From now on we are all brothers.'

He swallowed the vodka in one gulp, allowing a good part of it to wet his scruffy beard and run down his neck. With the movement of a victorious wrestler he came towards me and hugged me.

'Thank you, Mangi.'

We drank with joy. I kept shivering under my damp clothes. The bottom part was not yet dry. My feet were chilled and despair was reigning in my heart.

'From now on you are part of us. You can stay as long as you want.'

'Thank you, guys.'

'Hoorah!' Seatbelt shouted while lifting the steel cup.

There was another outburst of merriment among us. Regulator slapped his thighs. I was sitting next to him and he was chain-rolling joints.

'There is your corner to sleep near Airbag. Normally, the rent is five rand per night. You get a cardboard box to sleep in and a blanket with that. But for you tonight is free.'

'I appreciate it.'

'If you want to pee you go there to that tree, not on here or in our blankets.' He laughed at his own joke that I didn't get. 'If you want to do a number two you go inside that cemetery of white people and choose whichever sinking grave to shit on.'

'On a grave? Are you sure?'

'I've been doing that since I came here. There is also a tap inside there to wash. Or you can go to the one inside the old Braamfontein train station, which is a bit far.'

I was shocked to learn the connection between the city of broken dreams and the Braamfontein Cemetery. More shocking – even under the bridge, one had to fight for a space and a right to live.

Airbag removed some piles of books to make room for my sleeping corner. I could not read the titles because of the darkness. He spread out some boxes on the ground.

'So, you like reading, too?' I asked curiously.

'Yes, a woman gave the books to us. She passes here sometimes to give us food and old clothes.'

Airbag was of a peaceful disposition as he responded to my question. I liked him a lot. Bhoboza was busy rolling a joint, mixing it with butts of cigarettes that Regulator handed to him. He lit it and took several puffs before passing it around. It was the length of a thumb when it got to me. I took two puffs and quickly passed it over to Seatbelt. They laughed at me when I started to cough.

'Your first time smoking?' asked Seatbelt.

'Yes. I don't even smoke cigarettes.'

'Welcome to life under the bridge, grootman. You will need this if you live with us long enough to experience the cold days. You're lucky you joined us in spring.'

'I bet I'm lucky.'

'Being a homeless beggar is not a kind of profession you can do if you don't smoke or use drugs, grootman. It's like saying you're allergic to grapes but you want to be a winemaker.'

Seatbelt took the joint, sucking in a drag so deep that the flame reached his fingertips. But he seemed not to care. Those two puffs seemed to have an effect on me. I was stoned and everything suddenly changed. The tone of people's voices, the image of the city in the dark all seemed to be upside down. I didn't know what to think and whom to listen to.

'You know the chameleon, my brother Mangi?' Regulator was talking to me as he rolled another joint.

'Of course I know the chameleon. I'm from the village. What about it?'

Regulator looked at me for a few seconds as he formed the strip of paper into a trench for the joint. He was holding it between the thumb and third finger of one hand. The tip of his index finger was placed in the hollow of the trench, keeping it in shape.

'The chameleon, my brother, is the only rainbow animal in the world that becomes black, green, yellow or red, according to the place where he is found,' said Regulator.

'I know that.'

'Yes, but I want to congratulate you,' he said, lighting the joint.

'For what exactly?'

'For adapting so fast to the life of the city of broken dreams, just like the chameleon.'

'Alright, I get it now. I hope you're not saying I'm a chameleon.'

'No. This is meant in a good way.' He took a few puffs of the joint. 'You know, when Mandela and Tutu called this country a rainbow nation they were thinking of the chameleon. They expected us poor people to adapt fast to our poverty and homelessness. Look at us – we are living under the bridge of the city of broken dreams.'

Regulator was looking at me in the face hoping I would come up with a beautiful comment. He passed the joint to me and I took three puffs.

'Yes, the future is in the past, and the past is in the present,' I said out of context.

154

'You are right, my brother,' said Regulator. 'The whole nation of this rainbow has become a nation of madmen, including Mandela and Tutu themselves. May Mandela's soul rest in pieces.'

I saw the bridge swaying, tilting and climbing up the sides of the road. The sky was lower. A mist hung over the bridge. A few ribbons of vapour lay along the horizon, following the outline of the hills, while others, separating, drifted higher and disappeared. From time to time, the clouds parted on the distant roofs of Jozi. The whole city resembled a vast, pale lake evaporating into the air. At such moments something resembling happiness actually stirred in my chest, but it was not the sort of emotion I wanted to lean on very hard. I started to giggle, and everyone looked at me and laughed. We all giggled.

'Regulator is right,' said Airbag. 'Those two grandfathers sold us a fake rainbow with the colour black in it. A normal rainbow doesn't have the colour black.'

My confidence rekindled and my face glowed. Silently, I thanked the rain for awakening in me a sense of comradeship to help me escape from the abyss of isolation. Each drop that fell hard on the city that night drew out the positive side in me and stored it up in my heart as a reserve against the onslaught of loneliness.

The night dragged on until we didn't know what to talk about. Around us, in spite of the cold, mosquitoes buzzed or hummed incessantly. They took advantage of the fact that we were all stoned.

Past midnight we were surrounded by darkness and silence. The storm had been weathered. No cars passed for a while and it became colder. Only the ants, the mosquitoes, the flies, the rats, the rot, the smell invaded our silence. If I had not been heated by earlier walking, the fire and by the persistent glow of the vodka and the joint, I would still have been shivering. Seatbelt had offered me one of his two blankets. It was lice-infested, coarse and warmly itchy; it was very uncomfortable to sleep in. The whole night I kept slamming my hands together in an attempt to kill mosquitoes. Since I could not sleep, I watched from the bridge as the morning crept over Jozi, my city.

# 30

The next day of steady rain rolled on, wet. Grey skies, grey liquid. The signs of decay that had been blotted out by night were becoming visible again. Since sharing the bottle of vodka, joints and conversation, I had slowly begun to get used to the city of broken dreams under the bridge. I had adjusted to its ruggedness and everyone was becoming familiar with me, and I with them. Our conversations often stoked the embers of my memory and glowed in my mind afterwards.

That morning the air felt charged with tiredness. I spent about forty minutes killing the lice that crawled everywhere in my clothing. The lice and the mosquito scratches on me had turned black. We all looked hungry and tired. In our hand-to-mouth city, no one seemed to have a plan for the next meal. I assumed it was like that during the rainy days, but this year it was an unusual kind of rain. It was risky for homeless people to go out to beg. Very few motorists open their car windows to give alms.

Our heads were bowed, our faces full of misery. Only Airbag seemed to have energy as he sat against the wall and read from an old copy of *Drum* magazine. His eyes were fixed on a paragraph. Ghostface on the far side of the bridge was looking blankly past me. His nostrils kept sniffling convulsively. At one point

I thought he grinned at me so wickedly that I got quite a fright in case he was warning me over something I was not aware of. And then, there was Bhoboza next to him who rarely spoke and even then, only a word or two. He seemed introverted, almost cold. Regulator was washing his face with rainwater. I'd known as soon as I saw him yesterday that he was a ready-to-die type. The cigarette he rolled from gutting the cigarette butts from the night before was as thin as a pencil. Only Seatbelt pretended to be still sleeping as he twisted and turned while scratching his dirty head. The entire morning, two rats had been playing around the leftover food. A panther-rat ran out of a thicket, darted across a path and vanished into a small bush.

I went through Airbag's collection of books, which were about eleven books, all American novelists I hadn't heard of before. The love that I had for him for being a reader was like a fire that was fed on books.

'So, you read all these?' I asked while looking at the underlined pages in some of the novels.

'Yes, I love reading. Books are my companions in hard times.'

'I can tell.'

'How about you? Do you like reading?'

'Not like you, I think.'

'My dream was to become a literature professor at a university. But then there was no money at home to send me to school when my father died and my mother remarried.'

'Sorry about that. Where do you come from?'

'Marapong in Lephalale, Limpopo.'

'I'm also originally from Moletji near Polokwane.'

Airbag moved his eyebrows a lot when he was thinking, but they were still when he talked. The tips of his ears were slightly dirty. He couldn't have been more than twenty years old. He wore a red jersey that looked like the one I used to own, which had been stolen from Aza's place. The only difference was that his jersey looked old and dirty. For a moment I thought he and his gang were responsible for the break-in, but I immediately dismissed the idea when Airbag said he had never been to the northern suburbs. The fact that he was from Limpopo made me like him more and I trusted him to look after my things. I also felt a need to protect him.

By a stroke of luck, the rain paused abruptly. Fortunately, no one had changed their mind and asked when I would be leaving the bridge. Before Regulator influenced everyone to do so, I offered something special to the group.

'Gents, I want to go to Pick n Pay to get some food,' I announced. 'Who's coming with me? Airbag, let's go if you're done reading.'

That was enough to sweeten everyone's mood. The jubilation which beamed on every face filled me with joy.

'I'll come also,' said Regulator, uninvited.

'I'll tell you what, why don't you and Ghostface or Seatbelt go buy us some weed for tonight. I will give you twenty rand.'

I realised I would now be treated as a hero. I was deliberately taking over the reins of the city of broken dreams.

'Give me the money, I'll send Bhoboza and Ghostface,' said Regulator.

I gave Regulator twenty rand and he accepted it with a smile. I became suspicious that he might go through my bag while I was gone, so I changed the plan.

'Okay, I will go with Regulator and Airbag to the Pick n Pay.'

'I will walk to the snyman alone,' said Ghostface. 'The one at Melle sells the best weed, so I will go to him. No more the Bree Street fake.'

Ghostface jumped up and put his arms in the sleeves of his jacket, ready to go. The three of us, Regulator, Airbag and I, set off for Pick n Pay on Jorissen Street. As we walked, Airbag's worn-out laceless Nike shoes flapped.

Along the way, I asked Airbag about the lady who donated things to them. Maybe it was Aza. I didn't want her to find me under the bridge when she came again.

'A white lady, I guess?'

'No. She is an old black woman.'

'Okay, I see. Very old?'

'Sort of. About fifty and she drives a white Volvo.'

'Oh, okay.'

I looked at Airbag again, his jacket drowning his tiny body. His too-long sleeves hung over his hands and the fabric of his creased trouser legs bunched up over his dirty shoes.

I didn't go inside the shop for fear that somebody may recognise me. Instead, I gave Airbag two hundred and fifty rand to buy a two-litre Coke, a whole chicken, twenty-five vetkoek and a bag of wood. I then gave a hundred and twenty rand to Regulator to buy us a bottle of Smirnoff from the liquor store, the same vodka we had had the previous night. Of course he also bought himself a pack of twenty RG cigarettes, which was less than twenty rand. That was why he'd insisted on going with us in the first place. On our way back, I made Regulator carry the bag of firewood. The rain started to pour down again before we reached the sanctuary of our bridge.

There was a great feast that afternoon. Alcohol and weed made everyone talkative. We told one another all the vexations the week had brought, and we gazed at one another, laughing with delight as we exchanged stories. It wasn't because we were naturally cheerful that we made jokes. No. We kept cheerful because, if we didn't, we'd be unable to deal with our poverty and homelessness. Our restlessness was a result of happiness, not of suspense. Surprisingly, Ghostface was also in a cheerful mood and was pleading with me.

'You are welcome to stay with us, grootman,' Ghostface said while puffing away on the joint. 'I know you're supposed to leave but I wish you don't go.'

'Yes, please don't leave soon,' said Airbag.

'I will consider your requests and stay just a little.' I took a puff of the weed. 'Why do they call you Ghostface, by the way? Is it your real name?'

'Back home in my village in Kuruman, everyone thought I looked like a ghost with no face.' He grinned at me, revealing a mouthful of prematurely rotting teeth. 'And the name has stuck with me ever since.'

Regulator plucked another chicken piece from the plastic packaging and began to delicately strip it of meat with his teeth.

'If we don't finish and throw the bones far away, the ants and rats will soon invade our space and irritate us the whole night,' he warned, but we ignored him. 'They may even bite our feet.'

That made me a bit scared, but we continued to drink, telling one another fantastic lies about our experiences. Seatbelt told long stories about his past, embellishing, embroidering and dramatising in the manner of theatre actors. We had created our fantasy city that was so far off the scale that nobody was able to connect with it.

'They call me Seatbelt because they thought everyone has to fasten their seatbelt to avoid falling from laughter when I start talking.'

'Ah, is that right?' I asked while laughing.

'Yeah, I'm special because I'm like Julius Caesar. We both came through the rooftop in this world.'

'What does that mean?'

'My mother was so young when she had me. I didn't want to come when it was time for her to give birth to me. So, I blame the doctors for forcing me into this world through caesarean to live under this bridge. There was no path open for me after I was forced to be born.'

'And where were you born?'

He started talking non-stop. His mouth and nose looked too small for his face. He then brought out the dab of Vaseline he had rolled up in a twist of paper and smoothed it on his lips.

'In Vereeniging. I'm the only one here who is from this city. Actually, this city is mine. But I found Regulator here. If I had superpowers after I was born, I would unleash a storm of pain and suffering to those doctors.'

'But why would you do that instead of thanking them?'

'Thank them? No way. They led me to this broken-down, burnt-out, rootless life without a hope.'

'That's deep, bro,' said Regulator. 'I told you that you must consider writing poetry.'

'When life confronts you with grief and great confusion, you will always be a good poet, my brother,' he responded. 'So, I'm not surprised that you think I can be a good poet.'

'And you, Regulator, where do you come from?' I asked.

'Umtata. My friend, the Rock, and I used to live here before these ones came to join us.'

'Where is your friend now? He left you alone?'

'No. One morning he woke up dead. It was a very cold winter.'

162

'I'm sorry to hear that.'

'It's part of life. When death does come, you must open all your windows and doors and prepare to embrace it.'

'Still, that's sad.'

'Yeah. He was buried in a pauper funeral somewhere here in Joburg. I couldn't go because I left him over there and when I came back they had taken him to the mortuary.'

'Dying is only disappearing from view. At least he was buried in the city,' Seatbelt interjected. 'Imagine being buried in a cattle kraal in some Eastern Cape village.'

'But you can't say that,' I protested.

'But it's the truth, grootman. Have you ever been to Umtata? I once drove there with my uncle when I was still young.' He pressed his hand to his forehead in reflection. 'It's a neglected godforsaken place. The potholes in that town will change your radio station and unlock your car doors if you ride over them by mistake, they are so big.'

We all laughed, except for Regulator. From time to time he looked at me, coughed and sniffed violently.

'Well, in a fantasy anything is possible,' he said, feigning annoyance. 'You like speaking shit about my hometown.'

'I tell you. If you're a child like I was, those potholes will move you from the front seat to the back of the car.'

'Fuck off.'

'But that's right. And it's the government's fault and not yours. That's why young girls from that town look older. It's because of those potholes. They make the breasts of young women fall before puberty. And when you are wearing a bra, those potholes make breasts come out of it.'

There was more laughter. I had been watching Ghostface, seeing the way he had been constantly grinding his teeth and clenching and unclenching his fists. Airbag was resting his elbow on my backpack and listening to him.

'It's all lies,' said Regulator, lighting his cigarette and then shaking the match elegantly, one, two, three times, to extinguish the flame. 'As I was saying, Airbag was the first to arrive about seven years ago.'

'So, that makes him the second-in-command of the bridge after you?' I said as I took a sip of the vodka from the steel cup.

'You could say so. I used to see him carrying stacks of books and diaries and notepads around the city until he landed here. The others joined five or six years ago. Bhoboza here comes from Mpumalanga and he is good at catching the city pigeons which we roast here sometimes.'

'Bhoboza's pillow is also made out of pigeon feathers. And that's why he believes he can fly,' Seatbelt interjected.

There was laughter again. Ghostface and Bhoboza, on either side of Regulator, followed the movement of his hands as Regulator handed a burning cigarette to Airbag. How sad to think that a number of talented, self-styled survivalists and peaceful people were sheltered under the city bridge.

'How do you do that?' How do you capture city pigeons?'

'Simple, grootman,' explained Bhoboza. 'I feed them the crumbs of bread and catch them.'

'We are at war with hunger here,' Seatbelt said. 'You and I are misfits. We don't belong anywhere. Anyone with morals must be out of our way.'

In the early hours of the morning, while it was still dark, there was a commotion. A mob of fleeing rats stormed into the dugout and they ran along the wall. I shouted and cursed while trying to

hit the rats with a piece of wood. The rats squeaked and scur-
ried away. I couldn't sleep until the morning. I just stared in
front of me, trying to doze off. These people were right. A homeless person has no other choice but to fight, even against the rats.

# 31

Each day under the bridge brought with it more doubts and questions. I had learnt to find joy and happiness in situations and places where other people would go mad. The good news was that, little by little, I was forgetting about Aza. As for her memory, it was buried deep down in my heart. She was gradually being replaced by the people under the bridge. Whoever said that the only certain happiness in life is to live for and with others was right.

On Friday night, I came back from my SABS job in Rustenburg with Ndoda. We were dog-tired from driving and working under severe heat, checking every shelf of the shops we had visited. We might have done around thirty shops that day. I had officially replaced Thomas Moloto, whom the two white men thought was unreliable. Strangely, they had never addressed me by my name. I also didn't mind that they didn't bother to print my nametag with my real name on it. They even called me Tom, sometimes referring to me as 'my friend'. I was willing to let go of my own name and identity in favour of this new promised world I had assumed, which was glamorous but corrupt. I knew the two white men as Kobus, the chain-smoker, and Martinus Moustache. That was enough for me to separate the two.

I was sleepy and the lights of the car illuminated a little blur of the highway ahead. From time to time I would open my eyes, but then my mind would grow weary and, sleep returning, I would fall into a kind of doze again. My sleepiness would somehow mingle with my memory of Aza, my bag that I had left under the bridge with Airbag, our dog Popcorn, Moletji, The Royal and Braamfontein Cemetery. Sometimes I saw myself as many different people at the same time – as a boy herding goats in Moletji, as a first-year UJ student, and then as Aza's husband. What if I hadn't come to the city, I thought. Maybe I would have been a big livestock farmer in my village by now. The questions echoed back to an untouched corner in my mind where bits of my own childhood still lived.

One thought of Aza dominated me for about twenty minutes. One day Aza was angry with me because I had forgotten to defrost the fridge. She didn't talk to me for almost two days until I made a plan to force her into a conversation. I knew she was afraid of spiders, so I killed one from the tree and planted it on our toilet seat. Upon discovering it, Aza screamed. She came running to me in the kitchen and pleaded with me to come kill the dead spider. From that moment, we were on speaking terms again and she came and snuggled in bed with me. But it took her two days before she used our bathroom again. On the day that she first used it again, she asked me to stand at the door until she was finished taking a bath. That hilarious memory made me smile.

Kobus lowered the window and, driving with one hand, let his right arm hang over the side of the car. I started toying with the idea of a good sleep and comfortable bed. Maybe I should book a cheap hotel room at Formula 1. I had a box of eight pieces of KFC that we'd got for free so I didn't need to worry about food.

A sweet sky, full of stars, had descended when they dropped us off in Hillbrow. It was already midnight.

'Today you two have worked hard,' said Kobus as he removed his spectacles, rubbed his eyes, and breathed slowly and deliberately. 'I will give you a little more.'

'Thank you.'

'Next week Friday we are going to Witbank.'

He was polite, but I couldn't say he was also friendly. He gave me one thousand eight hundred rand and left. I didn't know how much Ndoda got, but he insisted that we go to The Royal for an hour before inviting me to come and sleep at his place on the corner of Pieterson and Quartz streets.

'Thong Song' by Sisqó was playing when we entered The Royal. We left our bags with the KFC inside with the Lord of the Rings. A group of four women stood around the bar smiling and holding their cider bottles. Another group stood at the periphery of the dance floor. I watched the dancers as they grinned and waved their arms. The disco lights flashed on and off. A few non-dancers blankly scrutinised the dancers or stood in groups laughing.

We didn't stay long at The Royal because we were both exhausted. The two of us walked slowly side by side to his place. Ndoda kept slowing his steps to keep pace with me. He looked this way and that, stopped walking, and listened to the sounds around us as if he were being cautious of the city criminals. In front of a lamp post, a swarm of flies buzzed in the heavy air. Each minute or so, he slowed to a stop, spat into his glasses and wiped off mist with the sleeve of his shirt.

We walked into a dilapidated dark building with the name 'Vannin Court' inscribed on it. Broken glass was all over the place and there were live wires of electricity connected along the corridor all the way up to the stairs. What used to be a lift in the building was now filled to the brim with a heap of rubbish, from cabbage leaves to empty bottles and tins. Huge city rats were busy scavenging. For a moment I wished I had a mask to put on my face so that I could avoid the smell.

We climbed all the way up to the fifth floor, jumping over leaking pipes and using Ndoda's cell phone torch as the only light. Several questions formed in my mind. If I'd known he was bringing me here, I would have said no, I said to myself. This place was not better than living under the bridge or the Braamfontein Cemetery. What if Ndoda's plan was to rob, kill and then dump me here? Why had I been so stupid? I remembered the building that I'd seen on TV burning about a year ago and imagined myself in that building among the dead.

The darkness was thick. It felt as though the light had never existed in this building. Some moments, Ndoda's phone torch would switch off for a few minutes and he would stick his hand out, touching the wall and rail on either side with his hand or fingertips as if he had become used to walking in the darkness.

We stopped on the fifth floor. Ndoda leaned his head against the rails after opening the door with his key and together we slid into the flat. The flat was partitioned about six times for six people or families. Pieces of cardboard had been used to patch where the windows were broken. Boxes, second-hand furniture and clothes hung in darkness, as if in a buried city. In front of me, Ndoda stumbled over things and cursed.

'Fuck. Who put these here?' he asked no one in particular.

Ndoda shared the kitchen, toilet and bathroom with five other people. At least they had running water and a dirty bathtub. There was a curtain that separated Ndoda's room and the bathroom. What used to be a balcony had been converted into some-one's bedroom and was closed off with zinc sheets.

'This is only a temporary arrangement, my brother,' he whis-pered. 'I'm moving out soon.'

'This is fine by me,' I lied. 'How many are you here?'

'I think we are six and we are from all over the country and outside. At the balcony is a guy from KwaZulu-Natal. We get along well. The others are from the DRC, Malawi and other places.'

'Sounds like a United Nations building.'

'Yeah, in a way it is. I have a very big house back home, seven bedrooms and two bathrooms.' His cell phone torch shone on his face and I caught a glimpse of him smiling with an air of complacency. 'Here in the city we are just visitors, my brother. You can't invest in this shit-hole of a city called Johannesburg.'

'I know. Where is your home?'

'Gwanda, Zimbabwe. And you, where is home?'

'In Linden,' I lied again.

'But where is your real home?'

'Oh, it's called Moletji, near Polokwane.'

'Oh, I see. The rent is very cheap here.'

'How much?'

'Four hundred rand a month. That includes unlimited water supply and electricity. But we have not had electricity for the past three weeks.'

'Well, that's affordable.'

The walls were brown and the room was dimly lit. Only Ndo-da's face in front of me was alive and clear. The flat smelled of tinned fish, air freshener, our sweat and the KFC.

I slept next to Ndoda, facing opposite directions in his single bed.

# 32

In the morning, the sun blazed down in fury when I left Ndoda's house. I walked fairly quickly down the stairs. When I got outside, the heat came with greater intensity, a stronger stench of the city reaching me. I could smell the smoke of a mbawula coal stove coming from a balcony and felt a sneeze growing inside me.

A flock of pigeons dropped out of the sky and landed on the parapet of the block of flats along Klein Street. I turned right at the Hillbrow Community Health Care Centre towards Esselen Street. A dazzling sun was creating mirages on the tarmac. On the pavement of a disused building along Esselen Street, I saw the lumps of sleeping figures.

I was not in a hurry, as I was busy eating my KFC from the previous night. The streets were already buzzing with humanity as if an ant-heap had been disturbed. My feet made a sucking sound on the pavement. I passed a group of workers who were relaxing under a tree, munching groundnuts near the Hillbrow Mortuary. One of them was peeling an orange, leaving its skin on the ground. The smell of fresh vetkoek at the nearby shop drifted to me. There were weather-beaten posters on the walls of the flats, on traffic light poles, tree trunks and streetlamps. I passed a woman selling overripe bananas and tomatoes. Another one was selling pig trotters and cooked sheep heads.

I arrived under our bridge after one. Bhoboza was on the other side of the bridge, leaning forward and making soft bird sounds, extending his ragged arm towards the pigeons. He caught one pigeon as it tried to eat out of his hand. Next to my backpack of junk was a huge black refuse bag full of shoes. Airbag and Seatbelt were nowhere to be seen.

'What's this?' I asked, pointing at the bag of shoes.

'That's my score. I need to sell them to the jumble sales people at Park Station. At least we will have something to eat for the whole week or two,' Regulator responded.

'Where did you get them?'

'From the mosque in Mayfair. I went there with Airbag and Seatbelt yesterday. When everyone was busy praying, we took their shoes.'

'What? You mean you stole these? Where are Seatbelt and Airbag?'

I looked at Regulator with an expression close to horror.

He gazed at me thoughtfully for a few minutes, finally saying with a wry smile, 'I don't know, bra. The security guy saw us as we were walking out and chased us. We went in different directions. I was lucky I escaped, but after they beat the hell out of me. Seatbelt and Airbag didn't come home yesterday, so I don't know.'

'So, almost none of you have a clean conscience.'

His cold stare unnerved me.

'What I do know is that almost every homeless person was born when God was dead. Only those who have been given more than they deserve by life worry about their actions and clean conscience. The rest of us who have been deprived by it have selective worries.'

'Is that your excuse to steal and put your life and those of others in danger?'

'This is a dog-eat-dog city.' He wagged his finger at me. 'Good morals can't be eaten and it doesn't keep you warm under this bridge. As soon as you understand that this city has no business or obligation tolerating a piece of shit like me and you, then you will know why we do what we do to survive.'

'You're not doing yourself any favour with that attitude.'

For the first time I realised that Regulator was injured as he covered a big gash on his foot with a handful of earth. I stood there with my hands folded and watched in astonishment. I could not conceal my unhappiness. He pulled his legs in, pressed himself against the wall and bared his teeth like a mad dog. That was also when I realised that he could not walk properly and that his ankle was badly swollen.

'I accept. We were unlucky this time, my bra,' he said, forcing a smile and shaking his head knowingly.

'You are damn right that you were unlucky. But what about Seatbelt and Airbag?'

'I don't know, bra. The last time we managed to hit a huge score I was able to buy food for two weeks. The shoes that we are all wearing here came from that score.'

'But who on earth goes to the mosque and steals shoes from praying Muslims?'

'I tell you, bra,' he said, 'this last visit we were reckless. I even told Seatbelt and Airbag that we must hurry up before security became suspicious.'

He touched his injured calf and I saw blood running from his torn flesh. He then coughed a little and winked at Ghostface. I had nothing more to say to him. He sounded like someone who was so sufficiently infected by the thinking and ethos of a criminal. He persisted in telling himself that stealing was a job that needed doing.

I was tired, so I sat there checking if my things inside the bag were still safe. An hour later I walked aimlessly around Braamfontein, sitting under the trees to take in the fresh air. But I was worried about both Seatbelt and Airbag. I returned to the bridge when it was dark. They were not back yet.

'Why are you not worried that they are not here?' I asked Regulator.

'There is nothing to worry about. It's not like it's the first time it happened. How do you think we have been surviving for over seven years before you even became homeless?'

'What if they have been killed?'

'We will all die one day, but dying of hunger is not an option. Stop with your morals. When you have nothing to lose like us, all you think about is hunger and your next meal. You don't even think about your life because it's not that interesting.'

Seatbelt arrived later that night with wounds from the beatings. He was limping badly. Chin raised, eyes widened and nostrils flared. To judge by the movement with which he snatched his foot back, you would think he had burnt his soles. He gazed at me with eyes full of terror and mumbled between sobs. He bit his lower lip and looked into the distance.

I sat frozen, silent.

'You came back alone? Where is Airbag?'

'He was arrested.'

'What? How did that happen?'

'The guards caught us and beat us up. They tied us with a rope and called the police. While waiting for the van to arrive, I managed to escape and ran away.'

I shook my head in bewilderment and sorrow, and sighed. Seatbelt's bruised mouth twisted into a parody of a smile. Two streams of tears ran slowly from his eyes onto his jersey.

174

'Where do you think he is now?'

'I think they took him to Langlaagte Police Station because that's the station they called.' He clenched his teeth furiously. 'Those bastards tied my arms with such violence that I thought the ropes had torn my flesh and cut off my circulation.'

I could read worry in his eyes, but there was also scorn. He moistened his lip and I could see his nervousness. I searched my mind for something good to say, and found almost nothing.

'But why did you steal from them?'

'Because we wanted the money for food, grootman,' he replied confidently enough to put on a show of indifference. 'Why does it matter? Unlike the brain, the stomach alerts you when it's empty. And what do you do when that happens? You can't think of the consequences because the brain is not working.'

'You guys must work on your souls. It is karma that did this to you.'

'Those Muslims and their Christian brothers believe in heaven, so they don't want to fix anything here on earth.' There was a helpless smile on his face. 'Starvation is not a pleasant way to die, grootman. God is like an absent father when it comes to us here under this bridge. In fact, He doesn't exist here. We have to look after ourselves by all means necessary, just for survival.'

'And I'm sure stealing is one of them,' I said sarcastically.

As silence again settled under the bridge, I felt abandoned, vulnerable and lost. That talk with both Regulator and Seatbelt had left me with an unpleasant taste in my mouth. As far as I was concerned they both radiated stupidity. As the darkness of the night closed in on every side, I thought about Airbag. What if the police beat him up until he named us as accomplices? *A fly that won't leave a dead body gets buried with it*, I heard my grandfather's voice warning me. Surely there was a misfortune lurking under the bridge, but now that it was really here, I could sense another one coming. I could no longer work out where reality began and where the illusion set in after what had happened to my fellow residents of the city of broken dreams. That night, I stole three of Airbag's books and marched off to the Braamfontein Cemetery with my bag on my shoulder, winding between the darkness and the black silhouettes of the cemetery's trees.

# 33

The cemetery was choked with weeds. Often I would hear a tiny flutter of wings quivering out from under a small bush, and the throaty cooing of pigeons as they flew up into the trees. It reminded me of life under the bridge and I wondered how everyone was doing. Sometimes I had sleepless nights worrying if I'd be alone for the rest of my life. When that happened, I would sit on the tombstone and not say a word all evening. Sometimes I would read one of Airbag's novels. Sometimes I would writhe and twist at night, thinking that swarms of ants and flies and rats were crawling over me, mistaking me for a fresh corpse.

Sitting on my own, I would sometimes see the shadows dancing between the trees and I would give them names. I would invent dreams and ghosts, but the fear became unbearable. I would not sleep except when I had a bottle of vodka next to me, which I often had. Some nights, nothing moved and there was no sound. I could not bear the silence of the trees. But above all, what was important to me was that the life which carried me through those bitter months of separation was still there in my hands and in my eyes. Whether or not I had mastered it, I was not sure.

I had managed to avoid the bridge for about a week and a half. My heart and mind throbbed with nostalgia and repentance. The thoughts of my brief stay there were the most dominant. That place had been the capital of the exiled, the hungry, the perpetually unemployed and the addicts. It consisted of different age groups whose relationships had gone sour like mine. The bridge had made it possible for me to forget Aza for a while. Little by little, the fire of love that I'd once had for Aza had been extinguished by her absence under the bridge. That longing I had had for her had been smothered by my mundane world of activities and routine under the bridge. In my mind her beautiful face had grown more clouded, gradually fading away. It was slowly replaced by Kobus and Martinus, Airbag and Seatbelt, Boni and Ndoda, Regulator, Bhoboza and Ghostface.

That morning I found myself thinking about my engagement to Aza, which I now thought of as a case of childish infatuation. Three months after we had met, Aza and I had attended her friend's wedding at Thaba ya Batswana in Klipriviersberg. When it was the time for the bride to throw her bouquet in the air, that was enough to convince Aza and me to get married too. A week later, under pressure, I proposed to Aza. Then we moved in together a year later. We kept on postponing the marriage because I was paying her rent, which I could not afford. She also kept on taking the little from our account that we saved, promising to pay it back. When I thought about this now, my heart was no longer cold and implacable towards her. Just a few months ago, my eyes would suddenly well up, but now I was too stubborn to let a single tear fall. I only felt a slight pressure, something close to regret.

Two weeks later, I decided to pay my friends under the bridge a visit. There was no cloud heralding hope in the hot sky, which was like the lid of hellfire on that day. I was carrying the food that I had bought at Pick n Pay.

The inhabitants of the bridge were not there, except for Seatbelt and Regulator. There was a funereal air about them. Regulator and Seatbelt were wandering around, both limping badly in different ways. I watched Regulator as he limped to the far end of the bridge, occasionally slowing his pace, like someone in deep thought. He was behaving like a man who was waiting for a terrible pain to pass.

Overcome by my imploring eyes, Seatbelt growled. 'You see, grootman, those Muslim people bewitched us. Look at how our legs are swollen.'

'No one bewitched you. You guys were negligent, that's all.'

'Whose side are you on?'

'I'm on the side of the truth, which is that you did something wrong.'

'What a rotten world it is that keeps good things away from us only to drop them in the lap of other people.'

'You need to work hard and stop blaming others.'

'Where can we find work in this city? Tell me, grootman.'

While Seatbelt was trying to put only the outer edge of his feet on the ground, Regulator was hopping irregularly along, trying not to put his weight on his lame leg. His eyes were wild, darting around frantically. I looked at him once more and he nodded agitatedly.

'Why don't you two go to the hospital?' I asked, fixing my eyes on Regulator.

'Hospital? You want them to finish us?'

'So, you'd rather rot under the bridge?'

'Even if we want to go there, we don't have IDs.'

'They will definitely take you in without ID. Try the Joburg Gen or Helen Joseph.'

'How will we get there? Our feet are rotting. We can't walk.'

'Let me figure something out tomorrow. You guys urgently need to see a doctor.'

Regulator groaned softly and covered his face with his hands. He then made a small movement with his mouth as he tried to find a gob of grease that he smeared on his foot. Suddenly, he jerked upright, opened his eyes wide and shouted. 'Fuck!' The veins in his neck stood out like taut cables.

'A pain for a man who ordered it himself is a good pain,' I said.

'A coward like you will always die a thousand deaths, a soldier like me only dies once,' said Seatbelt.

'Shut the fuck up,' said Regulator.

'It's not me, it's 2Pac. Have you not listened to his song "If I die 2nite"?'

'So, you are not saying what is really in your heart and mind. You are actually repeating somebody else's words.'

'It's in my mind, too.'

I had already figured out that Seatbelt was an intense man who possessed a streak of stubborn idealism that did not mesh readily with his existence. At the same time, Regulator had changed overnight. His voice had lost the rough edge I had heard in it since the moment I had met him.

'Any news about Airbag?' I asked.

'They sent him to Sun City Prison. His real name is Thabang Mashishi. Actually, his novels here are also signed with his real name.'

In the afternoon I left them with the food that I had bought for them: a chicken, a loaf of bread and a two-litre of Coke as well as RG cigarettes. By then I was living quite secluded around the city, with the possibility of being useful to people for whom it was easy to do good. I headed to the Braamfontein Internet Café at De Korte Street where I made a call to the Johannesburg Prison, which is also known as Sun City. They confirmed that

Thabang Mashishi was indeed being held at Medium A, together with the other accused who were awaiting trial, and they gave me his registration number.

# 34

The following day at ten in the morning, I was at the main gate of the Johannesburg Prison, registering my name and personal details as Thabang Mashishi's visitor. There were about ten people when I arrived, but the numbers kept swelling with each minute. In fifteen minutes, there were about fifty of us, cursing, pushing, shouting, grumbling, in general milling around while waiting for the prison visitors' bus. There were women who came with their babies, fathers with their children to see their imprisoned mothers, nephews and nieces who came to see their uncles and aunts, girlfriends and boyfriends who were there to see their partners and friends, grandfathers and grandmothers who came to see their grandchildren.

Approaching the registration desk, I studied the faces of the officers to find the best match for me. I wanted to walk up to the female officer with the friendliest demeanour, and was surprised when the male officer talked to me warmly.

'Your ID please?'

'Is a driver's licence okay?'

'Yes. That's fine.'

He looked through a file, then wrote my name in the register.

'Here is your entrance paper. Give it to the officers when you arrive at Medium A.'

I produced my ID to the officer at the gate of the prison yard. The officer searched me for dangerous weapons and cell phones, which were not allowed inside the prison. Those who had cell phones on them were asked to leave them outside, either inside their cars, or with the street vendors outside the gates of the prison. This, they were told, was at their own risk.

I was let inside the prison gates and then waited for the prison bus to take us to different parts of the prison: Medium A, Medium B, Medium C and the Women's Section. The waiting, wracked with anxiety and hope, continued. Why am I doing this, part of me was asking. Airbag and his gang were a bunch of reckless homeless idiots and narcissists who were bound to perish from their arrogance and stupidity. He was surely undeserving of my attention. That community under the bridge was beyond the fringe, a vision of post-apocalyptic South Africa.

The bus arrived about fifteen minutes later. I sat next to a lady who had come alone. She was in her late thirties, light-skinned, and had cheekbones that were like small hills. She was wearing makeup and her eyelashes were thick and long just like those of Aza. They spread like the feathers of a peacock.

It was the first time that I'd visited a prison so I struck up a conversation with her in the form of a question.

'Excuse me, sister. Do they allow us to give prisoners money?' I asked. 'I didn't know I could, so I just brought the money.'

At first, she stared at me with a pensive squint. It was as if she had been interrupted in the middle of an important thought and was annoyed to be wasting her time talking to me.

'Well, in some sections you can do that, yes,' she said. 'But you have to buy whatever the person you're visiting needs at the tuckshop.'

'Oh, thanks. I didn't know prisoners also have a tuckshop inside.'

'They do. They're called "clients of the state" nowadays, not "prisoners" by the way.'

'Oh, is that so? Thank you for the information.'

'My pleasure. Who are you coming to see for the first time?'

'A friend who was brought here a few weeks ago for theft.'

'Okay, good luck.'

She was silent for about a minute. Her neck was wrapped in a blue scarf that cascaded elegantly on one side over her shoulder.

'How about you? Who are you visiting?'

'My husband. He's also awaiting trial at Medium A for two years now for robbery. They keep postponing his case and denying him bail. They say he is a flight risk.'

'It sounds complicated.'

'It is.'

We both got off at Medium A. There was a queue at the gate as we were searched again. Then there was another queue at the tuckshop where I bought a few things like fried chips, a loaf of bread and a two-litre Coke, all for an inflated price. I entered the building where I submitted the card to the prison warder through the cubicle.

Medium A's building was divided into Section A, B and C. It didn't take long for the lady to be called at Section C while I waited on the waiting room bench for Thabang Mashishi's name to be called at the opposite Section A. That took about ten minutes. There were a few others at the reception area coming to see their people. I was sitting next to a woman of about eighty years of age, erect, without a tooth missing in her mouth. Opposite us were two ladies who had come to see the same man at the same time. They were already fighting with words until they were sent outside by the prison warder who threatened to lock up both of them. They were accusing each other, calling each other whores in front of everyone, including the children.

'A visitor for Thabang Mashishi, please come.'

The white officer looked around and met my eyes. I raised my hand.

'Follow me,' he said.

I stood up and followed him to the well-guarded Section A visiting room. Each person was allowed only one hour to accommodate other visitors in that small hall.

'Anything you've brought for him?' he asked, clearing his throat.

'Yes, I bought some stuff at the tuckshop outside.'

My gifts were registered in a book before I was allowed to speak to Airbag. I even registered the hundred rand that I'd left for him.

Airbag was so clean, I couldn't believe it was him. He stood up to greet me and took a few careful steps towards me, flashing a wide grin. His nose seemed to have grown larger and lumpier, his face broader. We went to a little private corner at the end of the bench.

'You're the only person that visited me, grootman,' he said, taking a step back with a smile of disbelief. 'Thank you so much.'

'I'm probably the only one who knows that you're in jail.'

'But Seatbelt probably knows.'

'Well, I'm not counting your friends under the bridge. They can't afford to come here.'

'I know.'

'Besides, it's dangerous. If they come here, they think they will be arrested too.'

'I know. How are they?'

'Regulator and Seatbelt can't walk properly from the beatings. They are still swollen.'

'They will be alright. They have suffered so many hailstorms to be bothered by raindrops.'

'This is serious.'

'That's nothing, grootman. I mean, that's the normal life of the homeless person.'

'I think you just don't understand.'

'I have been kicked violently by crazy and aggressive drunk people while sleeping inside the city centre. I have had my money taken away from me by the city thugs and homeless bullies. Some of them even urinated on us while we were sleeping. Some also burnt us for fun; some shoot at us. Worse of all they rape the homeless women. So, I know.'

'That's terrible.'

'That's life. You should have seen me, grootman, I was swollen all over.' He was grinning as he whispered. 'But at least I'm happy here. They first sent me to the hospital. I was released the day before yesterday from the hospital.'

He lifted his trouser to show me his healing wounds. His cuts had closed up, scabs had hardened and his skin gained back its lustre. He shifted about on the bench as though it were full of needles, blushing and looking down at the floor. I put a reassuring arm around him.

An hour later, the visit was over. There was a tearful and reluctant goodbye.

'I will come see you again next week, probably with the whole gang,' I promised, without meaning it. 'That's if I manage to convince them.'

'Tell them I never mentioned names,' he whispered. 'They tried to get a confession by beating me up but I never did.'

'That's clever of you.'

'Yeah, I'm not a rat. Please do me a favour when you come next week and bring me my books. I want to read. And maybe attend university from prison. I heard that education is for free here. This is my only chance.'

186

'That's a good idea. I will bring them.'

'But maybe you can have the books because they have a library here. I haven't checked it out yet. But if they do have the library here I will read their books. You can have mine as my gift for you.'

'Thank you. It's good that even here you still love to read.'

'Yes, it's a passion that will not die. I used to visit the Johannesburg City Library in 2008 when I first came to the city. But a year later they closed it for refurbishment. Even now, ten years later, it is still closed because the politicians don't care about books.'

'I'm sure they have chowed all the money allocated for it.'

I left Airbag with mixed feelings. Maybe it was good that he was in prison because finally he would have a meal every day and attend university for free.

Outside, I saw the lady I had seen on the bus again. She was collecting her cell phone from a guy called Pitso. Pitso had created a job for himself by guarding people's valuables, including cell phones, knives and other things that were not allowed inside the prison. He gave everyone a number written on a torn piece of cardboard to reclaim their valuables upon coming out.

The lady looked angry, but I greeted her anyway.

'Hi, we meet again. Sorry for being rude earlier.'

'Rude, where? You were not rude.'

'But I didn't introduce myself to you. My name is Mangi.'

'You call that rude?' She smiled and blinked. 'That's not being rude. Anyway, my name is Boitu.'

'Nice to meet you formally, Boitu. Are you in a hurry or can we have two drinks there at Tinties?' I offered, pointing at the establishment where a few cars were parked.

'Why are you inviting a stranger for a drink?'

'Because I'm so happy to have seen my little brother today. As you know, unshared happiness is not happiness. It would be great to exchange notes about our loved ones behind this terrible fence.'

'Okay, but only for an hour.'

'Not more than that, I promise.'

I bought three cans of Hunter's Dry for her and three Windhoek Draughts for myself. I also bought a hundred rands' worth of meat for braaiing. The guy responsible for the fire offered to braai for us for a small fee. We sat under the thatch, a little bit away from the fire.

'So, my little brother was happy to see me. He promised not to steal again once he got out. How about your husband?'

'How long is he in for?' she asked, ignoring my question.

'He is still awaiting trial.'

'My husband is facing ten to twenty years for robbery if they sentence him. So far, they have no evidence and that's why his case has been dragging on for two years. His name is Fox.' Her smile was at once bright and melancholy. 'But we will appeal the sentence when that happens. It was a matter of being at the wrong place at a wrong time.'

'I hope all goes well.'

She smiled again, but this time showing her even-sized teeth. The skin on her face was glowing and smooth, and she was more beautiful when she smiled properly.

'How old is this brother of yours?'

'He is very young, early twenties.'

The meat came. She ate slowly, thoughtfully.

'At that age boys experiment with everything for fun and as a result of peer pressure. They experiment with drugs, petty crime, everything. I have two boys aged fourteen and twelve. The other day the school sent me a letter to say my eldest son is not doing his homework. He goes with the wrong crowd.'

'It must be stressful for you.'

'Very stressful since their father is in jail.'

'I can only imagine.'

There was a great question in her eyes and I knew that she burned to have it answered.

'How about you? Do you have children of your own?'

'No, I don't. My girlfriend and I tried to have a child, but unfortunately we could not.'

'I'm sorry to hear that. Maybe you must try again.'

'Impossible. We are no longer together.'

'Oh, I see. I'm sorry. What's her name?'

'Aza.'

The mention of Aza's name unsettled me. I took a tissue from inside my back pocket and wiped my sweat with it.

'You can't hide her away from your heart, you know that?'

'I closed my door for her a few months ago. Not because I didn't love her. But simply because loving her didn't lead me anywhere I wanted.'

'I'm sorry that it didn't work between you. But you do not have to feel guilty for wanting to get your own soul back. Your soul belongs to you, for better or worse.'

'Thank you. I think God has a funny way of answering people's prayers.'

'What do you mean?'

'He gave me the courage to speak to you. Now I feel healed.'

I was being honest. Our meeting seemed to have soothed my bitterness and brought me peace. She looked at me with a quick, bright smile. I was struck by her calmness and certainty.

'Don't be silly. You were healed already. I was the one bleeding with emotions when we came out of that prison. So, thank you.'

'Maybe we saved each other from going mad. That's exactly what I mean by exchanging notes about our loved ones.'

Her words had triggered many sensations with me. Unfortunately she had to go to her home in Westdene because the kids had come back from their aunt's place. She stood up and kissed me lightly on the cheek. With that kiss, I felt as if I had passed the first inspection.

'I hope I will see you soon. Here's my number.' She handed me a piece of paper.

'Perhaps sooner than expected.'

'Just don't abuse my number,' she said playfully.

A blissful smile spread over my face as I watched her walk off to the main road to catch a taxi.

# 35

I woke up in the Braamfontein Cemetery with the first rays of sunlight. There was a line of tiny black ants on the ground. Tufts of clouds had drifted in and the sun had slipped behind them. A few minutes later, the sun emerged. It powered me up with its energy and goodness. The line of trees next to my spot had a few brownish-yellow leaves clinging to their branches. A gentle breeze blew. The trees swayed and the wind whipped a few dry leaves of the trees further away. I looked at the tree in front of me, at its straight strong trunk, its roots that struck down into the ground. I decided to visit my people under the bridge.

Things seemed to have taken a turn for the worse. Seatbelt sat on the ground in the corner gazing at the opposite wall. He was silent, sniffling at regular intervals and wiping his eyes. His foot was covered in flies. In fact, the shape of his whole leg had disappeared beneath a swelling of such severity that the skin seemed on the point of bursting. Cuts were hardened into scabs. He had lost so much weight that the arcs of his ribs showed clearly and his arms lay beside him like spindles. I watched him as he scooped up a small glob of Vaseline with the tip of his finger and put it on his leg. He stared uncomfortably at me, as if he had discovered for the first time my bitter and awful presence.

Regulator, on the other end, lay stretched out, mouth open, eyes closed, hands flat at his sides, as motionless as a statue. His flesh was melting away, his forehead higher, cheekbones more pronounced. A crust of dried blood made a dark line on the hard, broken skin. He was so thin that his favourite dirty jeans looked like a blanket over him.

'Ghostface and Bhoboza have left us,' Seatbelt said, sweat trickling down his sombre face.

'What do you mean? You mean they're dead?'

'No, I mean they are gone. We don't know where they are.' He lowered his head and looked at his swollen foot. 'They just took their things and left two days ago.'

He tried to stand up, feet apart, knees slightly bent.

'What happened to them?'

'I don't know. It's one of those things. I think they were tired of this place. I guess we had entered an experience of the city through the same bridge, but then they decided to wander off into separate tunnels of the city.'

'That's sad.'

'Yeah. My feeling is that they became scared seeing Regulator and me like this. They then decided to walk out through darkness alone because we are both ill, I think.'

'I thought you were friends?'

'I thought so, too. But one day we will both emerge finally at opposite ends of this hell city.'

'How is Regulator doing?'

'He is just like a dead person.'

When Seatbelt spoke, his voice was full of fury and relief and unshed tears. His half-opened lips produced the occasional bubble of saliva which burst when he breathed out.

'Let's be honest. What were you guys thinking when you stole those shoes?'

'What happened, happened. We can't reverse it, grootman. Engaging in risky behaviour is a rite of passage for every homeless and unemployed person.'

'A saying like that cannot be used as a justification for the crime you have committed.'

'Those Indians and their white counterparts are great exploiters who have grown fat on the neediness of many black South Africans.'

'It's fascinating that you can speak such good English with an empty stomach. Is that caused by the whites and Indians, too?'

He bit his lips in annoyance. I checked on Regulator. He looked like he was in the advanced stages of famine and his own body was beginning to consume itself. I looked around, shook my head and said in a low voice, 'Regulator, can you hear me?'

Slowly, he opened his mouth and closed it again. His eyes were half-open, but looking. Fear in me hung like a big rain cloud in the sky, ready to burst. The nervous energy left me and I became commanding and authoritative.

'He needs to go to the hospital immediately. You also need to see a doctor.'

'How is he going there?' said Seatbelt.

'I have to make a plan quickly.'

I tried to smile at Regulator, but a bolt of pain ripped through my lips. Already his cheeks were sunken. His eyes were also deep and sunken from the sorrow and hunger, and his arms were those of a skeleton. I bent down over his face and suddenly he groaned, and there was a rattling in his throat. He began to whisper in gibberish. It was impossible to understand anything, except that this jumble of words and thoughts always centred on the same thing – home. As he mumbled, tears spurted from his eyes.

'What do you mean? Speak slower.'

His words needed all the slow seconds to arrive. They sounded more like an echo of his anxious breathing as I pondered the best way of answering him. I examined him a little more closely, our knees almost touching. He looked condemned, separated from the world, his dark face weeping.

'He has been like this for three days now. Plus, there was nothing to eat. My leg is still healing so I can't help him. He vomited blood yesterday and when I gave him water this morning, he didn't drink.'

'Three days?'

'Yes, without eating. At night he just screamed for help all the time. On the second night he became feverish and started talking to his invisible relative and girlfriend. I only picked out the name "Mandisa" because he called it several times and smiled while hugging the air. This morning it got worse because he kept pointing at his stomach and I thought he was hungry.'

'Don't worry. God will provide.'

'That kind of hope is for the dead.'

'Stop being pessimistic and suspicious about everything.'

'That's right. No one can believe in God any more here. It is impossible to believe that a kind and humble God would tolerate this widespread wickedness on earth. What kind of a God causes hunger and homelessness like this? Please don't tell me that this is the work of the devil. I'm tired of that lame excuse.'

'Just shut up, will you?'

There was a strange rattle in Regulator's throat again as he struggled for breath. He was frothing at the mouth, the foamy spittle soaking his beard. The faint smell of rotting flesh became more insistent. He was so thin that his ribcage was visible. The skeleton was working its way to the surface. His eyes were wide open now. His forehead sank in at the temples, his mouth all teeth now and his nose flatter. Only his mouth continued to tremble.

Thirty minutes later, his silence felt harder for me to bear than his groans. He had been lying on his back with a face that remained absolutely motionless, even when a fly buzzed around his face. All of a sudden, his glare looked permanent.

'Let me quickly try to get some help,' I said.

'Sometimes it is not necessary to lie to the dying,' Seatbelt said. 'There's no person left here.'

'What do you mean?'

'I don't think he will make it.'

'We need to take him to hospital.'

'God only prolongs a life where he deems such a delay appropriate for the individual's salvation. Not for hobos like us.'

The fly landed on Regulator's nose. I thought I saw his nose twitch, but he didn't raise a hand to swat it away. I spread a blanket over him, fear coursing through my body. I looked at Seatbelt and saw his hollow cheeks and the pale chapped lips he moistened with many licks of the tongue.

'You have an obligation to think positively, my friend.'

'It's funny how the truth makes us uncomfortable, but a lie gets us excited,' he said, his hands clasping the back of his head. 'I'm speaking the truth when I say this guy won't make it. He is already in another world.'

I left the two of them and walked towards De Korte Street. I lifted both my hands to my face and smelled them, the odour of sickness still on them. I surprised myself at the strength of my grief. What if Regulator was already dead? I shuddered at the prospect. Had he ceased to exist and now become a memory under the bridge like his friend?

I was trembling all over and could feel a cold sweat on my brow. At the internet café I made a call to 10177 for an ambulance and 10111 for the flying squad. I directed both of them to the bridge. Within an hour, and from not so far away, I saw a police car and ambulance under the bridge. A police officer was redirecting the traffic while the paramedics used a stretcher. A crowd galloped towards the bridge to witness what was happening. I was among the crowd as a spectator. I kept my eyes open for some kind of a signal that would confirm something to me. But there wasn't any signal. Even so, I knew he was dead.

A man next to me looked on, gathered saliva in his mouth and spat. Why do most Africans spit on the floor when they witness or talk about death, I wondered. Another man shook his head sadly. Later I saw one of the paramedics carrying a big piece of shiny foil. The foil was the confirmation. Regulator was gone, just like that. It felt as though I had an enormous stone crushing my chest. My world seemed vast and emptied of meaning. Standing by a wall, I wept quietly as I watched the ambulance's departure with a pang of regret. I kept weeping out of sheer shock, but I knew I couldn't make myself that conspicuous. That was my last time anywhere close to under the bridge.

# 36

One day followed another, days filled with pain and fear, fear of remembering Regulator's death rattle under the bridge. In those days, I did a lot of grief-walking inside the city. I kept finding myself in places without knowing where and why I was there. Sometimes I read with compassionate attention the signs pasted on the city walls.

On this particular day, my memory seemed to creep through the cracks of my everyday life. It overpowered other memories that had formed a tapestry, woven from forgetting and recalling in my mind. I could summon my friends under the bridge, Aza's name scornfully intruded, and my late mother and grandfather in Moletji also usually crept in. Those days I liked delving into my village memory as it helped me in my search of the lost pictures of my childhood.

Considering that I only spent a few weeks under the bridge and in Regulator's company, it amazed me how much I was bothered by his death. I was still shocked and needed to recover. One of the many lessons that I had learnt from my grandfather was that unshared emotions pulsate like an abscess, accumulating cancerous pus. In order to heal, he said, the abscess needs to burst and discharge, taking the weight from your emotions. I knew that when someone we care about dies, the archaeology of grief is born. Regulator's death, however, affected me in an unusual way. I started blaming myself for his death. I thought that if I had visited the bridge earlier I could have at least saved him. I should not have hesitated to call an ambulance and the police. I should not have been distracted by Seatbelt's crazy philosophies. I should have known better that hunger knows no philosophy. I should have forgiven him and Seatbelt for stealing.

All these fragmented thoughts made my nights long as they flooded my mind. Regulator's voice, his face, his life, his death, the bridge, the smell of the blankets, the liquor we shared, the joints, the rot of his wounds rising, his body supine in that state of complete immobility – all invaded my mind. Everything was pressed and dried in the dark vaults of my memory.

I knew that if I shared with someone this agonising pain of my loss, it would help me to come out of my grief and make it possible for me to continue living to tell the story of the bridge. But who was willing to share this weight with me? I was alone in my life – this had been my own choice. But now my choices were beginning to run out when I lost my friends under the bridge. Through them I had managed to swim across many of my sorrows.

While walking in the city, I began to search for people I knew. I settled on Boni, but her cell phone was off. Then, out of the blue, I thought about Boitu, the lady I had met at Sun City. It was with a mixture of desire and pity that I thought of her as a second option. Her face had sprung clear to my mind amid the roars of the engines, the hooting taxis and the sound of tires against the city streets. I pushed down the idea for a little while, but then it sprang back, even more urgently.

Eventually, in a bid to battle the emptiness, I tried to make contact with Boitu at the nearby internet café.

'Hi Boitu, it's Mangi. We met at Sun City the other day and we had a few—'

'Yes, I remember you, Mangi. How have you been?'

'I'm good. I was wondering if we could meet over a few drinks. There is something I want to share with you and I want your honest opinion on how to go about it.'

'For sure. When?'

'The sooner the better. Are you free this afternoon?'

'I'm at home in Westdene. You are welcome to visit.'

'Wonderful. What drink can I bring for you?'

'I'm actually a wine person. Red wine, Porcupine Ridge. But anything red is fine really.'

I went to the nearby second-hand clothing vendor at the Park Station and bought a T-shirt and jeans. With my backpack on my back I went to the toilets and freshened up. I put a lot of roll-on and perfume that I'd bought the other day under my armpits and came out smelling new and fresh. I then entered the nearby bottle store to buy the drinks before taking a taxi at Bree Street to Westdene.

It was also the first time in a few months, except for Sun City and my work in Rustenburg, that I had gone anywhere beyond the circumference of the bridge. As soon as I opened Boitu's gate into the yard, glum thoughts vanished from my mind. There were weeds in the joints of the paving of her driveway. I noticed marks of rain on the facade of her house and it needed painting. The grass was growing untended in her yard. I knocked on the door while studying the peeling plaster on the walls.

'You look very beautiful,' I said as she opened the door.

She winked merrily and then laughed a joyless sort of laughter, dry and empty. Her hair was short and she wore a pair of pretty earrings. I heaped praises on her while looking at her face and her slender hands, which could belong to a pianist. Her long nails were painted cream. I stole looks at her behind as she ushered me to a couch in her dining room. The couch and two chairs were covered with a floral-print cloth, probably to disguise how old they were.

'Thank you. At my age, men don't notice me any more.'

'I don't believe that. You still have it and I suggest you flaunt it. I saw men looking at you at the Tinties braai place the other day and forgot to tell you.'

I realised that she had defective hearing in her right ear, as she always tilted her head to the left and brought her face forward each time I spoke.

'Perhaps I just don't know how to engage in subtle flirtation to get attention from men any more.'

'Why? I don't think even one man passed you by without showering you with compliments on that day.'

'Maybe it's because I'm focusing on raising my two sons. It's hard to be a single parent.'

'It makes a lot of sense.'

I poured my vodka and soda in a glass with ice. She poured her wine and we avoided catching each other's eye. I took a sip and also crushed an ice cube between my teeth. The ice clinked. She smiled and squinted, as though trying to help herself to remember. I wiped moisture from my face with a finger.

She looked at me for a long time, like she was waiting, her eyes hinting at an unspoken secret between us. Her brow furrowed. She then weighed her words before clearing her throat.

'So, what was it you wanted to talk about? You sounded serious on the phone.'

'Yes, it's something serious,' I said as I took a sip from my glass and then put it down on the table again. 'So, three days ago I lost a friend and there was no one I could talk to. I thought I needed to speak to someone.'

'Was this person close to you?'

'Yes. This is a friend who was dear to me. We have known each other only recently though.'

'Male or female?'

I told her the whole story, rapidly and incoherently, exaggerating some facts and inventing others, and including so many parenthetical irrelevancies that she was unable to make head or tail of it all. But she listened, nodded and took an occasional sip from her glass of wine.

'How did you know these friends of yours under the bridge?'

'Well, when I still had my car I used to drive under the bridge to give them food and old clothes,' I lied to her. 'They were very nice. But last week or so, I decided to take a taxi to the city since I no longer have a car. That's when I found out that they were dying of hunger. It traumatised me. I can still see his picture.'

Boitu shook her head pityingly. I evaded some of the questions as best as I could, but in the end, I was forced to submit and tell her a few stories that had roots in the truth, although the details were invented.

'I used to have a car, but it was repossessed a few months ago. I used to load food and clothes to bring to the people living under the bridge,' I repeated the same lie.

'That's so kind of you. Sorry about your car.'

'Thank you. It was a terrific scandal – if you were on social media at that time, you certainly heard of it.'

'I missed it. Not that it was important anyway. I'm not that active on social media.'

'Okay. But yeah, it's the kind of a story that stirred up my fear and disgust of social media.' I took a sip of my vodka. 'I never imagined it would happen to me one day.'

'You have seen a lot in a short time. Maybe it will help to see a psychologist.'

'I will consider that advice. But perhaps I don't need a psychologist. I guess I'm just lonely.'

'I insist you consider a psychologist if these visions recur. You know, no matter what we think, there is no escape from stories in which we become entangled. But a psychologist will help you carry the weight.'

'Thank you. I know we've only known each other for a couple of weeks and you are not obliged to listen to my problems.'

Looking gently at me again, she was surprised and saddened to see that there were tears on my face. The vodka was beginning to loosen my tongue as I talked about what I still saw in the grimy pages of my mind, the particular scene that worried me.

'Witnessing Regulator's death, the images repeating in my mind, feels like being nailed to the cross in my imagination.'

'I can imagine.'

'Every day that I'm forced to pass by that bridge, I recall those bitter memories. Regulator's brown complexion was drained of life and tinged with grey.' I took another sip. 'His mouth was forcibly closed, his jaw clenched shut, as if pinned together.'

'Horrible. Can we talk about something else?'

'His body was small and shrunken in on itself. It was all bones, veins, skin and muscle, with not a single scrap of fat.'

She flinched, as though struck by a whip, but said nothing in reply. She seemed to sink immediately into deep thoughts and then looked at me. I popped an ice cube in my mouth.

'Please let's not talk about it.'

'You are right. Let's find something interesting to talk about – relationships, marriage, sex, anything.'

She looked at me, a bit taken back. She did not say anything. Instead, she leaned back to drink and, with her head tilted, her lips pushed forward and her neck taut, she burst out laughing while still holding her glass.

'Sex, really? Didn't you say you broke up with your girlfriend?'

'Yes, I did.'

'You think that's a good topic? I mean, you just broke up with the love of your life.'

The tip of her tongue poked between her beautiful teeth, and delicately licked at the bottom of the glass. We were both getting tipsy.

'Seriously, I don't mind.'

'Perhaps all you need is an orgasm that will fill the holes in your body,' she said. 'It can be a best therapy in your situation, I think.'

'I know. But I do get sex sometimes.'

'You have found a new girl? Good for you.'

'Not really. To be honest with you, I sometimes buy sex when there is an urgency. I mean, the city is full of sex workers.'

'I love your honesty.'

'How about you? What's the thing that you miss most about your man, besides sex?'

'Let me think. Going out together, I think. I love his taste in music. So, I would say going to music concerts like the Cape Town International Jazz Festival with him is what I miss the most. I think I might have been there three times with him. We have also been to the Bushfire Festival as well as the Standard Bank Joy of Jazz Festival.'

'That sounds wonderful.'

'And yes, like you, I do have sex,' she said. 'At least you were honest to say that you do buy it sometimes. With me, I have it in the house.'

'With who? I mean, your husband is in jail. Are you cheating on him? Not that I judge you.'

'Well, yes, I have always lived alone, but I've never been lonely. Even in case of emergencies there are toys. So yes, sometimes with my toy.'

We both laughed. Her presence was soothing to me, in spite of an irritating habit she had of biting her thumb.

'With a toy?' I repeated. 'That is not enough. And by the way, that's not cheating either.'

'Maybe it is not the same as a dick, but it is awesome.'

'Does it fill your whole body with rapture?'

'What do you mean?'

'I mean, are you tingly and full of energy for days to come after using it, or do you sometimes get tired? Does the orgasmic feeling pass through you within a few seconds?'

'So many questions. Are you doing some research, or what?' She took a sip of her wine.

'Well, it's because I don't see muscles in your arm, so you are probably not good at using a dildo,' I joked and touched her bicep briefly.

The sun had almost sunk behind the hills, the dusk painting the sky pink and purple. Shadows started to lengthen. Her bottle of wine was finished. She helped herself to my vodka. Her pupils dilated with pleasure.

'Thank you for your good company. I think you're funny. I mean it as a compliment and not in the wrong way.'

'No. Thank you. You made me feel human again after my trauma with Regulator's passing and my breakup with Aza.'

'Never let people's negative opinions pin you down. Dirty water never prevents plants from growing.'

'That's very nice of you to say. But I think my state of mind is getting worse all the time and I can't control my thoughts.'

She reached across my seat, slung her arm around me and pulled me close. A focused look came over her face. I took her hand and squeezed it. Her eyes continued to bite into me.

'It would be a shame if you did not take the opportunity to revolutionise your life and move into an entirely new realm of experience. Remember, you are still going to live for a long time.'

My face broke into a radiant and understanding smile. She went quiet and assumed a serious air, lowering her voice to suit the gravity of what she was going to say. Outside, the sky went dark and the wind grew anxious, but the clouds passed and it didn't rain.

'It was terrible for me at first when my sons' father went to jail. I thought that I needed a man in my life to protect, save and hold me. Now I realise how naive I was.'

'When did you realise that?'

'It takes time. It took me years – nearly two years? Then I realised that the purpose of human life, no matter who is controlling it, is to love whoever is around to be loved.' She paused and stared at the darkening evening. 'Women should not define themselves by a male partner. To depend on a man is a sign of weakness.'

It was as though I were returning after a long suspension of consciousness. She took my face between her hands and kissed me on the forehead. Releasing me, she smiled and stroked my cheek. We kissed each other with desperate anxiety while taking off our clothes. I was moved by courage, reckless innocence and the urgency of my desire. She pulled up her blouse and unhooked the front clasp of her black bra. There was nothing and no one to disturb us, no cares, no obstacles. My lips began to tremble and my knees shook a bit. Her eyes were very close to me. I kept my gaze lowered. I could not look at her.

205

'I think I'm falling for you,' I said out of the blue.

'Why are you so set on spoiling the brief duration of your visit with such useless words?' she said while smiling.

I ran my fingers along her neck and down her back. We looked into each other's eyes without blinking. I caressed her jaw line and then massaged the side of her head. This type of affection and sensation woke up our senses. We were lost in our nakedness.

In the morning she lent me her man's clothes while she put mine into the washing machine, including the dirty ones I always carried in my backpack. I was astonished by the affection I felt for her. Until now, I had believed myself only slightly attached to her. Her face wore an expression that was so composed. No make-up, just plain sensible good looks handed down by the gods. I was filled with unspecified hope, vague happiness, and I thought my face was more attractive when I brushed my teeth in front of the mirror.

# 37

One Friday, in the endless succession of grim days, fortune seemed to smile on me again through Ndoda. We had just come back from our SABS stocktaking job in Witbank and were standing in front of The Royal. As per usual, Kobus and Martinus had just dropped us off on Smit Street after giving us our money. I was given two thousand rand and didn't know or care how much Ndoda was getting. We were walking happily towards The Royal.

'Do you wanna make more quick good money, bro?' Ndoda emphasised his words with his hands.

'Come on. What kind of a question is that?' I replied. 'December is around the corner. Of course I want to make good money. Everyone wants to make good money.'

'Are you prepared to work irregular hours?'

'Anything, bro. Anything. I can even clean your penis before and after The Royal for a fee. Not sucking it, though.'

He opened his mouth and burst out into uproarious laughter.

'A man needs washing and disinfecting after talking to you. You're vulgar.'

'It's one of those desperate days where I cannot refuse anything asked of me.'

Around us, the city shimmered with lights and pleasure. But, one step away there were people who were sleeping on the pavements and filth. A man in a suit drifted past us on his way to The Royal.

'Okay then, let's meet tomorrow morning at nine in front of The Royal. From there we go to the FNB Stadium for soccer. The following day there is a music concert. We have four events lined up and I will be selling booze at all of them.'

'Sounds big. I'm up for the task.'

'It's a Boyz II Men concert at The Dome. Black Coffee will also be performing.'

'Wow, wonderful. You just made my day, my brother.'

'But first we have to go to a derby at the FNB Stadium. Chiefs and Pirates are playing and we have to be there by twelve.'

'It can't get better than that.'

A spring of hope sprouted in my heart. I felt as if a weight had been lifted off me. This victory was so huge and overwhelming and it had come after so many setbacks.

'Do I need to buy a ticket for the match tomorrow?'

'Don't worry. You're my guest.'

'This is getting better and better. The last time I saw a live derby was about ten years ago.'

'But remember, you are coming to work and not only watching football. You are working for three people at the bar – myself, Lina and Joshua. You must only buy from one of us.'

'Okay, deal. Ndoda, Lina and Joshua,' I mentioned the names as if practising their sound.

'Good. Always use twenty- and fifty-rand notes. Come every twenty minutes to buy and you will get a change of three hundred and three beers in a can with a plastic cup. We will share the money after the game.'

'Sounds good.'

'Don't ever get drunk. Actually, I encourage you to give away the beer. You must have a small bag to put the money in. I will give you a specific bag.'

'I get you.'

'We will give you ten per cent of the amount we make.'

'That's fair.'

'Remember, we don't know each other tomorrow. I don't want anyone to suspect anything about our transaction.'

I nodded enthusiastically, delighted by this unexpected caution and prudence. Now and then as he spoke, his hands jabbed at the air for emphasis.

'I buy only from Joshua, Lina or Ndoda every twenty minutes. I got it.'

At the entrance to The Royal, two security guys had blocked the door with their imposing size, legs astride. It seemed the Lord of the Rings had taken the day off. One bouncer had wide nostrils, and he would take deep breaths as if hoping to smell those good city smells from the nearby street vendors. The other guard had a grave, pugnacious face, but nothing sleek about it. We paid the cover charge at the window where there was a huge sign written: 'Check your ego at the door'. It was not the first time I'd seen it.

'You know why they put up this sign?'

'No. But I assume it's for violent people.'

'Well. It's because controlling your anger is very important in places like this. A friend of mine one day got so upset with his girlfriend that he reported her to his wife.'

'You're talking bullshit now.'

'You see, he was married, but essentially a bachelor at heart and in character. That's what places like The Royal do to you.'

Ndoda was completely absorbed by the music playing and he began dancing with his hands.

'Okay, I will see you tomorrow at eleven o'clock sharp. We will take the Rea Vaya bus together to the FNB Stadium. For now, let me look for a good company that will take me nice and slow.'

'I hope you find one with your specifications.'

'There is always someone for everyone in The Royal. And don't forget that the purpose of life is to journey towards its conclusion, my friend.'

On our way to the bar, Ndoda saw a light-complexioned lady sitting on a stool and stopped to talk to her. He winked at her as she pulled him from me through the crowd. After a small talk, she wrapped her long arms around his waist. I left him there and continued to the bar, where I bought myself a Windhoek Draught. I was thinking of Boni and hoping to see her. I wanted to thank her properly for introducing me to Ndoda. Perhaps pay double for a round.

'Nobody's Body' by Monifah turned my thoughts from Boni. A number of women were dancing and singing along. I saw Ndoda and the girl walking onto the stage. They danced slowly, their hips swaying from side to side.

The minutes ticked by. I sat there in silence, my thoughts lost among the dancing crowd. In front of me, a man was sleeping on a chair. His head was thrown back, eyes closed, mouth half-open. I felt tired, so I sneaked out of The Royal and went to book a room at the Formula 1 on Wanderers Street. My stomach had been pleasantly warmed up by a couple of beers. I called Boitu that night asking if she would like to attend a music concert at The Dome with me and she excitedly said yes.

At noon the following day I was already at the FNB Stadium, running through the crowds, crashing into sweaty bodies at the gates, rubbing against breasts with my shoulders at Ndoda's beer stall. I was filled with euphoria and an overwhelming sense of relief. I couldn't believe that it was me among the ninety thousand people at the stadium and not under the bridge or at the Braamfontein Cemetery. Me, Mangi, the homeless. It was amazing how quite suddenly, when I'd given up hope, new horizons were stretching before me.

It was a very noisy atmosphere with whistles, vuvuzelas and sirens. There were people shouting, children crying, and loud music drifting in and out of the stadium, pounding against my ears with its obnoxious beat. Thousands were in their team colours, black-and-white for Orlando Pirates and gold for Kaiser Chiefs. Some had painted their faces with their team colours. Team merchandise was sold everywhere. Other people sold last-minute tickets, biltong or loose cigarettes at double the price. The derby was a sold-out affair and VUSI's HUB was licensed to sell alcohol exclusively. They occupied the two corners inside the stadium near the north and south entrances. They also had an exclusive but expensive suite upstairs where they served only their clients with very deep pockets.

An excited rumble went through the crowd. Ndoda worked behind the counter and operated a till at the north wing beer stall, which is where I was. In that stall they sold only two South African beer brands: Castle Lager and Black Label. They only came in a four hundred and fifty-millilitre long tom can, which was sold at thirty rand each and was supposed to be opened before giving to customers. Each beer came with a plastic cup that one could take inside the stadium, as tins were not allowed inside.

The chorus of voices swept across the stadium as fans cheered for their respective teams. It was an honour to return to the profane world of soccer again amid nudges, where fans fought, hugged, cried, laughed and shouted at each other. While in the queue to buy beer, I heard the angry murmurings of the impatient crowd at the bar as they tried to get the attention of the waiters and waitresses who they thought were servicing only one side of the bar. Pickpockets also targeted people's cell phones and wallets. As I'd rehearsed with Ndoda, I bought three beers for sixty rand and he gave me three hundred change.

When the game started at three in the afternoon, a good number of spectators were already drunk. Some did not even watch the game and slept throughout, while others vomited on their seats and so on. By the end of the game, which was a draw, my bag and pockets were full of money, something I had never experienced in my life. I made sure that I didn't drink much. I resold whatever Ndoda, Lina and Joshua gave me at forty rand to people who didn't want to stand in the queue when the game was already playing.

When it was all over, and the stadium was mostly empty, I returned to the Formula 1 in Wanderers where the four of us – Ndoda, Lina, Joshua and I – had agreed to meet and share the money. I didn't show them the money that I had hidden inside my socks, which amounted to about four thousand rand. I had made about six thousand rand that day.

Ndoda had come with a suit, shirt, shoes and tie that he gave me to wear for the following day's assignment.

'Tomorrow I want you to wear this.' His voice, when he spoke, was a loud whisper. 'You must look professional.'

'It sounds like there is a big fish to catch.'

'Yes. I want you to look professional, like you have all the money in the world.'

'Can I bring someone, please? She loves Boyz II Men.'

'Bring her along. As long as you stay focused on your job. And please don't tell her what we do. Otherwise those people will kill us.'

'I already figured that out.'

'Yeah, just remember that courage and strength are not without prudence,' he said with a voice faint with exhaustion. 'A momentary negligence may destroy the happiness of a lifetime.'

'I understand.'

'But your girlfriend has to go home after the concert. We are working until the morning.'

'I got it.'

# 38

Women like Boitu always happen to you suddenly. Since I had met her my confidence had improved and my feelings of inadequacy were reduced. Through her I had realised that we can endure any misery if we have someone to share it with. Her mere presence injected a massive dose of joy into me.

In the afternoon I went to Boitu's house to pick her up for the concert at The Dome in Northriding. I found her trying on different dresses and posing in front of the mirror in her bathroom. She was wearing orange lipstick.

'How do I look?' she asked, spinning around.

'Fabulous, exquisite. The world is yours, babe, especially when you're backed by my love.'

While waiting for the Uber at her Westdene home, she kept checking her teeth in her compact to make sure they weren't smeared with lipstick.

With about eight thousand rand in my pocket, I felt confident enough to take an Uber to The Dome, which was quite a distance from Boitu's. I was carried away on a wave of optimism.

Around two in the afternoon, Boitu took my hand and led me out of the house with authority to the waiting Uber. I was wearing Ndoda's suit and shoes, which I felt symbolised the severance from my previous homeless life under the bridge and in the cemetery. The shock of holding Boitu's hand in the back seat of the car made me feel that my hands had been empty and without love since I left Aza. A thousand tiny fires lit up in my body.

I pulled Boitu to my side and she rested her head on my shoulder.

'I will be working inside there until late. It's a pity I won't be with you all the time.'

'I really don't mind that. You have already made my day by bringing me to my favourite band. It's an early birthday present.'

'I'm glad to hear that. We will have a great time. When is your birthday?'

'December 23 and yours?' she answered.

'No way! Mine is December 22.'

'So we are both Capricorns? That makes a lot of sense.'

We both laughed. Sweat was beading on my brow. I opened the window for a minute and breathed in the city's air. Boitu's fingers were playing with her dangling earring.

'What will you be doing, if I may ask?'

'I manage the bar during the events making sure that everything is running smoothly, including the stock that they may need to replenish.'

'Oh, I see.' She smiled and her teeth glittered like polished pearls.

'It means I will be moving about to the bar a lot. But I will make sure you never run out of drinks.'

'Drinks or no drinks, I'm super excited,' she said. 'I know most of their songs by heart.'

'I can't wait to hear you sing along.'

We arrived at the venue shortly before four. I took one step at a time, trailing Boitu's high heels as we walked towards the mall.

She was clutching her orange leather purse with her orange fingernails. She looked gorgeous and confident, I thought, as I gave her a kiss. Her arm slid around my waist from the side as we entered the Dakota Spur at the mall where we sat down and ordered ribs and buffalo wings.

When we were done, we met Ndoda at the venue where he had two tickets ready for me. He was working with Lina and Joshua and three more people at the bar. I bought two beers from Lina for fifty rand and she gave me a change of three hundred rand. The beers were expensive there, at forty-five rand a can. I also bought a small bottle of red wine for Boitu, which was served with a plastic cup. Boitu and I then walked to the venue, heads close together, arm in arm, in intimate conversation. A few necks twisted in envy to look back at us and there were a few inaudible whispers.

# 39

Boyz II Men were on stage and I was happy to see Boitu's throat throbbing and bobbing as she sang along to their songs. When they performed her favourite song, 'End of the Road', Boitu raised her hands above her head, with her eyes half-closed. It was hot inside and drops of sweat trickled down her jaw and into the hollow at the base of her throat, the tip of her nose gleaming. Every now and then she wiped herself with a tissue.

Halfway into Boyz II Men's performance, a miracle happened. I saw a ghost from another time: Aza. She was standing there, not so far from us. My mouth opened wide and I shook my head in disbelief. Since I'd met Boitu, Aza had existed as a memory. Now I saw her dancing with a dude with a belly as round as the earth. My heart started to beat faster and sweat broke out over my body. A pain stabbed my heart, as it did every time I saw a girl I'd loved who was going the opposite direction. I could not move. Our eyes met. I smiled at her, but she did not smile back. I felt her glare on me like the heat of a blistering sun.

If there were a thing called 'face crime' in South Africa, Aza would have been found guilty of looking at me that long without blinking or smiling. From the corner of my eye I saw and imagined her huge, blazing eyes fixed on me, with a terrible gaze. The man she was with looked like he had little sense of taste, or rather had a great tolerance for bad taste. At the end of the song, the man gazed at the inside of his Dobbs hat he was holding, tapped it, gazed inside again and put it on his head. My heart was pounding and my feet hurt from standing. Indecision paralysed my legs and I kept looking at the man with jealousy that I could not hide.

Outside, the night had fallen and the moon was high in the heavens. The Boyz II Men concert had ended and Black Coffee had started his set. It was nine pm and Boitu wanted to leave. There was a constant motion of people heading in all directions.

'I'll see you when you come,' Boitu said. 'That's if you're planning to come to Westdene after work.'

'Thank you. I will be there. But I warn you, it will be in the morning hours.'

'I'll be waiting. Thank you for a great time.'

'It's only my pleasure.'

I pulled her closer, held her around the neck tightly with one hand and kissed her. She called an Uber and I gave her two hundred rand from my bag. As the Uber slowly drove away with her, she opened the window, pointed at her orange lips and sucked the air in a passionate kiss.

I knew that Boitu was the kind of person who was ready to see me only if it suited her pleasure and convenience. Otherwise, she was still close to her man, Fox, whom she said may be out soon. I saw her only when her boys were not home and I respected that.

As soon as her Uber had disappeared from my view, Aza's image floated up from the recess of my memory, panning shots of her into my mind. My eyes were flying from face to face as I walked to the bar, searching for her, or for someone I could recognise from my old life. I began making imaginary preparations, planning in advance how I would talk to Aza if I saw her again. In my mind she was still so beautiful to look at, to think of.

At the bar I felt soft hands touching my shoulders. I looked behind me and recognised Sonto. She waved and smiled widely, like she was seeing a celebrity. The last time I'd seen her had been at Aza's house many months earlier.

'Hey, Mangi, it's me, Sonto, Aza's friend. Do you remember me?'

'Hi, Sonto. Of course I remember you.'

'Can I please give you the money to buy drinks for us since you're already next to be served? I have been standing here for too long.'

I had learnt early the effectiveness of politeness, so I agreed.

'Oh yes. What do you want?' I asked, taking her money.

'Six small bottles of red wine, please. I will be over there.' She pointed towards the light.

At the bar, Lina caught my eye and asked for my order. I gave her fifty rand and she gave me three-hundred-rand change in return. I walked with my order to Sonto who was already standing on the side with Aza and two friends. Aza wore a beautifully fitted red dress, and thick black eyeliner that gathered in blobs in the corner of her eyes. She had a lovely blue handbag on her shoulder. She stared at me intently. There was no sign of the fat guy I had seen her with earlier.

It was an awkward moment when I greeted them all. I started with her friends. I could tell that Aza wanted to speak, as she was looking at me from head to toe, heaving a sigh of impatience. My chest tightened with a surge of unexpected anxiety as I looked at her out of the corner of my eye, studying her expression. It was almost half a year since we'd separated and I was not sure whether I should talk or ask for a hug first.

I tensed as I walked to her with a smile. I felt a brief tremor and quiver all over my body. I was not ready for rejection and the very notion that such a thing might happen made me shudder.

To my relief, Aza gave me a welcoming smile. Involuntarily, my eyes flinched when her arms came close, but we lost our fixed gaze and my tension eased. We then briefly embraced each other tentatively like strangers. She hugged me as if she were afraid to ruin her makeup. Every curve of her body spoke of beauty and perfection. Her full-lipped mouth smiled at me and I felt my passion reawakened.

Her friends were busy talking to one another as if to allow us time and space to talk. We stood facing each other for a long while, a vague smile of reminiscence playing on our faces. I saw love in her eyes with all the old fears and demands for reassurance. She looked down and shook her head. She looked at my face again, blinked, unable to believe her eyes.

'You look good. I didn't know you're into suits these days.'

'Thank you. I'm preparing for my thirty-sixth birthday so that I no longer fall under the youth category.'

'Oh yes, I remember 22 December is your birthday.'

'Your memory was always sharp.'

When she smiled it was with the same radiant smile I had always associated with her.

'How is everything?'

'It's getting there. Like they say, time crumbles into a myriad of tiny pieces when you spend your days unwisely by drinking, getting old and watching life go by,' I said, trying to impress her.

'I can see you have been taking care of yourself. Have you been working out?'

'Yeah, a lot of walking, I guess. And how have you been doing?'

I had to control myself so as not to be hypnotised by the sight of her cleavage that peeped out of her dress.

220

Her face suddenly smoothed down, her smile disappearing, and she said, 'Well, so much has happened since you've been gone. Where do I even start? We buried my mom last month and I've been diagnosed with depression. Popcorn also died about four months ago.'

I'd forgotten about her voice, how resonant it was, a trace of nervousness in it now. I nodded in acknowledgement.

'I'm sorry to hear that. You have had a rough time.'

'I'm sorry that it never worked between us,' she said, glassy-eyed and clearly angry with herself. 'It was my fault.'

A feeling of triumph flared up in me. I nodded at her to keep going.

'At least we tried, didn't we? But don't worry. Anything should be forgiven in a woman who has experienced a loss like you did.'

'I still don't understand how it never worked,' she said. 'I mean, we were so much in love with each other.'

'Well, sometimes it is the very thing we cannot understand which makes life worthwhile.'

'I agree. It is what it is. Nothing is lasting in this world – even joy begins to fade after only one minute.'

I liked how she could hide all our history and talk to me as a new person.

'Yep. I will see you guys around, there's something I'm attending to. Shall I bring you more drinks?'

'That would be super nice of you.'

I smiled and walked off slowly, slightly bent forward, my hands in my pockets, as if I had discovered the secret of being success-ful. In reality, my heart was racing and my mind whirled. I felt guilty and irritated and full of love and pain at the same time.

# 40

'I have a special request,' Aza said as I brought the ladies eight small bottles of wine. 'I'm wondering if it's appropriate for me to ask you.'

'Please do ask.'

She coughed, quite unnecessarily. Her voice was as feeble and throaty as possible. Her eyes were dancing between us, as though she was unsure of where to land them. I just closed my eyes and took a long and slow inhale of my roll-up.

'My friends and I are already drunk, so I was wondering if you could do us a favour and drive us home.'

It wasn't an unreasonable question, but the predictability and agitated delivery of it was annoying. They were expecting me to leave what I was doing and take them home.

'But I'm also drunk. Besides, you can leave the car here and take an Uber home.' I arched my neck and scratched my throat. 'And I'm still here drinking.'

Aza opened her mouth wide, offended. Her friends were looking at us as we talked.

'You're not drunk. Don't forget that I know you.'

'Things have changed. I now get drunk without being noticed.'

'Please, please, please. I'm begging.' Aza pretended to be slurring, 'We drank a lot with the girls and I think it's too late to stop now.'

She then smiled, sad and strained, but sort of affectionate, and put her hands on my shoulders.

'Okay then. I will drive you guys on the condition that you will wait for me to finish my job.'

She cupped my face with both hands and kissed me lightly on my forehead.

'Thank you so much. Now I'm relieved. I can drink.'

'Where have you parked?'

'Opposite the Spur.'

'I'll find you there when I'm done.'

I watched her as she walked to her friends dancing to the music by rotating her hips a little and sticking out her tongue to show them everything was in order.

From then onwards, I started drinking more water. The party ended around three in the morning. I had arranged to meet with Ndoda and others at one that afternoon. I found Aza and her three friends sleeping inside the car. They were all drunk and had locked themselves in. Aza was in the passenger seat and the driver's seat was empty, obviously reserved for me, their designated chauffeur. The other two ladies were in the back seat; Sonto was not in the car. I knocked on Aza's window and she unlocked the car for me. The keys were placed on the cupholder next to the gearstick together with a parking ticket. Luckily, the boom gate was malfunctioning so I passed through without paying.

I moved my hands up and down the steering wheel, squeezing it anxiously. I then wiggled my toes to remind myself that I was in my body, alive and not dreaming. From the rear-view mirror I could see one of the girls' long legs sprawled awkwardly over the seat, half-open and tenting her tight silk dress so you could almost see between her legs. Aza's head and backrest had been adjusted to the back and she was sitting there, her dress slightly pulled up. The strangeness of it all delighted and fascinated me. Aza dropped her head against my shoulder as I was driving. I smiled tolerantly and stroked her neck. I couldn't help but squeeze her hand when she took hold of mine. She averted her eyes and then placed her hand awkwardly on my back. I could feel the heat of her breath in my ear.

The girls slept most of the way. At regular intervals Aza raised her eyebrow suggestively. She would sit up and look at me with a smile. For a few moments I would let go of the wheel with one hand and stroke her head. As we approached Beyers Naude Drive the two ladies in the back sat up and smiled, holding their purses with tight fingers, their legs pinched together at the knees.

'Can we please drop off Carol and Nozi in Honeydew.'

We stared at each other for several seconds.

'Can't they Uber from your place?'

'It's not far. Come on please. Let's make sure the ladies are safe,' said Aza. 'I don't trust these Uber drivers nowadays, especially when the ladies have been drinking. They may take advantage of them. You know our country – when it comes to gender-based violence, we top the world.'

She was looking directly at me, holding my gaze. Slowly, she touched my face and traced her hands down my core before leaning over and kissing me lightly on my left cheek. Her warmth put me at ease and I stared back at the road.

'Okay, I understand,' I said as I joined Beyers Naude towards Honeydew.

'Thank you,' the ladies at the back said simultaneously.

Driving back to Linden, there was a comfortable silence between us. Aza was busy changing the radio stations.

'Thanks for driving us home safe.'

'My pleasure.'

'It means a lot to me.'

I smiled at her and all the tension in my body was replaced with warmth and comfort. I had no idea how to respond properly.

'I'm tired. Can I crash at yours for a few hours?'

'Of course you can.'

We arrived at Linden around five in the morning. I followed her, carrying my small bag with cash. I realised that the front door was different from the one I had left behind and the lock had been changed as well. I stood in the middle of the dining room where I expected to sleep on the couch. There was a big new fifty-five-inch Samsung TV set on an oak stand in front of me. The walls of the house smelled faintly of a fresh paint.

'I still can't believe I met you today and that we drove together here,' she said. 'Anything to drink?'

'No thanks, it's too late, or rather too early for me.'

'What do you mean? Somewhere in the world it is the afternoon and time to drink. Just one drink.'

She didn't wait for my approval, but went to the fridge and came out with a bottle of white wine, which she poured into two glasses. Carefully, I put my small bag behind the couch.

'I know you're a beer person, but this is all I have in the house,' she said as she came towards me and handed me a glass.

We took a sip at the same time and put our glasses on the small table. I sat down on the couch, and Aza came and sat next to me. She moved very close and she put her arm around me. She began stroking my head and then my arm. She had a seductive touch. It had been a long time since anyone had touched me like that. I experienced a disorientating sense of comfort and safety, and I became totally vulnerable to her. She moved her head towards mine and we kissed. My penis was already so hard that I thought I might pass out.

While still kissing me, she unzipped my pants, and I felt her hand flat against my penis through my trousers. She was gentle, patient and attentive. I was a bit disappointed with too much foreplay. She then pulled her dress off over her head. I stripped off my clothes and dropped them in the middle of the floor. I lay on my back and she put one hand on my penis. I fastened my mouth on her breast and played around the nipple with my tongue. Adjusting my position on the couch, I took her head with both my hands and pushed it between my legs. As she performed fellatio on me, my body wriggled and stiffened with pleasure. I then put my fingers on her back as if they were soft claws.

The couch creaked as we hurriedly changed positions. I lay on top of her, gripping her firmly about the hips with her legs parted. I entered her with overwhelming force and we started screwing each other. My body seemed full of unnatural energy and purpose. It felt as if I was taking revenge on her as I heard her short and stifled screams.

Five minutes later we broke apart and regarded each other warily. Our breathing was rapid and I could feel the rhythmic pumping of my heart. I put my hand on hers tentatively. We lay there in silence. She then held my face and kissed me, staring me dead in the eyes for at least three seconds without a word. I stared back at her. Was this an official rebound, I asked myself.

# 41

There is an African idiom that says love is like rainwater. These two entities, love and rainwater, have perfect memories. Even after a long, severe drought, when it rains, the water is forever trying to get back to where it once flowed, and it always finds its previous trail. This was my situation with Aza.

When the sleep wore off, a pleasant shock passed over my face. It was only at that moment I realised that I was sleeping in Aza's house, in the very same bed I'd once slept in. The only difference was it was now covered with designer sheets and a duvet patterned with beige and tan dolphins on blue waters. What also became clear to me was that what I had previously considered to be my past with Aza was never dead. It was not even the past, but an unending action.

That morning, she lay on the bed watching me, her mouth slightly open and her eyes like lights. I was ready for the second round, so I moved my legs slightly and my hands started working on her breasts. She let me take her nipple in my mouth and I rolled my tongue around its perimeter. Her moaning became louder and louder. I extended my tongue and kissed her on the neck. It seemed we were tied by cords of shared intimacy. Her flushed cheek was resting on my wrist and she looked down at me languidly. I was already erect.

Without warning, she gently pushed me away, twisting her arm a bit and rolling her eyes.

'No,' she said, as if she had finally come to her senses.

'I don't understand. Why? I thought we had a great time this morning.'

'What happened this morning was a mistake. I was still drunk.'

'What do you mean?'

'We should not have had sex. But that doesn't mean I didn't want it to happen then.'

'Why this sudden change of mood?'

'I think we have to take it slow.'

'Okay, why?'

She paused, searching for the best way to express her feelings. She was trembling a bit. I was confused and my erection had suddenly waned.

'Is it because of anything I've done, said, or not said?'

She rolled away on her side, her body curled tightly. She sniffed once, turned on her back, and looked at me with puzzled eyes.

'I just don't feel like it,' she said, disinterested.

'Of course. It's not for me to tell you how to feel.'

I tried to caress her thighs, squeeze her breasts, but she seemed so virtuous and inaccessible that all hope, even the most remote, deserted me. Reluctantly, I gave up. Whatever reason she had for not wanting to have sex with me again, I figured it must be a good one. She took my hand and for a while our fingers inter-locked.

'Why is it that whenever a woman refuses a man sex, refuses him sincerely and wholeheartedly, he persists in believing she is being coquettish?'

'I don't know. Maybe we are operating with a hope that you'll change your mind.'

I didn't want to say anything that would make things even worse. She traced my thigh with her finger and then squeezed it.

'But I need to be sure that you are not a new wine in the old bottle,' she said.

'When do you think you will be ready? How will you know that I'm still the old wine?'

'When the sky is ready, the rain will fall. Now it's still too early. What if you break my heart again? This time it will be difficult to put it back exactly in the same position.'

Her polite tone filled me with a rising lust. Her fingers crawled to the back of my neck, caressing the back of my ears, and then the lines of my jaw.

'But love is not a choice. There is no way to avoid it,' I said.

'I know. But you need to be patient. Patience and courage are the key to everything.' She spoke dreamily. 'I would do anything with you when the right time comes.'

'And I'll be waiting patiently.'

I put my hand on her thigh. She ignored it. My hand sweated on her leg and I took it away. We kissed and touched each other a little and then broke apart to talk some more.

'I'm glad that we finally found each other again,' she said. 'You have no idea how much of me is lost along with those memories.'

'What happened is in the past. There is no time to wallow in self-pity. Everything passes and time covers the history in rust.'

As we clasped our hands, it seemed as if our past and future, memories and dreams, were all merged together again in the sweet rapture.

'Who was the lady you were with yesterday?'

'Oh, it was my friend Boitu.'

'I thought she was your new woman.'

She laughed and squeezed my arm. The bright day outside

came streaming into her room in three immense shafts of light. My head was propped in my hands and my eyes were directed at the door.

'Are we becoming jealous now?'

'Not really. I just wanted to know if it was something I should be worried about before I commit myself to you again.'

I scanned the room to check what else was new in the house. My sweeping glance took in the walls, the shelves, the new forty-inch Samsung TV on the white stand, the new Acer laptop on the bedside, the boombox, a fan and oil heater. I saw my trousers, actually Ndoda's trousers, hanging at the foot of the bed.

Aza took my arm and was leaning lightly against my shoulder as she stared at the ceiling.

'So, this Boitu, are you friends with benefits?'

'Well, yes. Something like that.'

'Don't get me wrong. I'm definitely not angry that you chose to continue to live your life after we broke up,' she said, stroking my chin. 'I think I would have done the same if I was in your corner. I'm not going to contest your judgement. Here I have nothing to give you except my tears of joy.'

'I know.'

'Of course I didn't mean that you should give up or share the privileges you had. Your happiness with her should also afford me some happiness as well.'

'Thank you for your understanding.'

'It would be unfair for me to expect you to suddenly abandon somebody you are with.'

'I guess that's the correct attitude needed to deal with our situation at the moment.'

Her demeanour had changed and it revealed the maturity of a woman who had suffered, and the generosity of a woman who had transcended greed. Overwhelmed by the love that swelled in my heart, I took her hand and showered it with kisses. Stretching out her other hand, she grasped hold of mine, planting kisses on it, then held it on her knee, and she toyed gently with my fingers while mouthing an endless succession of sweet nothings.

'I love you so much. I hope you won't leave me again.' Her voice shuddered.

'We have to guide and take cues from each other.'

'Maybe we can try what we had before. This time we have to improve our communication. You have to communicate with me all the time so that I know if you're up to the task again.'

'I agree. As you said, we have to take it moment by moment and slowly. At this point we have to agree that it is still a steep path that we both have no strength for.'

Most of the time her face lay against my ribs. She then turned her head away, but I did not let her go, encircling her waist with my arms. I wanted to tell her that I still loved her, but my courage abandoned me.

'Tell me it is still possible to love each other.'

'I would not be here if it were not.'

'So much has happened since you've been gone. I have learnt that as you grow apart from the person you love, you realise that love and happiness are not like a hairstyle you can suddenly cast off.'

I listened and allowed the words to sink in. I then held her tenderly, like a big ostrich egg that might break and make a mess on the floor. I felt her eyes on me and heard the pulse of her breathing. The memory of the past hung uneasily over us.

'And who is the guy you were with yesterday?' I asked.

She was caught off balance by my direct question. All she could do was to give me a distorted smile.

'Oh, you mean Tony?' she said with a gleam in her eyes. 'He is Sonto's colleague. He organised the tickets for us.'

'I see. He disappeared too early.'

'Yeah, he was only there for the Boyz II Men performance. He is trying to hit on me but he is married. I don't date married people.'

'I understand.'

There were many strained silences between us, many unspoken things. The words settled in my mind and scattered my thoughts. In the silence, I began to dig through my feelings, searching for my true desire. Aza kept sighing deeply, her eyes half-closed. I breathed in the cooling breeze coming from the slightly open window. I was tempted to tell her that after the break-up, she had been floating in and out of my mind like a butterfly. I wanted to tell her that in the mornings and evenings, her scent had a perverting influence on me.

'I guess some hopes you can never easily let go of,' I said.

'What do you mean?'

'I never stopped hoping that one day we would lie in bed together again like this.'

I stretched my hand and Aza gave me hers. She intertwined her fingers with mine. It was as if we were taking revenge on our lost time. She was now facing up with legs spread apart. The thoughts scuttled around my head. I crossed my legs, uncrossed them again, rubbed my hands, rubbed my hard penis.

'Oh, the insurance finally paid for the stolen goods.'

'Good. I'm glad they did.'

'I also took out a policy for my mother and when she died they paid some money. It was enough to pay off the car.'

'Wonderful.'

She ran a finger up and down my arm.

'Did you miss me?'

'Yes. A lot.'

'Do you still love me?'

'Yes.'

I suddenly felt caged inside the house. Like an outsider who'd got accepted to a dinner party in a borrowed suit. I got up and put on my clothes. I remembered that I should have slept at Boitu that morning and that I had to meet Ndoda and the others at the Formula 1. I had to leave.

'I'm sorry, I'm late for work,' I told her. 'I will call and come see you later.'

She shook her head unhappily.

'Where do you work? What kind of work do you do?'

'All over – Joburg, Witbank, Rustenburg, everywhere. I do stock assessments for different companies,' I lied. 'At least it's a rewarding and meaningful work that fills me with a sense of purpose and mission.'

'Okay, I'm happy for you. Do you still use your cell phone number?'

'No. I don't have a phone any more. I lost it recently and I've been meaning to buy another one soon.' Another lie.

'Oh, I see. But you will call me, right?'

'Of course I will. Do you still use the same number?'

'Mine has not changed.'

'Okay, I will call you.'

In the dining room I picked up my small bag full of money, I opened the door and went out. The amazing coolness greeted me and my eyes could see clearly. My thoughts were fleeting, conflicting. I was sure that my short-lived love for Aza was now about to evaporate like steam. The fantasies I'd had earlier melted as soon as I came out of that haunted house. My initial sex cravings were also gone. As I walked down the street to catch a taxi to Joburg City Centre, my mental powers returned to me. My cheeks burnt and guilt coursed through me, the guilt of indulging myself at the expense of Boitu and my emotions. Somehow I was relieved that I had evaded the second threat of intimacy with Aza. I realised that it would come with messy emotional baggage. I could not just ignore, repress and pretend I'd forgotten everything between us.

# 42

I was in a taxi on my way to Westdene to see Boitu. She had told me earlier that she would start at the Johannesburg Prison that morning and would be back in the afternoon around three. After sharing the money with Ndoda and his colleagues, I was eleven thousand rand richer. Ndoda had taken his clothes back, so I decided to kill time by doing some shopping at the Newtown Junction Mall by the Market Theatre. I bought myself a new pair of blue sneakers, a pair of jeans and a T-shirt. I also got Boitu her favourite Porcupine Ridge red wine and vodka for myself.

But my mind was being pulled in a different direction. I was now officially dating two women, one from the past and another one from the present.

At some point I even thought of taking a trip to Moletji, but reasoned against the idea when I thought about the expenses I would incur at home. Maybe I would go there over Christmas when I had accumulated enough money, I told myself. Anyway, December was just a few days away. At the same time, I realised that I no longer had any *home*. Moletji was no longer my home, but only my birthplace. After my mother's death, my family and I only maintained a relationship out of obligation. It no longer qualified as home. After all, what was home and family to me?

Nowadays, a family didn't need to be blood-related. I had Ndoda as my family.

My home was every place I missed. Aza's place was my home again, but an unreliable home, although I thought about her all the time. Boitu's house was my home for the time being, as long as her husband was still in jail. The cemetery and the bridge were my makeshift homes in case Boitu and Aza showed me the door. The Royal and Formula 1 were still my temporary homes, but expensive ones. Home and family to me meant everywhere I could run to with my legs or see with my eyes. It was a place that felt like sunshine and warmth. Home meant being safe and far away from warning signs and red flags. Home to me was whatever direction the wind blew me and right now it was blowing me to Boitu.

A lot was going on in my mind as I exited the taxi at Westdene. I thought of taking the rest of my clothes from Boitu's and maybe relocating them to Aza's. I tried to search for good excuses for doing that. I thought about how awful Boitu's kitchen looked compared to Aza's. In my mind I could see the balls of dust and tiny crumbs around the edges of Boitu's floor. How about the oily pots and pans in her sink and the top of her refrigerator that was black. These were the excuses that visited my mind when I tried to choose between Boitu and Aza. Maybe I must just be brave and date them both at the same time, I said to myself.

Maybe with the money I had on me I could finally buy a decent tombstone for my mother. I thought of my mother and how her grave looked. Shall I ask Boitu to come with me on Christmas? Or maybe Aza? But Boitu was not into me. She had her husband. What kept us together was the fact that neither of us belonged completely to the other.

Boitu had just come back from Sun City when I arrived at her home. We sat outside on the camp chairs in front of her house, drinking the wine and vodka.

'The festival ended very late this morning and I could not come,' I said to Boitu.

'I know. I hope you had fun. Sorry I couldn't stick around. When are you visiting your brother in Sun City again?'

'I'm not sure.'

'I just found out that my husband may be released soon before Christmas.'

'I guess that is good news for you, but bad news for me because it could mean we won't see each other again.'

'I'm not sure about that.'

'What do you mean? Will we continue to see each other?'

A startled look flared in her eyes. She tilted her head back and dropped her eyelids. My back began to sweat. She shrugged and looked at me. The feeling came over me that she was saying good-bye to me.

'What do you think?' She coughed gently into her fist. 'We will cross that bridge when we come across it.'

She seemed to scrutinise my face for signs of acceptance. I did not press for details. Unconvinced by her answer, I took a sip of my vodka and pinched the base of my nose between my thumb and forefinger. In the meantime, the events of the previous night with Aza unreeled inside my skull without producing the slightest reaction. Boitu could not go on looking at me, and she let her gaze drop and took a sip of wine.

'My feelings are hurt,' I said.

She stood up, took my head between her hands gently and kissed my lips, making a smacking sound.

'Don't be angry. I'm sure you understand. Of course things just happened between us. I don't know how it happened.'

'So it was a mistake?'

'No, don't get me wrong. I'm not saying it was your fault.'

Her eyes started to beg for an explanation which I didn't have either. I let her do most of the talking and didn't interrupt her. I just let her go on about the things happening in her life. I couldn't stop watching her as her eyes closed and lips parted.

'I'm not trying to blame you, and I'm also not saying it was my fault because it wasn't. It was our fate,' she said. 'Maybe it's also our fate to call it quits. But let's be practical here. I don't see how we can continue.'

That night, I undressed and got under the sheet with her, wrapping us in a ball. We were drunk. When I touched her hips, I thought that I could feel her innermost life on the sensitive surface of her body. She shoved her pelvis against me, threw her arms and one leg around me and squeezed with all her slippery might. We didn't talk after we made love. We were both sticky with sweat from the summer heat. She curled her body against mine and I squeezed her a bit harder. It lulled her to sleep, her naked body sprawled out next to me in bed, her heavy breathing evidence of deep sleep.

In the morning when I opened my eyes, I looked at her to reassure myself that she didn't have regrets. I asked her for the time. When she told me it was past eight, I adopted a panicked expression, jumped to my feet and quickly dressed. It was as if she had read my mind that I was not coming back when I dashed out, feeling a wave of relief. I opened the door and stood there silently. Then I was gone.

# 43

Rumours were flying around like bats within Aza's circle of friends and family that we were back together. Some of Aza's nosy friends had seen me driving her car on my way to the pharmacy to get her antidepressants and had phoned to confirm if it was true. Others had spotted us holding hands while doing grocery shopping together at the Cresta Mall.

What people did not know was that it was no longer the same between Aza and me. She was different from the Aza I'd known before, the one I had initially fallen in love with. She talked to herself a lot, cried often over small things and she looked permanently worried. Our reunion was ruined by her fretting and hypersensitivity. I felt it was all desperation and depression masquerading as reunion and love. She had developed a disturbed personality characterised by brooding silences and constant sloppiness. This sometimes came in the form of dirty clothes on the floor, dirty dishes in the kitchen, strands of hair in the bathroom and outbursts of irrational violent anger.

One day, I found Aza sitting up in her dishevelled bed wearing her old blue velvet robe, surrounded by fashion magazines. I sat next to her in bed.

'Did you by any chance see our engagement ring?' She screwed up her face. 'I have been looking for it all over the house. I think it got lost when you left.'

'Not at all. The last place I saw it was on your finger.'

'What do you mean?'

'I mean, I expected you to always wear it.'

'I know. I have been trying to look for it in the past few days. I thought since we are now together I want to wear it again.'

'Me too. I expect you to wear it again. Didn't it get stolen with other items when there was the break-in?'

'That's what I'm also wondering. But I will look for it properly.' She paused. 'By the way, when are we going to your village so that we can start arranging for our marriage?' she asked while stroking my cheeks and kissing me tenderly.

'When the time is right. We will do it properly this time.'

'I'm now ready to be Mrs Mangena.'

'We need to take it slowly. I mean we just reunited three weeks ago.'

Her voice faltered and I recognised a prelude to tears. The truth was that my view of marriage had changed. I was of the opinion that marriage was the only excuse for love. I was afraid of marriage, as it often meant the end of love.

'You know I love you, right?' she said.

'I know,' I replied, a little confused by the thoughtful gaze being levelled at me.

'There was something so aimless about our days and our drinking in this house in the past.' She suddenly leaned back, a satisfied look on her face. 'If we have to be serious about life and each other again, we must get married soon.'

'Before we can even think about marriage, you need to heal from your loss first.'

'I know. I just miss my mother sometimes. It's nothing serious,' she said, but her face crumpled and she dabbed it with the back of her hand.

I felt my heart pounding harder and harder at my inability to afford her the slightest comfort.

'I know that feeling. I miss mine, too.'

'When she died, I learnt a big lesson,' she continued. 'I learned that one may have a mother who gives love and good upbringing, but you can never replace a mother, never. And of course, I suffered from depression after that. But I'm working on it.'

'That's a normal feeling. In most cases mothers and their children are not only umbilically attached in the womb. The bond is even stronger after birth.'

'I think you're right. I will work on getting right.'

'Love, I'm sure you understand that I'm not here to belittle your pain and what you have gone through. I also understand that the path you travelled was difficult. But it's important that you are in the right frame of mind before we can even entertain the idea of marriage.'

'But I promised I'm working on it, and I'm serious,' she said and fixed me with a fierce glare from her bloodshot eyes.

What Aza didn't know was that to me marriage was now an institution in which I no longer recognised myself with her. I had changed a lot over the past few months. Since I had become a lone wolf, I no longer believed in pairing for life. I could only see marriage as boredom, a permanent contract based on temporary feelings. It was about two people depending on each other and babysitting each other and defending each other against the world outside. I didn't want that in my life. My approach towards life these days was that it had no plot or order of things. I felt life was far more interesting than the template that had been drilled into us by our parents or society. If I saw a woman I liked, I could move in with her today. But if things did not work out, I could also leave today. That was my strength now. I was always

241

waiting for something to happen. Sometimes my intuition was very accurate. I knew that I was a coward, but from time to time I suffered from outbreaks of bravery. When it was time to leave, it was like moving from one kind of world to another. The adventure was inexhaustible.

# 44

That second week of December was very hectic. On Thursday we worked at Witbank with Kobus and Martinus. The following day was another concert at The Dome and then a soccer match at the Orlando Stadium between Orlando Pirates and Mamelodi Sundowns on Sunday. I alternated my nights between the Formula 1 on Wanderers Street and Aza's home.

At the same time, Ndoda had told me that his wife, Phindi, was here visiting him from Gwanda so he would not frequent The Royal until further notice. I could not even mention the place when I called him on the phone, he warned. As a result, I decided to take a break from The Royal for a while too. There was no one to see because Boni and Ndoda were no longer there. I assumed Boni had found someone to marry, maybe the last guy I'd seen her with.

On Sunday, coming back exhausted from the soccer match, I found Aza crying. She was lying in front of the TV screen with a soundless picture on it. All I wanted to do was sleep; instead, I had a very disturbed night. Aza had been to the dentist for a filling and her face was still numb. But she forced a conversation which was difficult for me to participate in.

'I want us to set a date for our marriage today so that we can start planning. That's if you seriously love me.'

'Is that an ultimatum? I thought we had already talked about this.'

A small frown of irritation showed on her brow.

I no longer felt the love that I had had before and it was all her fault again. She had different mood swings now – cold, jittery and dysfunctional. She would talk about her mother and start crying while drinking her wine. When she cried, it felt like it would never stop. Then, after a scene full of sobs, she would make me swear that I would never leave her again like I had the last time.

'Of course it's not an ultimatum. You sound like I'm forcing you to love me. Am I forcing you?'

'No, you're not. I'm just tired. I have been standing the whole day, working. My mind is really not working right now.'

'Let me run a bath for you.'

'Please don't, I just want to sleep.'

'But how are you going to talk seriously about our marriage if you keep avoiding the topic?'

'I'm not avoiding the topic. Maybe you should find the engagement ring first before we talk about marriage.'

'The engagement ring served its purpose. Now let's talk about the main event of the marriage.'

A host of realisable fantasies paraded through my imagination. I was now sharp and dangerous as a polished spear after learning from the city streets. I was no longer the Mangi who was looking for a clever, outstandingly pretty woman to marry. My excessive politeness of the past had changed. These days I no longer troubled myself with expressions of courtesy. I came to her house in the morning, noon and evening, whenever I wanted, and didn't trouble myself to apologise for anything like I had in the past. Though we still loved each other, we could no longer tune in to each other's heart channels and share the pain and new challenges that came with us. Every time I visited Aza, I found myself reliving the emotions of our previous life. I had stopped taking pains to please Aza.

'Can we please talk about this in the morning when my mind is working.'

'It's just a date,' she said while opening her phone that was lying next to her. 'You can simply say on Good Friday or any date, and we are done. It doesn't mean we can't change that date in the morning. I see no problem really.'

'Sweetheart, we'll make it work.' I patted her back affectionately. 'Love is the best of ambassadors.'

'I love you. You are my only hope, the sole recourse remaining to me.'

'I love you too.'

'All my love and all my dreams are yours.'

I nodded absentmindedly, then frowned at the strange words. I was conscious of her crying silently. When I didn't say anything, her weeping grew louder and was transformed into a fierce sobbing that shook the emptiness between her and me. Her head was buried in my chest, so I could smell the scent of her weave hair, feel her hot hands stuck to my back, the dampness of her tears on my chest.

'We have to take it bit by bit. Being in love has a lot of draw-backs,' I said.

'What do you mean?'

'Never mind. It's just something that slipped out,' I said with a clumsy tongue that felt heavier and heavier in my mouth. 'It's all my fault.'

To be honest, I now approached everything with such detachment, with amiable words and unpredictable manners, that even

I failed to distinguish egotism from love, depravity from virtue. There was some indefinable gap that existed between myself and Aza. I felt no particular fondness for her, neither affection nor dislike. She sometimes worked herself into a froth of excitement that in the end only repelled me. I got bored with her constant praise over my looks and manliness. I was amazed at the transformation in her – she was submissive and artificial. She even brought me breakfast in bed, which she'd never done before.

'You still love me, right?'

'Very much.'

'You're never going to leave again?' She rubbed her eyelids, making no attempt to hide her helplessness.

I wiped her tears with my finger and squeezed her shoulder. She got up, walked away to compose herself in the bathroom. I followed, her mumbling a lame apology.

'No, babe, I'm not going to leave you again.'

'You swear you still love me?' Her eyes glazed with tears.

'I swear.'

Her eyes were red and puffy and her face was pale. I wiped tears from under her eyes and held her tightly. These were the kind of emotions that I'd had to deal with since we got back together and I always felt guilty. While in the bathroom, Aza burst into sobs in my arms. I could feel that the love, which had once existed between us before, had now vanished from my side. In the early chapter of our lives together, I had found her enchanting and utterly irresistible. She'd sometimes fill our home with her sweetness and her laughter. Not any more. Now, I'd become nervous of even touching her.

Was I condemned to share my life, day after day, hour upon hour, minute by minute with such a person, I asked myself. With her antics, Aza had over-wound the screw of love that I'd once had for her. Since I could not avoid seeing her and her sad face, I decided to shut her off from my mind's eye. I realised that I had made a grave mistake by getting back with her. What was the least amount of time I could spend with her without being rude to her or making her cry? I tried to reason with myself. I felt I was sinking into time, as if I were moving against the currency of history. There had been a point when the weight of my sorrow was far too much when I thought of being away from Aza. That was then, but not this time around.

There was nothing left for me to share with Aza. I felt my romance with her might ruin my life again. I had to stop it. It had been a long time since I'd felt my life was in danger of further ruin. My heart had grown indifferent towards her clamorous love, whose delicate nuances I could no longer distinguish. Even when we finally made love, it was without passion. Sometimes we would kiss for a long time, her tongue making dizzying circles in my mouth. But no matter how long we went on kissing, my penis would stay flaccid. Our intimacy had evaporated and I didn't even want to say to myself that her face was no longer beautiful. Some mornings she would wake up with giant bags hanging beneath her eyes as a result of crying. She ate infrequently. In fact, most days she didn't eat at all. The loss of her mother was the loss of her happiness. It was because of faith alone that she could be strong in spirit even when she was weak in her body. I tried to just embrace her, in some way or another, bite into the muscle to remain sane in her company. But no, I didn't have the strength that I used to have before. I had to leave her again. It was time for me to release the past from my hands and mind. Aza's weight was no longer mine to carry.

# 45

After a third concert at The Dome and another soccer match at Orlando Stadium, Ndoda and his people did not come back to me to reclaim their share. I had more than fifty-four thousand rand in the bag for three days of work. Christmas was around the corner, I was scared of always travelling the city with a bag with such a huge amount inside. After two more days, I tried to call Ndoda and a woman answered the phone.

'It's his wife, Phindi, speaking. Who is this?'

'It's Ndoda's friend, Mangi.'

'Okay. He told me that when you call I must tell you to deliver the parcel to me.'

'Where is he?'

'Oh, you didn't hear? He is in casualty ward at the Charlotte Maxeke Hospital, ward six.'

This shook me out of my fantasies. Panic flooded my body. My heart thumped so wildly, I could feel it in my throat.

'What? Oh no, what happened?'

'It's complicated. Some people at his work accused him of stealing money and they beat him so badly that he suffered a concussion and broken ribs.'

'It can't be.'

'Yes, very cruel bastards. He has a brace on his neck and a

bandage on both arms and legs. IV tubes were plugged into his arms yesterday and his head wrapped in layers upon layers of bandages.'

'Who did that to him? Who are these people?'

'I don't know. But it's something connected to his work and his colleagues. His whole body is covered with bleeding welts and both his eyes are swollen shut. I wonder if you will be able to recognise him.'

She spoke so fast, eventually running out of breath. I realised she was sobbing. What if he had already told them where I stayed and they were already following me? But I didn't remember telling him where I stayed with Aza or with Boitu. I can't put the two ladies at risk, I told myself.

'Okay, I will call you tomorrow again. Did he specify what this parcel is that I have to give to you?'

'Not really.'


The sun had started reddening in the west and I walked off from the call box, not caring where to. I knew that in our line of work with Ndoda, danger had always held a certain allure. This is the part of the plan when the two or three unavoidable risks came into play. Since Ndoda and his colleagues had been accused of stealing, what would stop them from pointing at me as their accomplice, I asked myself.

I made the decision to leave right there and then. The urgency of this idea grew as I remembered the harsh days of sleeping under the bridge. I remembered what had happened to Airbag, Regulator, Seatbelt and the others. Only then it made sense how they'd got into their unfavourable situations. I didn't want to end up like them and the only alternative left for me was to invent a new life for myself in a different city. Maybe the grass would be green somewhere else; if not, I would just have to water it myself. I had suffered years of frustration and disappointment thrown in my face. I wanted a new life in which I would be free to wallow in unfiltered experience. But this new idea weakened again, overwhelmed by the thought that I might lose Aza and Boitu forever this time. Why did whatever I depended on turn instantly to dust in my hand, I asked myself. I decided to call Boitu.

'I'm glad you called,' she said. 'This thing of you not having a phone is not good. There have been some developments.'

'I'm listening.'

'My husband is coming home this week.'

'Oh my god! How soon?'

'Are you not listening? I said this week. So, I want you to come take your backpack with clothes that you asked me to throw into the washing machine for you the other day. I don't want him to be suspicious.'

The reality had struck me, as if up to that point I had been dreaming. There was too much sadness inside for me to know what to say.

'So, when can I come?'

'Actually, no. Tell me where we can meet today or tomorrow so that I can bring them to you. His relatives are already here and they are planning a surprise party. I've already put your backpack in the garage.'

It was over between Boitu and me. I was not even going to bother to meet to get my clothes. They were old anyway and I had enough money to buy more. But what about Aza? She had become baggage I could not carry. She could be emasculating or endearing as it suited her. There was no better time to leave her

250

than now. I was convinced that nothing had changed. I must never forget how she'd made me feel in the past when all I'd needed was her love. I wished that time would have a better timing for both of us then. If I allowed her to spoil me with a house and a car now, it would be as if she were buying a dog. She would not let me off the leash.

# 46

My life in Joburg City had become evocative and risk laden. After I had spoken to Ndoda's wife, the excitement turned into paranoia. My forehead was pouring with sweat. I felt madness taking hold of me. I was afraid and confused, but then I managed to pull myself together in order to stay focused. I felt weird, unsafe, like there was someone watching and wanting to hurt me. I was breathing heavily through my mouth and my throat was getting dry.

I couldn't sleep at the hotel that night for fear that the people who beat up Ndoda might come to get me. I had already told Aza that I was not coming home since I worked the night shift and slept near work in Rustenburg, which was a lie. Of all the things I ever wanted to tell her, goodbye was not supposed to be one of them. I thought about The Royal and then remembered the incident when Ndoda's money had been stolen.

Fortune had deserted me, I thought. I had to make a decision right away. I had to leave Joburg immediately. I was thinking of either going to Cape Town or Durban. I had never been to Cape Town, but I had been to Durban once with Aza and I'd liked it then. I didn't know anyone in both these cities. The joy of life comes from our encounters with new experiences, I convinced myself. There is no greater joy than to have an endlessly changing horizon, for each day to have a new and different sun. I was propelled by a desire for a change in life, or perhaps it was the nervous condition produced by Ndoda's hospitalisation.

I was heading towards the Wanderers Taxi Rank, walking fast, not looking behind me. As I walked down the street, I could not suppress the feeling of dread that welled up inside me. It was as though I sensed that something evil was going to happen. My joints ached, not having had the time to recover from attending three big events in a row, the two concerts and the soccer match.

I had suffered enough in my pursuit of happiness, I thought to myself. Now, when I thought I held it within my grasp, it disappeared just like that in front of me. Until now, I could not believe that this placid existence of mine was the happiness of which I had dreamt of in the past. In order to savour the little that was left of it, I had to travel far away, where I hoped life would be sweeter, even for a few days. Misfortunes seemed to be chasing me everywhere with fury. All I wanted was to live a normal life, love and be loved.

I stood for a while in front of a fish and chips shop, filled my lungs with air, and made a half-turn towards the entrance of the taxi rank. A sameness coloured all the details – the dirt, the faces of the homeless, the smells and shards of broken glass winked in the late afternoon light. I was on the brink of retching because of the smell. The filth, the hunger, the dirt and despair. I saw my face reflected in the backlight of a window as a taxi drove past. I frowned to myself behind sunglasses which I'd pulled over my eyes, not so much to soften the glare of the setting sun but as a disguise to my unknown pursuers.

Reaching the Wanderers Taxi Rank, I was consumed by exhausting thoughts, with the names Cape Town and Durban racing back and forth in my mind. Joburg belonged to the brave, I thought. I was an anomaly and unhappy in this city. I had experienced much sorrow in the past few months and now it was starting again. I knew for certain that it would never end. Perhaps I was a man of chance rather than destiny.

The smell of fried chips and the towers of braaied chicken from the street vendor sharpened the edge of my appetite. Chicken bones littered the ground. A homeless man was rummaging through an overflowing rubbish bin next to the street vendor for the bones and pap remains. He was barefoot, his clothes in shreds. His scalp was covered with ringworms, his arms and legs scarred with sores. He smiled as he saw a bone with some meat on it. His thin face flushed. He picked it up together with the cigarette butts on the ground. He then coughed and moved away.

To one side, some men played cards on an upturned crate. A man with a toothpick in his mouth and his newspaper under his arm was shouting, and he looked like he was a taxi rank marshal.

'Four more, Durban. Durban, four more,' the man shouted near the Iveco bus, and he looked burnt and salted by the many suns of the city. Near him was a rubbish bin choked with waste. 'Are you going to Durban?'

He was looking at me in the face when a green fly landed on his nose and then on his lip before he swatted it away. I longed to escape like that fly, to somewhere I could recapture myself, far away from Joburg, out in immaculate space. I was determined to search for another city that would restore laughter to my lips.

'Yes, I'm going to Durban,' I said with a nod.

'Come,' he commanded as he retrieved a notebook from the front of the taxi. 'Your name and contact number, please.'

His eyes were rimmed with red. I thought of Airbag's name and gave it to him.

254

'Thabang Mashishi.'

'Contact numbers of your relatives just in case anything happens?'

I gave him Ndoda's cell phone which I knew by heart as mine. The man lifted his cap, scratched his hairless head and pulled it back on.

'Do you have any bags?'

'No, just this small backpack.'

'That's okay. You can put it between your legs on your seat.'

'Thank you. Do we have any stops for food? I forgot to buy.'

'Only in Harrismith,' he replied in a calm, detached tone of voice, licking his lips. 'But you can buy food here if you want. This taxi is not yet full. No alcohol drinking inside the taxi.'

'Thanks,' I said as I entered the taxi.

The smell of the sweat was heavy and cloying, and I opened the window. I then took off my sunglasses and wiped the lenses clean with the hem of my T-shirt. The open window invited street vendors who came to sell their wares to me, including water bottles, cool-drinks, food, electronics and clothes. I bought two bottles of water, a half-litre of Coke, biltong and a hot dog. I stepped outside the taxi and began to eat. I would see everything else in Harrismith, I thought. I got back into the taxi and sat next to a huge woman with big thighs. She was silent, biting her nails and looking ahead. Her brain seemed to be engaged elsewhere and she began fidgeting on the seat. Leaning at the front of the minibus, the taxi rank marshal kept repeating the same spiel to potential travellers.

'Two more, Durban. Let's go!'

A man who sat impatiently in front of me kept turning his head as if he wanted to disconnect it from his body. About two or three hours later, the taxi left the rank, turned east onto a crowded Bree Street and on to the N3 highway. Shwi Nomte-khala's 'Ngafa' was playing at high volume. I sighed with relief. Maybe in life one has to be completely shaken up like I had been in order to relocate to another place. I ate what was left of the hot dog, which scraped painfully along my throat. I was itching with curiosity to see one of the greatest sights on earth: the ocean. At long last I thought I was unburdened, emancipated from the stifling Joburg City and Aza, a city in which I felt cut off from the raw throb of existence. I was thrilled to be on my way to the coast.

Drifting towards sleep, it came to me with cold clarity that a whole day had passed in which I had not thought of Aza. An anticipation for what would happen in Durban while inside the taxi was what helped me to fall asleep until Harrismith.

At Harrismith, halfway between Joburg and Durban, the taxi came to a stop. The driver announced that we all had twenty minutes to stretch, buy food or use the loo. I went to the crowd-ed loo first. I was ravenously hungry. I then went to the Steers to buy some chicken and two Cokes.

The atmosphere was grey and thick with fog. The taxi left half an hour later. The sky was threatening rain and lightning began to flash. On the side of the road, the trees twisted as though the wind were tickling them. My ears were filled with the sound of Soul Brothers' 'Bazobuya' played by the driver and the little snatches of conversation coming from the other passengers. It struck me that out of all the various sounds I could hear, it was that of the crying baby in front of my seat that stood out.

I levelled my gaze as sharply as possible at the window, but unfortunately there was little solace or encouragement to be drawn from the sight of the fog, which was thick enough to obscure even the opposite side of the street. As I fell asleep, I enjoyed travelling in a dream to a distant planet. I dreamt of myself as a powerful man. As I woke up, I grinned at the dream in fore-glimpsed delight at future abundance.

# 47

One's entrance to a city usually doesn't lie. Either the city embraces you from the start or it shuns you forever. I know it was still very early to draw conclusions, but from that moment I felt as if Durban gave me clear answers that I was looking for. It allowed me to be reborn. The coastal city became my dawn. Real life was just beginning. Unlike Joburg, which I thought had many faces, Durban was a city that didn't have the luxury of choosing between the many faces it had day and night. Maybe its true face was yet to come. I had no right to judge a city within an hour of arrival. The ocean, the homeless, the drug addicts, the green landscape, the hills, the beach, the sex workers, the criminals, gqom music, the maskandi, and the rest gave Durban its identity.

Here, finally, I was able to surrender myself to a new city. The ocean was there to make me happy. Here at least I could confront life on my own terms. I could buy the future by forgetting about the past. I could start on a clean slate with no love, no belief, no ambition, but only thinking of myself.

The faint smear of dawn was already bleaching the rim of the northeast sky when we arrived at the Durban Taxi Rank. The city was fast asleep. A dank humid stench filled my nostrils as I stepped outside the taxi. I decided to wait inside the rank until the city was back to life again. My fellow travellers and I lay on the floor, our heads leaning against the building, looking up to the approaching morning sky and thankful to be alive and safe. The pale moonlight covered the place with a ghostly light. The pillars of the taxi rank building cast long shadows.

I could not sleep and felt a bit disorientated. Anyway, who would sleep with such an amount of cash in their bag? When it was clear to me that I'd never fall asleep, I decided to get up, stretch a bit by walking a few steps. It was so humid and warm that it seemed you could reach out in front of your face, grab a handful of humidity, fling it at the wall and it would stick. Flies were clustered on walls, gleefully rubbing their legs together as they slept. There were countless stars looking down on the city, the almost visible silence, and the trees overhanging the houses and buildings. The trees and fences turned even darker and cast deep shadows. I savoured, most of all, the inviting smell of the Indian Ocean. My twitching nostrils gratefully sniffed the salty air blowing in off the ocean which I could not see, but could feel just at the end of the city.

Dawn slid by as if it were a liquid. The first birds began to chirp as the sky gradually lightened. Then the sky leaked light. The new day brought fresh delights for me. With a triumphant smile on my face, I followed the city signs and walked towards the ocean. A sheen of sweat on my forehead, I sighed with happy exhaustion as I looked at the vast ocean. A new life was beginning. I had never felt better physically, mentally and spiritually. The universe, with its past, present and future, was gathered together into a single point before and after which nothing existed.

Every fibre in my body was savouring the kindly warmth of the early morning sun. The sky was an endless blue slate. The circle of red on the shining white morning mist of the sky was like a yolk of an egg that had been broken onto a white plate. The lights of the massive ship anchored in the harbour were seductive. A few ships, both large and small, were going by in the distance. I have never been on a ship in my life. Maybe one day I would sail away from here. For a time I let my mouth hang open, so that my excitement might take the opportunity and come in and out. In that stretched moment, I was carried by the wings of memory back and forth, between Aza, Boitu, Ndoda and Airbag. There was a tiny warning pain in my head. In order not to think about what had happened to Ndoda, I removed my sneakers and carried them in my hands. I began to look back at the footsteps I was making in the sand, but the waves broke over them shortly after I had made them.

# 48

The first thing I did was to look for a cheap place to stay. At the nearest internet café, I googled and found a backpackers house in the Musgrave area at four hundred rand per night. It had a swimming pool. While waiting for my place to be ready, I went to Ace Butchery and Restaurant to buy pap and braai meat. After that, I went to the nearest bottle store to buy two bottles of vodka and tonic. From there I took a minibus taxi to Musgrave. My aim was to relax alone for a day or two before I figured out what to do.

The house looked old, but was coated with fresh paint. It was concealed behind high walls and security gates, and backed by small forests. It was between the Musgrave Mall and Durban University of Technology. The tiny room I'd rented smelled of past ancient rain that was still in the old carpet, but I didn't mind. I took a slow bath, till the skin on my fingers became white and spongy. I then fell asleep and woke up at about eleven at night.

I opened my eyes suddenly, not because the first bout of tiredness had ebbed away as a result of my retiring early, but because I sensed that somebody was moving outside my outer door. I opened the door and saw a group of people swimming outside. They were all white. I went outside, paused, stood still for a moment, before I decided to join them. They all spoke a language I could not understand until I learnt later that they were backpackers from Germany. They were two guys and three ladies, swimming, drinking and smoking weed by the pool. They saw me and invited me to join them. I thanked them before letting myself be persuaded to have a drink with them.

'Hi, I'm Paul. This is Anna, Heidi,' he said, pointing to his companions, 'Hans and Ingrid.'

Hans saluted me with a finger to his forehead. He had wet hair on his arms and chest. I acknowledged them all with a nod.

'I'm Mangalani.'

'Hi, Mangalani,' they said simultaneously.

'Where are you from?'

'Joburg.'

'We are from Germany.'

'Nice meeting you all.'

That's how I came to meet Ingrid by chance, but it later felt as if we had known each other forever. I liked her because she kept repeating my name again and again under her breath, as if delighted by the sound it echoed in her ears.

'You can all call me Mangi.'

She gave a short laugh. Her eyes in the dark were bright and brown and full of humour.

'Mangalani sounds nice.'

I fell in love with the way she could smile, just with her eyes. Her voice had a huskiness that deserved to be on the radio.

'You can call me Mangalani. The rest must call me Mangi.'

Everyone laughed. Ingrid was sitting a little apart from the others, her face lowered, and regularly polishing her gold-rimmed spectacles.

We sat there by the pool drinking and when we ran out of alcohol, I went to fetch the two bottles of vodka and tonic that I had bought earlier that day.

I felt sufficiently rested and restored. The air was filled with merriment. The glasses clinked and the vodka gurgled. We laughed, splashed water on one another, sang, danced, and smoked cigarettes and joints. It was bliss, a true bliss I had not had in a long time.

Around midnight we decided to take our drinks and weed and head to the beach. Two Ubers were ordered. I sat with Ingrid in the back of one of the Ubers.

'So, which part of Germany do you come from?'

'Berlin. Have you ever been there?'

'Never. I've never been overseas before.'

'I see.'

We were tipsy, but not drunk. I found her intelligent with an easy-going personality. Her forehead was broad and generous, her eyebrows set well apart and forming crescent moons above her eyes. Our knees touched and my heart beat fast.

'So, what brought you to this country?'

'Happiness, a search of a good summer and the sun.'

'Interesting. You don't have the sun in Berlin?'

'Not this time of the year. It's dark and cold. You won't like it. Always raining and sometimes snowing. The sun makes me happy.'

'I get you. I have not experienced a long period without a sun.'

'Believe me, it's not a good experience. That is why my friends and I like to scrape up a few crumbs of happiness everywhere by travelling every now and then to enjoy the sun.'

She flipped her waist-length hair from her face with a toss of her head as she spoke and chopped the air for emphasis with small, expressive hands.

'Last year we were in Senegal, the previous year in Kenya. I guess we like following the sun and happiness.'

The taxi dropped us off next to Joe Cools by the beach. Paul, Heidi, Hans and Anna immediately ran in and out of the ocean. Ingrid and I followed. I felt good and washed clean of sin after that.

It was already two in the morning and Ingrid and I were still talking. We separated a bit from the group, alone, surrounded by promenade lights, water and silence. The heaving, restless ocean whispered intimate secrets to the beach. We spent dawn there talking about our dreams.

'And you visit here often?' she asked, looking at me until I lowered my eyes.

'It's my second time here.'

'It's amazing what the sea does to the mind, isn't it?'

'Yeah. I came here just for that after breaking up with my girlfriend for the second time.'

'I'm sorry to hear that.' Her bright kitten-like eyes were dilated.

'It's no big deal.'

'Second time sounds like a huge deal to me?' She raised her eyebrows.

The light on the promenade penetrated the lids of her eyes, which from time to time she blinked. Hans lit a joint, blew smoke rings and passed it to Ingrid before he ran into the ocean again. The way she blew the smoke upwards from her nose and mouth indicated in particular a great pleasure on her part. I was staring at her inches from her face and she looked right through me. I was filled with a strange calm which seemed to radiate from her.

'Well, we quarrelled over marriage and there seemed to be nothing I could do at that moment to recover her affection,' I replied. 'So I decided to come here to cleanse myself in the ocean.'

'How long have you two been together?'

She passed me the joint and wiggled her toes on the thin plastic sole of her flip flops. I shuddered at the thought of opening up to a stranger about things not even my sisters knew about. How do I reveal my fears, insecurities, skeletons and shady past to strangers, I asked myself. I knew myself as a placid and slightly withdrawn character. But Ingrid had unmasked the gaping void in me.

'The first time was just over eight years. Then we broke up for just under six months. The second time we dated for less than a month before we broke up again.'

'Wow, it sounds a bit complicated for me to make sense of it.'

'Kind of. But better to be alone than live unhappy permanently with someone.' My tone was final with a rare touch of pride.

'What was she like?'

'Intelligent and very independent.'

Ingrid stroked my cheek. A boat hovered into view, rising and falling with the movement of the waves.

'I believe our hearts are like the ocean,' she said, putting her hand on my shoulder and looking intently at me. 'Oceans are deep enough to bury our sorrows, anger, countless secrets and hide our past.'

She picked up a small shell and held it in her hand, stroking it with her fingers, then rubbed it across her lower lip.

'I guess you're right. Certain places and things on earth are there to produce happiness.'

'Yes, most importantly, oceans fill our hearts with the capacity to give and forgive. Maybe that's the reason we are all here today.'

'Well, it's always a great thing to go somewhere and snatch life with both hands and feel no remorse or guilt for anything.'

She took my hand in hers, squeezed it. We burrowed into conversation that skimmed over the present, then tunnelled back through five years of her life.

'My ex-boyfriend from high school dropped me to marry another girl. I'm also trying to reform my personality by travelling.'

'Sorry about that. At least we have something in common,' I said with a grin. 'Break-ups.'

'Maybe we do.'

'I think it's unfair that a man can marry and leave his girlfriend heartbroken like that.'

'It's part of life,' she said. 'Of course a woman decides who to sleep with, but a man decides who to marry. It seems men have long figured out what to do to make themselves wanted by women for sex. But women cannot figure out what to do to make themselves wanted by men for marriage.'

'What is meant for you will always be yours. That's why it's important to give people space and not to beg anyone to stay. We are not the rejected ones. We are the ones who broke free.'

'That's a good point you're making.'

'How about, if possible, tomorrow we explore Durban together, just me and you? We can go to Umlazi Township if you like. I've heard good things about a place called Max's Lifestyle and Eyadini Lounge. I've never been there before.'

'That sounds like a great idea. The only places we have explored so far are the ones along Helen Joseph Road. Two nights ago we were at a place called Amsterdam in the Davenport area and it was fun.'

'Great, say around two in the afternoon?' I suggested.

Heidi came over to us, the scarf tied round her head flapping in the breeze. Her eyes were full of delight as she hurried along the beach. Ingrid joined her. As I watched them running towards the water, Aza's image came to my mind. I thought I had forgotten about her. In fact, while trying to forget about her, I was subconsciously always thinking about her. I was filled with despair at how her image kept coming into my memory at the very time when I was struggling so hard to let go of her.

I lay on my back and looked at the glittering stars in the sky. I stayed like that for a while, my eyelids shut, listening to the sound of the ocean and lost in a reverie. The thought of Aza kept crossing my mind. I hated getting flashbacks of the things I didn't want to remember about her. How strange to still dream of her even when I was wide awake in a faraway city. In my thoughts and dreams, she always found her way back to me. But this time they were only thoughts and not regrets. I did not lament the mental state I'd left her in. There was no way I could change that – it was beyond me. For the first time, I thought about her not as my lover or fiancée, but as another close human being I knew who was suffering from health issues. A strange, friendly pity for her entered my soul. I felt sorry that I'd left as suddenly as I had arrived back in her life again. Our dreams together had vanished into the desert like a mirage.

I thought about Airbag, relieved that he was in jail. At least he would be able to realise his dream to be a literature professor if he stuck to his plan of studying for free in jail. What if he had planned the whole jail thing in order to get access to an expensive university education, I asked myself. Anything was possible. Anyway, at the core of a person's spirit is their passion for adventure. I was not unhappy that Boitu's man had been released from prison and I didn't miss the life under the bridge either. I thought about Boni and Ndoda, the only two people who had been good to me when things were really tough. It is true that after a certain age or experience, we do not move on from the people we loved. We may be physically away from each other, but in our minds, we remain in the time, experience and company of the people we care about. Boni and Ndoda had reinforced me

267

in the view that my life, my person, had no less meaning and value than others. I would never forget Ndoda. He came to me with a torch when I was in the dark. In the process, I tried to repress the memory that I'd failed to give Ndoda's wife a share of the money. What if he died and she didn't have the money to carry his body across? With that feeling came a sharp pang of remorse.

It takes strength to remember; it takes another kind of strength to forget. It takes a hero to remember only the good things. Generally, people who remember are those who caught madness through pain. Some memories can be so comprehensively silenced that we forget that those invisible experiences are, in fact, lives of our own.

(Photo by Alet Pretorius)

NIQ MHLONGO is a South African novelist, short story writer, travel journalist, essayist, editor, and educator who graduated from Wits University with a BA degree (African Literature and Political Studies) in 1997. He has written five novels and three short story collections. He also edited an essay collection and two short stories anthologies. His first novel *Dog Eat Dog*, published in 2004, won the Spanish Literary Award called Mar der Letras Intenecionale in 2006. He has also won several literary prizes in South Africa for his work, including the Herman Charles Bosman Literary Prize, a Humanities and Social Science Award and the K. Sello Duiker Literary Award. His work has been translated into several languages, including French, Dutch, Flemish, German, Burmese, Spanish, and Italian. Niq is based in Berlin, Germany.

**Other titles by Niq Mhlongo published by Kwela Books:**

*Dog Eat Dog* (2004)
*After Tears* (2007)
*Way Back Home* (2013)
*Affluenza* (2016)
*Soweto, Under the Apricot Tree* (2018)
*Paradise in Gaza* (2020)
*For you, I'd Steal a Goat* (2022)


*The City Is Mine* celebrates Niq's twenty-year anniversary with Kwela Books.